"With Hearts of Honor"

A Family's Story of WWII

Kathy S. Howell

"With Hearts of Honor, A Family's Story of WWII," by Kathy S. Howell. ISBN 978-1-63868-005-5 (softcover); 978-1-63868-006-2 (eBook).

Published 2021 by Virtualbookworm.com Publishing Inc., P.O. Box 9949, College Station, TX 77842, US. ©2021, Kathy S. Howell.

Dedicated to:
Jack Daniel Sprunk and those who loved him

Chapter 1

INNOCENCE IS A FRAGILE THING. Shattered at a moment's notice, impossible to replace. Many people don't treasure its presence until it is taken from them.... sometimes by circumstances well beyond their control.

It was raining cats and dogs in Mountainview, New Mexico that mid-September night of 1940. At Skippy's Diner, the weather didn't seem to dampen the customers' enthusiasm one bit. Fords, Willys, and Dodge pick-ups pulled in as fast as Studebakers and Chevys pulled out. The local high school football game had just concluded, and people began streaming into the small town diner. Rain-soaked cheerleaders squealed while ducking under their boyfriends' letter jackets.

Inside Skippy's, someone turned up the radio, so that Don't Sit Under the Apple Tree blared in the background. Gwen Mackenzie surveyed the scene from the diner's front window, wondering if she'd make enough tips from this Friday night's youthful crowd. Barely twenty and a college sophomore to boot, Gwen considered herself well above the high school fray. She'd only recently decided to moonlight at Skippy's because her day job on the college newspaper didn't pay enough to make ends meet. Gwen's father, a widower, worked for the railroad, supporting a family of four kids. It was fine if Gwen, the oldest girl, wanted to go to college, but her family couldn't afford to help her.

The diner door flew open, letting in three young men who were sopping wet. Puddles of muddy water followed their every step. Gwen rolled her eyes and ran her fingers through her carefully coiffed brunette curls. The trio had chosen a booth in her station. Grabbing her pen and order pad, the young woman made her way to the booth. Her customers looked like three drowned rats.

Suddenly, Gwen did a double-take, as she realized the tallest one was Charlie Murdoch, one class above her in school. Charlie was someone all the girls had swooned over in high school. In a nutshell, he was smart, gorgeous, and athletic. At the moment, however; his bangs were plastered to his forehead and rivulets of water trickled from his ears. His expressive eyes managed to mesmerize her in spite of that.

He needs a towel and a little TLC, thought Gwen, trying hard not to smile. Charlie must've read her mind because he ordered a Coca-Cola and ducked into the men's room. After they removed their parka hoods, Gwen also recognized the two remaining in the booth. Mike and J.D. Sommers, brothers of her good friends Margo and Elise. Mike was also Charlie's age, though not as dazzling, while J.D. was four years younger; just a kid, really.

She couldn't help noticing the brothers' resemblance to one another, with their dishwater blond hair, dark thick brows, deep set eyes, strong noses, and intensely serious expressions.

"Hey, Mike. What's Margo doing these days?" Gwen gave him a perfunctory smile. Mike was okay; someone you'd think of as a brother.

Mike's face lit up when she spoke to him. "She's looking forward to her basic training in Georgia, at Fort Benning. Still can't believe she's gonna be in the Women's Army. I wonder how they'll get her out of bed so early in the morning." He felt like he was rambling. "So….what about you? Haven't seen you lately."

"Yeah, Elise told us you were workin' here now," J.D. chipped in.

"Oh, did she?" Gwen blushed, showing her dimples. Maybe Charlie had decided to come in here and see her. "To answer your question, Mike, I'm going to college. In my second year now." She politely poised her pen, indicating it was time to order.

"See, Mike, she's a coed now." Charlie's deep voice boomed throughout the diner. He walked up, not bothering to disguise a hungry look that enveloped the young waitress from the top of her head all the way down her lovely figure to her slender ankles.

This time it was Gwen's turn to light up. She forgot what she was doing, continuing to make eye contact with the handsome young man. He gave her a little pat on the shoulder as he jumped into the booth. This jolted Gwen like a bolt of electricity and she came down to earth.

"So, what'll it be for the three of you tonight?" she asked, flashing her dimples at him.

"When did the burgers go up to fifteen cents?" J.D. drawled unhappily, digging in his tight cowboy jeans for extra change.

"Don't worry, J.D., I'll cover you this time." Mike elbowed his fifteen-year-old brother hard in the ribs, never taking his hazel eyes off Gwen.

When she arrived with the meal, the young men summoned their will-power by sitting patiently until all were served. Please don't let me spill the sodas down anyone's back, Gwen prayed as she tried to gracefully place Charlie's in front of him. He chose that moment to grab her hand.

"Sit with us awhile," he begged.

"I-I can't. I'm on duty."

"Hey, everyone gets a break now and then. Take one now," he urged.

Gwen looked across the diner. The place had cleared out it was true, and she had been on her feet all night. Why not? She signaled, Louie, her boss. A break it would be.

Charlie moved over to make room for Gwen on his side. Disappointment evident on his face, Mike shifted away from his little brother, who was crowding him in.

Again, Charlie touched Gwen's shoulder. "So how do we rate the company of a good-looking college girl anyway?"

Gwen didn't know how to answer so she leaned forward, pretending to daintily sip her chocolate soda. When she finally looked up, Mike caught her eye and coughed in a fake sort of way.

"We're trying something new---starting today," he mumbled.

"Like what?" Gwen asked.

"We've enlisted in the military---Army that is. We're gonna defend our country---when it comes down to that." Mike sat up straight in the booth, shoulders squared.

"You did what?" Gwen exclaimed. "Did you sign up too, Charlie?" When Charlie nodded smugly, she continued, "You know we could go to war at any time, right? It's all my professors talk about these days, The president is cooking up some kind of plan to lend guns and boats to Britain. We've already traded 50 destroyers with them this month. It's all a way to get our foot in the door."

Charlie stuck out his chin proudly, raised his eyebrows and began to open his mouth when J.D. jumped in. "I'm getting in, too. Recruiter was at school today. I'm signin" up first thing Monday." He then threw his head back defiantly, and Gwen was splattered with a few renegade raindrops.

Mike gave his brother a shove, his eyes flashing with fury. "Don't be crazy, J.D. You're too young. What'd you do, lie about your age to the recruiter?" The younger boy didn't answer. "I knew it! You're only a sophomore in high school, for crying out loud! For another thing, Mom will kill you if you don't finish school, and for another thing, Dad needs you at the dairy."

"I've had enough of cows, and enough of book work. I want to be a real man."

Mike sighed, scrutinizing his younger sibling. "You don't fool me, J.D. Not for one minute. I know why you really want to sign up. The recruiter said everyone who signs on gets a free trip to the rodeo in Las Vegas, Nevada."

J.D. reddened and slumped down in his seat.

"I knew it! I knew it!" Mike hooted.

"Go on, laugh all you want. I'm gonna do it. No one's gonna stop me. My birthday is right around the corner. I'll be sixteen in time for boot camp. Besides, it's not that big a deal. The National Guard means just that---protecting our country right here at home. I won't be on an active tour like you and Charlie. I ain't going nowhere, so cut out the complaining"

"I still think Mother and Daddy have to give their permission for you to enlist and leave school. Good luck with that one. I suggest you hide instead." Mike acted like he was joking, but his eyes were not smiling. He lapsed into silence.

Gwen listened to the give-and-take in conversation, mainly upset that the military would take Charlie out of flirting range. He looked very attractive to her at that moment, wet hair and all.

"Gwen, it's getting busy again!" Louie snapped his fingers at her, gesturing to the late-night surge of people. Reluctantly, she complied.

After waiting her tables, Gwen snuck a peek at Charlie's booth. Empty. Her eyes went to the door. She saw their three familiar heads ducking out.

"Good night, Gwen," one of them called out.

"Good night, Charlie," she managed to squeak. That sounded desperate, she reprimanded herself, wiping off the guys' table. Great, no tip. I wonder what that says. Then she saw the ashtray, and an unbidden smile crossed her lips.

Loads of shiny pennies lay in the ashtray. She looked around. No one was watching as she briskly counted them. 100 pennies! Double what the total meals had cost! What a wacky, yet sweet thing to do! She knew Charlie had a little more money than most, but times were still hard! And what forethought it took to walk in here and surprise her this way. She couldn't wait until she saw him again.

She dumped the pennies into her apron, letting the heaviness remind her of the giver. She knew it wouldn't be easy regarding Charlie. After all, he dated a lot of girls. Now he would be in uniform, making him more attractive than ever. But on this rainy night in 1940, she pledged right then and there to make him hers.

Chapter 2

THE MOON SHONE BRIGHTLY on the four young women jumping out of Gwen's '33 Ford. Gwen giggled as she teetered dangerously on her new black pumps. Her heels were nearly as high as her spirits. She noticed Elise, Margo, and Caroline were in the same predicament shoewise. *Oh well, at least they make our legs look good,* she thought cheerfully, *and if any guy gets fresh, then heaven help him.* She smiled to herself, remembering the time a fellow had come on too strong with Margo. Was he ever sorry! She clobbered him with her spike heels in nothing flat. He'd disappeared into the night like a puppy with his tail between his legs. *We might be ladies, but wimps we're not.*

Inside the Mountainview Community Center, the music of Benny Goodman could be heard for miles around. Young people from all walks of life lined the walls. Mostly nervous looking guys were clustered on one side of the big room, while girls pretending to be interested in social chatter huddled on the opposing side.

Elise, the eldest of the four friends, spoke up, "I hope this isn't another dull night, girls. It looks like the same old crowd. What we need is some new blood around here." Her eyes sharply scanned the darkened hall.

Margo suddenly giggled and elbowed Elise hard in the ribs. "Check out that sailor at the end of the counter. Who is he? Now *that* is a real hunk."

Caroline narrowed her green eyes and patted her sassy red hair which was upswept in pompadour fashion. "Let's make a bet. Which one of us can meet him first?" She arched her eyebrows for emphasis. With a sway of her hips, she started for the bar.

A brazen and determined look crossed Elise's face. Quickly she scampered in front of Caroline, careful not to crash, in her high heels. She paraded across the room in her sparkly shirtwaist dress that was fashionably tight across the hips. Careful not to lose the flower in her plaited brunette hair, she plopped herself on the stool next to the sailor with the dark wavy hair. She tried not to notice his big biceps sporting requisite tatooes of Hawaiin girls doing the hula. His big lazy blue eyes lit up when they set on her; a grin slowly crossing his tanned face. The bet was over and the winner was taking all.

Gwen and Margo laughed hard, trying not to spy on Elise for too long. Shrugging, Caroline turned away from the new couple, and rejoined her friends. "One down and three to go."

"I don't care if I meet anyone or not," Margo stretched out her long limbs as she spoke. "After I'm through with basic training, I'll be shipped out any day. What I really want to see is Europe. The heck with the men around here. There'll be plenty more where I'm going." Her sultry red lips formed a distinctive pout.

"You'll have your hands full, I'm sure," Gwen said. "Just take care of yourself, that's all I ask. I don't want any thing happening to my best friend."

Caroline tapped her heel to the music. "Somebody needs to stay stateside. That's what I'm going to do. Back up our soldiers right here." At that moment, a very tall, lanky cowboy approached the petite redhead.

"Hey, Carrie, I've been lookin' for you all night. It's about time you got here." He hunched over and put his hands around her waist, and away they went, jitterbugging into the night.

I wonder if Charlie Murdoch is here, thought Gwen. She reached into her pocket and felt for the lucky penny she'd placed there earlier. It was one of the pennies he'd left for her the other night at the diner. *If he* really *liked her, why hadn't he called?* She caught herself hoping for a glimpse of the darkly handsome young man.

"Hey Sis, have you seen J.D.?" Gwen looked up to see Mike addressing his sister, Margo.

"J.D.'s here? Since when did he enjoy dancing?" Margo seemed incredulous. "I thought he lived at the barn with his horse."

Mike laughed. "Yeah, well there's a lot of things you don't know about our little brother. He's got stuff to tell Mother and Daddy that will knock your socks off."

Margo furrowed her elegant brows together. "What are you talking--" Mike interrupted her query by pointing at the dance floor. A broad shouldered, narrow-hipped youth in a cowboy hat was awkwardly spinning a cute high-school girl across the floor. Margo watched her little brother speechlessly for awhile. "Now that I think about it, he did beg Elise for a favor the other night. I thought he wanted her to iron that crease in his jeans that he can't live without. I'll bet it was really dance lessons he asked for. She *is* the best in town." Margo shook her head. "Our little brother is growing up."

"In more ways than one," Mike muttered under his breath, stealing a knowing glance at Gwen. The young woman felt an unexpected twinge of guilt, because she knew J.D. had signed up for the military, something his own sister had yet to find out.

"How about a dance, Gwen?" Mike casually asked out of the blue.

"Why not?" she replied lightly, hoping to escape Margo's puzzled eyes, which were presently boring a hole right through her. It was not her place to tell Margo about J.D., even if she was her best friend. Anyway, J.D. said he'd just be in the National Guard, which meant staying on the home front. And it wasn't as if the country was at war, after all. The European conflict was miles away. Yes, that Hitler person was a power hungry dictator, but the problems *were* across the ocean.

Now that the radios were reporting the Germans had turned their full attention to knocking out Russia, maybe Europe could actually relax and regroup. Gwen felt pretty sure they'd straighten it out, one way or another, without direct American involvement.

Moonlight Serenade filled her ears, while Mike demonstrated his own fine dancing moves. Gwen was pleasantly surprised. The quiet young man had always just been her friends' big brother. Nothing more, nothing less. A nice guy, alright, but definitely not her type. She wanted Rocky Road ice cream, and he was only vanilla.

She used the time on the dance floor to peer over Mike's shoulder in search of Charlie. Her efforts were soon rewarded, but not in a good way. Charlie was in the far corner, laughing and cutting up with a group of young women who appeared to hang onto his every word. He looked like an ad for an aftershave commercial.

Now a dark cloud hung over Gwen. How could she have ever believed she stood a chance with such a popular man? How was she supposed to compete with gorgeous platinum blondes and curvaceous brunettes?

She couldn't and wouldn't. Who needed him anyhow? She feigned a sexy smile and suddenly pretended to pay close attention to Mike. He did not let on if he noticed a difference in her demeanor. In any case, he appeared content with the current arrangement. Many more songs played and they danced to them all. Against her will, Gwen peeked over to see if Charlie was noticing how much fun she was having. He wasn't even looking.

She finally gave up altogether. Her high heels no longer seemed like such a great idea--- her feet were aching, as was her head and her heart. The song, *In the Mood,* was coming to a conclusion. She was tired of this silly game and was about to tell Mike she was through for the evening when someone lightly tapped her on the shoulder.

A rich, deep voice asked, "May I cut in?"

Gwen looked at Mike apologetically and he reluctantly understood. He stepped back and she turned to Charlie, face flushed and spirits renewed.

"I like your hair like that. It makes you look gorgeous." Gwen touched her hair self-consciously. She'd let down her wavy, brown hair instead of holding it back with combs. Truly, Charlie was the gorgeous one, but she couldn't say that.

"I was hoping I'd see you tonight. That's why I came." He tightened his grip on her while staring into her eyes.

"Oh, really." Gwen couldn't help herself. "You look like you were doing just fine without me. What I mean is--- You seem to know a lot of---*people*."

"Oh, if you mean the ladies in the corner, they're all friends. I was merely killing time, hoping you'd show up." He pulled her close to him, and she offered no resistance. What girl could say no to those strong arms and broad shoulders?

They danced in silence for awhile. For once not even Charlie was attempting a witty line.

"So when do you ship out with the Army?"

"Probably next week. I'll go to basic training at Fort Wheeler in Macon, Georgia, and then we'll see where Uncle Sam puts me next. I can't wait until we throw our hat into this war."

"When do you think that will happen? So many people are against it."

"It's only a matter of time, Gwen. Somebody has to stop Hitler and it's going to be the United States of America!"

"I-I hope not. My uncle was in WWI and it left him a different person." A shiver went down her spine.

"Well that won't happen to me. Just give me a clean shot at one of those Nazi Krauts. That's all I ask for. They'll be sorry they ever started this world domination crap. Oh, excuse my language in front of a lady, but you get my point."

"Settle down, soldier," Gwen said with a laugh. Secretly, she wished she'd skipped the military talk. "We're not in it yet, and there's a fair chance we'll stay that way. Let's talk about something else. Now: what were you saying about being glad to see me?"

Shyly, she looked into his eyes for a response. He looked like he might kiss her right then and there, but something stopped him. Ambivalence filled Gwen. She wanted him to, but was also glad he didn't. The prudes who ran the dance hall would've talked about her for days on end. Public displays of affection were frowned upon this year of 1940.

Oh well, she thought reaching into her skirt pocket to touch her lucky diner penny, *I'll collect that kiss when we're alone later.*

And she did. And it was better alone on her doorstep anyway. Much better.

Chapter 3

J.D. WHISTLED AS HE PACKED. He picked up the starched skivvies his mother had carefully laid out on the bed for him. Longingly, he looked over at his well-worn cowboy boots. There wasn't enough room for those. The army said to just pack the bare essentials. He could only wear the black and white high top tennis shoes currently on his feet.

He got the feeling someone's eyes were on him. He turned and there was his mother in the hallway, miserably watching the packing process. Her lips were pressed together; her eyes shiny and red. She looked away and quickly rubbed them, though she was already caught by her son.

"Hey Ma, it's not that bad." He gave her a big bear hug; then bent his lanky frame down to kiss the top of her barely graying hair. "I'm only going to Fort Bliss, not the end of the world. It's *El Paso,* Ma. Three hours from Mountainview. They'll train me for six weeks and I'll be back here before you know it, serving and protecting our country starting right here in the Southwest. The National Guard works that way---it's all explained in this manual."

He snapped the leaflet against the table for emphasis. "I'll be in a cavalry regiment-getting paid to work with a *horse*, Mother. You'll look back and laugh at your worries. You always worry too much anyhow." He resumed packing and whistling.

"I know you're right, J.D. It's just that Margo and Mike are already gone. I can't see why you had to hurry and sign up. Your friends are finishing high school and you should, too. I wanted you home at least one more year, son. Call me selfish."

"Elise is still at home to keep you company. And I wasn't the only one my age to sign up. Besides, they gave us that trip to the National Rodeo in Las Vegas as an incentive. It was worth it for that alone."

Mrs. Sommers turned away, shaking her head and murmuring, "...the rodeo... We should have never given in and signed the papers."

Gwen popped in the next morning, bursting with news, until she noticed her friend Elise's downcast expression. "What's with the glum face? You'd think someone had died or something." She reached over to tousle her friend's perfectly waved hair, but Elise pulled away and made a face.

"No, it's just that J.D. is leaving today for his army training at Fort Bliss. Mother isn't very happy---him being the baby and all. You get it."

"So J.D. talked her into it. Well, she's still got you," Gwen teased. "Steady and reliable Elise. The young schoolteacher staying near the home front to educate impressionable minds."

Elise gave Gwen a light shove. "Quit it, Gwen. You make me sound more boring than I already feel." A dark look crossed her face. "I'm tired of being the dependable one, tired of staying home while everyone else is off on an adventure. I feel left out."

Gwen bit back her own news for the moment, knowing it would make Elise feel even worse. "Oops, Miss Sensitive, shake it off! You've got to know how much everyone admires your tenacity. You are the glue that keeps your family together, the glue our country needs right now. Besides, you've got that sailor-boy, Joe Howard, on a short leash. He'd probably die if he didn't get those wonderful daily letters from you."

The sound of horse hooves clip-clopping nearby interrupted the young women's conversation. Near the cedar trees in the yard, J.D. sat perched atop his prized horse, Star who was aptly named for the white star emblazoned on her roan forehead. The youth removed his hat and waved shyly at Gwen, then strolled to the front porch where his parents were eagerly awaiting his arrival.

Lainey Sommers gave her son a tight hug. With swollen eyes and trembling lips, she tried to ignore a strange sensation in the pit of her stomach. Mumbling something about having dishes to do, she ducked through the screen door back into the house.

"Make us proud, son," Jesse gave J.D. an extra hard handshake. "Remember, the dairy is always here if the army doesn't agree with you."

"Daddy, I'll take J.D. to the bus station. Wanna come with us, Gwen?" Elise jangled her keys while climbing in the family's trusty green Ford pick-up.

"Sure, why not?" Gwen squeezed in the middle after throwing J.D.'s belongings in the truck bed. The threesome soon sped off down the bumpy dirt road, leaving Jesse Sommers in a cloud of dust. Turning toward the house, he swallowed a lump in his throat. He supposed he was catching a cold.

"Hey Elise, I came over this morning to tell you some news of my own," Gwen said above the hum of the motor. "I'm taking a hiatus from college for the time being."

Elise took her eyes off the road to turn and glare at her friend. "Are you crazy? Whatever for? You're doing so well and don't you almost have your journalism degree sewn up?" Elise's lower lip stuck out in a sulk. Everyone knew how she felt about education. Plus, she didn't want Gwen to leave Mountainview like everyone else had.

"I need a break Elise. I want to put my craft to the test. I've got a gig with the El Paso Journal, one of the top newspapers in the Southwest! It's too much of an opportunity to let it slip by."

"El Paso, huh----" J.D. interjected. "Maybe we'll bump heads in the next few weeks."

"Well, it's a pretty big place, but I'd love to make contact. Maybe you can give me an insider's scoop on the prospects of war, if you know what I mean...."

J.D.'s ears turned slightly red. "Well, I doubt that someone like me is going to be handed any classified information, but I'll do my darndest for you." He looked pleased in spite of himself.

Elise swung in hard at the bus station. It was hard to say if it was because of her mood or because she was a new driver and not a smooth one at that. J.D. jumped out before she'd come to a complete stop. "You girls go on home now. I don't know how much longer it'll be till the bus pulls up."

"I'm in no hurry, little brother," declared Elise.

J.D. retrieved his meager suitcase and worn duffel bag, propping them against the station wall. Gwen's journalistic instinct surfaced and she pulled out her trusty Kodak 35 mm rangefinder camera. "Go stand by your brother, Elise," she commanded. "Say CHEESE, everyone!"

The two siblings posed awkwardly for the camera----J.D. exuding excitement about his impending adventure, Elise, glum about being left behind by her little brother, as well as her girlfriend. The photograph would be a reflection of opposites.

Too soon, gasoline fumes filled the air as the big, clumsy Greyhound pulled up. "Don't forget to make me a fresh apple pie when I get back from training," J.D. called back to his sister, smiling.

In the time it took to punch a ticket, the bus carried J.D. away. The driver was running late, so there were no more protracted farewells. Emptiness was all that was left in the air.

"It's just training for the National Guard," Elise said to her shoes. "It's not the end of the world. He'll be back in six weeks. That's what Mother doesn't comprehend."

Chapter 4

HUMMING TO HERSELF, GWEN SPED CONFIDENTLY down the streets of El Paso, pushing her old second –hand Studebaker beyond its capabilities. Ever since arriving in this border city that was part Texas, part New Mexico, and part Mexico; she had done her best to stay afloat. The transition from small-town girl to "city slicker" hadn't been as hard as she'd imagined. Plus—for one so young, she was demonstrating her wise, old soul when it came to chasing down news stories. Anything interesting, provocative, or suspicious was fair game for her reporter's nose. Even *Gwen* herself was surprised at her bold approach---she just wasn't shy when it came to news. And the news was WAR at this point. She wasn't sure where the words came from, but they flowed on the subject.

That's where her thoughts were as she turned her car into the entrance of Fort Bliss. In contrast to her clunker, Gwen herself appeared sharply dressed in a navy blue skirt, blazer, and crisp white ruffled blouse, finished off with navy pumps that tapped importantly on the street pavement. Thank goodness she'd scraped together those tips from the diner to purchase one decent business outfit!

Flashing her journalism credentials at the front desk, Gwen straightened up to her full height of 5'3" and looked gravely at the man before her. "Yes sir, I'm here to speak to the family of Private Edward Porter." The young man had been killed in a recent training exercise.

"I'll have to call his mother first. It's our protocol to notify families before we allow the media to approach their homes for interviews."

Gwen tapped her toe impatiently waiting for the officer to dial. Why did they always have rules and regulations for *everything*?

"I understand completely, Mrs. Porter. I will convey your wishes to the reporter." The man hung up and turned back to Gwen, brushing his hand across his buzz-cut. "Mrs. Porter does not want to speak to anyone at this time." He tried to conjure up a sympathetic expression for the smartly dressed young woman facing him. He wouldn't mind taking a girl like her for a cup of coffee sometime.

Crestfallen, Gwen walked away. All the starch had gone out of her sails. Now what? Truthfully, she'd been dreading the interview with the grieving mother, but at least it was *copy*, and that was the game at the El Paso Journal. She sunk down onto a bench in front of the commissary, to review her notes and remaining options.

"Gwen, I told you we'd run into each other sometime."

Gwen looked up from her work to see a tall, slightly gangly soldier with ruddy cheeks and hazel eyes looking down on her. All he needed was a cowboy hat and he'd look the same as that morning he'd dismounted his horse, Star. The only thing different about him was a fresh crew cut and a little more muscle.

"J.D., what a surprise! It is so good to see someone from Mountainview."

"Same here, Gwen. Nice to see a familiar face. Sure wish I could make it home for Christmas. For one thing, I miss the snow." He cocked his head meaningfully toward the brown mountains that looked more like mounds of dirt than anything else.

"So when *do* you expect to be home, J.D.? I'm sure it will be none too soon for your mother. She looked a little frantic that morning you took off." Gwen half-listened to herself as she peeked at her watch, already worrying about deadlines, when J.D.'s next words jolted her into the moment.

"Yeah, about that----I'm probably not supposed to talk about it, but the skinny is that we aren't going home."

"Aren't going home? What could you possibly mean, J.D.? Aren't you a member of the National Guard?"

"They've promoted us to active duty, Gwen. The word is," and he leaned in, lowering his voice, "we might be in the running for some kind of special mission."

Gwen's jaw dropped. Could she really trust this boy who was still wet behind the ears? She knew he was supposed to be at least sixteen, but he certainly didn't look it. "Surely you're mistaken. I'm around the war news office at the paper all the time, and there's been no talk of anything that extreme."

"I don't know, Gwen. It's just the scuttlebutt…" J.D. looked at her uncertainly, his ears turning every shade of red. So much for maintaining his cool!

Gwen suddenly jumped up off the bench and gathered her belongings. "This will throw your parents for a loop, if it's true. Well, I better get back to work. Good luck, J.D. and Merry Christmas." She started to stick out her hand in a cordial manner, but there was something a little lonesome in the face of her best friends' little brother. She hugged him tightly instead.

Soon she was back at the Fort Bliss Public Relations Department, staring squarely into the same sergeant's eyes. "Is it true, Sergeant, that the 200th Coastal Artillery has been upgraded to active duty? Could they be training for some special assignment? Because if they are, I think at the very least their families deserve to be informed."

"Excuse me, ma'am, but I am not privy to that information, and even if I were--- I couldn't give it to you." The sergeant began to look tired of the pesky, no longer charming girl.

"Sergeant Guthrie, what does this young woman need today?" Joining Guthrie was a very distinguished looking, well decorated fifty-something year-old man. He didn't look the sort you'd want to fool around with. Gwen took a step back from the desk ready to flee. Maybe she really was overstepping her boundaries. At the worst, she'd leave empty handed, and have to look elsewhere for a story.

There was a protracted silence, while the sergeant carefully chose his words.

"It's just that I---" Gwen burst out.

The sergeant interrupted, "She thinks she has inside information about military plans, Colonel."

"Oh really, and what might that be, Miss----?"

"Miss Mackenzie. I have reason to believe the 200th Coastal Artillery has been upgraded to active duty and has orders to remain at Fort Bliss for one year of active duty.. Can you confirm or deny this rumor, sir?"

The colonel sighed deeply and turned to the sergeant. "Dismissed, sergeant." Then he sank into the sergeant's chair and motioned for Gwen to pull up an adjoining one.

"Young lady, you need a story, and I can save a call to the paper. We were going to release this story in the next few days anyway. All I ask is that you wait until after Christmas day to print it. "I can confirm that the 200th has indeed been promoted to active duty and will stay at Fort Bliss for additional training. Is that enough for you, Miss Mackenzie"

Gwen ignored the loud buzz entering her brain, and grabbed her pen and pad with trembling hands. "Sir, how many of these men are New Mexicans......."

As the sergeant looked on with astonishment, the green reporter and the veteran colonel put their heads together to compose a story sure to make ripples across the Southwest.

ELISE walked in the house, shaking the mud and frost off her boots and looking like the cat who ate the canary. "I just picked up the El Paso Journal. I guess Gwen got her big break in journalism." She unfolded the newspaper and handed it to her mother. The dat was January 7, 1941 and the bold printed headlines jumped out at Lainey.

FDR Federalizes National Guard, 200th Coast Artillery Promoted to Active Duty for One Year, by Gwen MacKenzie.

Lainey felt ambushed as that strange sensation in the pit of her stomach resurfaced and churned hard. She slowly sunk down into her chair. "No---I don't believe it. Gwen must have gotten her facts wrong. No…." She put her face in her hands, trying to pull herself together.

Elise looked at her father doubtfully. Brows furrowed together, Jesse grabbed the paper and read every word like his life depended on it.

"Let's not overreact, everyone. True, J.D. wasn't supposed to be on active duty. We all thought he was only serving on weekends here in Grant County. So now he's risen in status." Jesse looked reassuringly at his wife, who wouldn't meet his eye. "He'll be a real soldier. Lainey, we should be darn proud of our boy." *I should have tried harder to talk him out of joining the Army. He was too young,* Jesse thought guiltily. *Oh hell, who am I kidding? I was still shy of fourteen when I left*

*home in Texas to make my own way. Is it really so
different for J.D.?*

"I want to visit him at the base if he can't come
home. I still haven't given him his Christmas
presents," Lainey announced tersely. It was bad
enough that Mike and Margo were gone; now so
was her youngest.

" Lainey, you know the military has rules and
regulations. You can't just go bustin' into Fort Bliss
looking for J.D. He's busy with Basic Training,
remember? We'll mail his gifts." He tried to
squeeze her hand, but she pulled it away.

"I don't see why we can't go, Jesse. Why not?"
Lainey tried not to whine as she dabbed the corner
of her eye with her apron .

"They'll let him out on furlough sooner or later.
You know that. Just have patience." He pointed to
a quotation in the news article, " Remember, this is
only for one year—— see, it says so right there."

Chapter 5

SHE FELL UNDER THE SPELL of his liquid brown eyes. They both smiled before she willingly fell into his arms. He kissed her so hard it almost took her breath away..

The wind-up alarm clock on Gwen's night stand began to ring incessantly. She tried to ignore it and keep the dream alive, but neither worked. Still, her heart was pounding so hard she wasn't sure which had caused it: the alarm or the dream about Charlie.

She'd stayed up typing until 3a.m. the night before and now here it was 10:30 in the morning. Yawning, she let her fingertips glide across the jar full of pennies she kept on her top of her bureau drawers. Impulsively, she grabbed one out. *I'll always carry this in my pocket for good luck until Charlie gets home safely from the army,* she vowed to herself.

Opening the curtains covering the window of her small downtown apartment, Gwen was hit by the bright El Paso sunshine. It never failed to disappoint, not even in February. And she loved the hustle bustle of this place. She was not one to look back sentimentally on much, including Mountainview. Instead, she plowed forward, full steam ahead.

She pondered what to have for breakfast, until a funny feeling came over her that she was forgetting something. Reflexively she checked her work calendar.

Ah-ha- that's it; I'm supposed to meet Captain Jake Noble from Fort Bliss for lunch today. He's giving me an update on the 200th Coastal Artillery. I wonder what their mission is....maybe I can wrestle it out of Captain Noble. But not looking like this, she thought as she surveyed herself in the mirror.

What time are we meeting? Her finger landed on an entry that said "noon", so she knew it would be a close call. *That's okay,* she thought ruefully, *that's how I live these days.* After black coffee and a hot shower, she performed magic on her hair and make-up. *Now what will I wear*? she thought scanning the tiny closet that was looked emptier than usual. She hadn't picked up her things at the dry cleaner's and the pickings were extremely slim.

A red linen A-line skirt jumped out at her, as did a white blouse that tied at the neck. After she tied the blouse, she pinned it down with a cameo brooch. Then digging through the closet, she retrieved matching pumps and a belt. She considered a hat, but decided that would be overkill. He wasn't a colonel after all.

Though she was in a hurry, she slowed down to carefully pull on her silk stockings without running them. Darn things were getting more expensive and harder to find by the day. Next she meticulously clipped them to her garter belt. *What a hassle! If only men could understand what women go through to look presentable!*

She hustled down to her old car and started the engine. It sputtered a few times, but didn't turn over. *Come on—not today.* Over and over she tried, but to no avail. Gwen had needed to buy a newer car for sometime now; however her meager news reporter's salary wouldn't allow for it.

She checked her wristwatch: 11:45. She prided herself on being prompt—what could she do? It was too late to walk. She sighed audibly before entering the apartment building to call a cab. Maybe the newspaper would pay for it.

The young woman peeked out the cab window as she passed the Plaza Theatre. The marquee boasted that "Citizen Kane" starring Orson Welles was currently playing. Soon Gwen's ride pulled up in front of the Camino Real Hotel, one of the taller buildings in the downtown El Paso area. Gwen craned her neck to admire the wonderful structure. She'd remembered that Zach T. White had first imagined the hotel in the late 1800's, and his painstaking work had finally come to fruition in 1912. The brick, steel, and terra cotta building was similar to those that withstood earthquakes in San Francisco. The interior walls were made of gypsum from White Sands.

She tipped the driver before entering the historic hotel. What had originally served as the lobby was now the Dome Bar. The bar had gotten the name due to its Tiffany glass dome-shaped ceiling. Gigantic arched windows showcased scenic views of El Paso. Usually, Gwen never tired of reveling in the architecture, but today she scanned the fine cherry wood bar and surrounding tables, looking for the Captain. He hadn't arrived yet.

Relieved, she threw herself into a corner table. Trying to look sophisticated, she ordered a dry martini. *I hope they don't card me,* she thought as she gave the waiter a disarming smile. After she got over the relief of not being late, Gwen felt new irritation rising within. Was the Captain standing her up?

She opened her purse and used a compact to inspect her lipstick. As she replaced her compact, a neatly folded letter with sprawling handwriting jumped out at her. Making sure she was still alone, she pulled it out to re-read it.

"Dear Gwen," it began, "I miss you so much. Your beauty always stays with me and keeps me from being lonely. I count the days till we can be together." He went on to grumble about the stark discipline of Army life and the politics pointing to the real possibility of war. Gwen skimmed over that part to reach the end of his letter: With all my love, Charlie.

Gwen marveled at the fact that Charlie was throwing the "love" word around so quickly. After all, they'd only been together a few times. She found this man unpredictable and exciting, a lot like her new career., She thought of her dream earlier that morning and something stirred from deep within.

"Miss Mackenzie, I presume?"

Gwen emerged from her fantasies, and tried not to blush.

"That must be one fascinating letter, based on your level of concentration." Extending a hand was a very fit young man in his late twenties looking ever so handsome in his military uniform. He met her guilty expression with a dashing grin and twinkling eyes as he sat down to join her.

Flustered, she quickly replaced the letter in her purse and dug around for her steno pad and pencil. "Captain Noble, I'm so glad you could make it. I'm writing a piece for the Journal concerning the 200th Coast Artillery's future . We believe families statewide need more information in that respect." She thought of Margo and Elise's little brother, J.D.

"Their future, as you refer to it, remains classified, Miss Mackenzie. I've heard they serve delicious green chile enchiladas here. Would you care for some?"

She narrowed her eyes at him, allowing a pregnant pause. "Well, I wouldn't want to leak top-secret information, Captain. I can't emphasize enough how the families of these young soldiers have been on pins and needles wondering where their sons and brothers are going next. Remember, it's all been very new and unexpected. These boys only signed up for the National Guard. And, no thank-you, I'll pass on the enchiladas. I'm still working on this for breakfast," she said nodding to her martini.

"What I can tell you is that we are training everyday in the desert--- training rigorously with anti-aircraft, for example. I'm sure I can depend on you to soothe people's nerves by assuring them that we are training their boys to be the very best soldiers possible—even in the case of war. And you'll be sorry for passing up the enchiladas." Noble proceeded to give Gwen a hand-out detailing the training exercises at Fort Bliss.

The P.R. folks are good on base, Gwen admitted grudgingly to herself as she perused the papers. "Captain, can I come out and photograph the men in action?"

"Probably. It all depends on Army approval.... *and* whether or not we could meet for--- say--- dinner to discuss this further." Noble polished off his bourbon on the rocks before issuing his signature charming smile.

Automatically, Gwen's eyes went to his left ring finger. No wedding band. And the man was persistant. She was tempted. He seemed very nice, as well as extremely attractive. Yes—she was lonely. She hadn't been on a real date since the dance with Charlie, if you could call that a date. Her mind reverted to the letter in the purse. She did have that to hold onto. Charlie sounded like he really cared about her. It wasn't his fault he was so far away, working for the good of the country. She reached down to feel the penny in her pocket.

Awkwardly, she began, "I'm sorry, but I can't. I'm seeing someone else."

Noting his crestfallen expression, she added, "I do appreciate your offer." Standing up, she smoothed her skirt, and tossed her brunette waves. "I better get over to the news desk or heads will roll. I'll be waiting for approval on those photographs, Captain, and I promise to write an article reflecting the dedication of your men."

Without further ado, the young woman walked out of the bar, leaving Noble to stare longingly after her.

Chapter 6

THE FRANKLIN MOUNTAINS ROSE above the desert terrain where the Fort Bliss soldiers trained. The sky was azure blue while the air was bone dry. J.D. couldn't remember a single late February being this warm in Mountainview. Must be near 80 degrees. And rain was *never* in the forecast around here.

Since army boots hadn't been issued yet, J.D. still had on his old high top sneakers from home. He shook them out daily to make sure no scorpions or centipedes were lodged inside. Today he wondered how much protection they would be if a rattlesnake were to come crawling out from a nearby yellow- blossomed prickly pear cactus

The young soldier noticed that his friend, Pat, was vigorously rubbing his temples . "You guys have too much fun in Juarez last night?"

"I'm tellin' you, J.D., you shoulda come. The beer flows like water and the senoritas—well, there's no words to describe them!" He winked at J.D.

"That's okay, Pat. You're the one with the hangover in this 100 degree heat. I feel fine."

"Face it, J.D. You're just jealous. What are you afraid of, buddy? Don't tell me you're afraid to raise a little hell."

J.D. pretended to ignore him as he reloaded his gun. The truth was a little more complicated than anything Pat could imagine. Yes, he *was* afraid. He was one of the youngest at age sixteen. He'd promised his folks he would do his best. He knew that didn't include drinking and carousing in Mexico. The closest he ever got to the place was right here , where he could squint across the Rio Grande River at the poverty-stricken shanty towns sprawled over the dirt hills.

Still, he was curious. The thought of fooling around with a woman made him blush. He'd only just now learned how to dance with one. What did he know about the birds and the bees? Basically nothing. He never even had a high school sweetheart. Sure, some of the girls were quite friendly, but he kept his mind on his horses. He wasn't tongue-tied around the horses.

Maybe he should try Juarez. Just once. If he could overcome his shyness, that is.

"J.D. Sommers. You're next, private!"

J.D. grabbed his 30 calibre rifle and got in position for his turn at target practice. Because he'd always hunted with Daddy, he was comfortable with guns. A circular target on a paper 200 yards away was different than a dodgy animal, and not necessarily easier, for some reason. His head moved at the last second and he missed altogether.

A red flag dramatically emerged from behind the target.

"Maggie's drawers!!" J.D. hated to hear the slang term for "total miss". Everyone joined in, hooting and hollering. J.D. reddened; laughing with the others. One more try. Taking a deep breath, he aimed his gun and stilled his body. Time to clamp down. This time he almost hit the bull's eye. *Whew,* he thought with relief. *What a difference a little concentration could make.*

"Okay, Sommers, better. Take a break. Miguel Armendariz, step up."

Gratefully, J.D. grabbed his canteen and headed for the shade of a tarp strung between some higher brush. Sitting on the rocky sand next to his rifle, J.D. sipped the lukewarm water carefully, assessing his situation.

Basic training was almost behind him. It had run on an extremely disciplined schedule. First thing in the morning was reveille, which began with that damn bugle player rudely disturbing his sleep before it was even light outside. The men rolled out of bed, put on their fatigues, and got into formation for roll call.

Next, J.D. had to make his bed according to Army regulation. At first, he was no good at it. It didn't help having the top bunk either. After thirteen weeks of tough inspection, he'd finally gotten the hang of it. He couldn't wait to see the look on his mother's face the first time he tried it on his bed at home.

After bed making came breakfast. It was a good idea to arrive early in order to get seconds. J.D. had learned that early on. It seemed like no matter how much he ate, he was bound to burn it off or turn it into lean muscle. His newly sculpted physique was a testimony to that.

The dreaded rifle inspection was next . If there was even one speck of dirt on a soldier's gun, he'd be sent to clean the latrines. J.D. found this out the hard way. Now his gun remained spotless at all times. Still, the biggest part of the day was spent on calisthenics and close order drills. *I bet we walked 500 miles drilling,* J.D. reflected.

Yeah, thirteen weeks he'd been here, and he hadn't washed out yet!! The young man couldn't help but wonder what lay ahead for the 200th Coast Artillery. The government had asked them to stand ready for a solid year. He could do that. And after all the predictable drills, J.D. was hungry for a little excitement and adventure. Maybe his unit would get sent somewhere besides this barren desert.

Life was a book, and he couldn't wait to turn the next page.

Chapter 7

IT WAS A LAZY SUMMER SUNDAY in El Paso. The temperatures had cooled thanks to the dramatic monsoons that blew in over the Franklin Mountains. The thunder and lightning were spectacular, and rain came in sheets, flooding the parched city streets. It was well past mid-morning, and Gwen felt no compulsion to get up, so she lay there in her summer pajamas, contemplating life and its options.

Gwen thought about what was going on at Fort Bliss, and nationally as well. The country was on the verge of war. The president knew it, most of the Congress knew it, and the citizens knew it, too. Of course, no one really wanted it, but as the days went by, there seemed to be fewer and fewer alternatives.

She couldn't help but think of Hitler. She knew he was a power hungry dictator who was attacking other countries without provocation, but she wondered if the rumors were true about the atrocities he was committing against the Jews and other people he deemed subhuman. She shivered just thinking of the man.

Then there was Japan with their rapidly growing imperialism, and their inhumane treatment of the Chinese people. Gwen also realized Italy and Spain weren't far behind in this new coalition of world terror.

So many people she knew were already headed overseas, helping the world stand up to these enemies of peace. Like many of her school mates, Margo and her brother, Mike, were on their way. The boy, J.D., would soon follow. She let her mind come to a firm rest on Charlie. She pictured him in uniform, so drop-dead attractive and spirited. She smiled as she remembered how many times he said he couldn't wait to "kick some butt".

She idly wondered what he was doing as she lay in bed, holding onto his good luck penny. She'd only heard from him sporadically, and his letters gave away little. He didn't wax poetic about his feelings, beyond the word, "love" at the end of each letter. She forgave him for not being more forthcoming, concluding that writing wasn't his forte.

I want to be in the heat of things like everyone else. El Paso is too tame for me. It's time to move on to bigger things. I need to go overseas. Involuntarily, Gwen pictured her dead mother. What would she want her to do? Her siblings were in high school now; one even had a part-time job. Her father would soon be remarried; he seemed happy enough. Still, she knew he wanted her to stay nearby and "be a good girl."

Without warning, her mother's voice burst through her brain, loud and clear: Follow your dreams, Gwendolyn. Live life to the fullest. You know that's what I want for you.

Gwen remembered her mother's fondest hopes and wishes. Mary Wright was developing a passion for photography when she met Brian Mackenzie, a very charming and hardworking young man employed by the railroad. When Mary wed Brian, she put aside her photography dreams, and had a family instead. The roaring twenties offered a lot of opportunities for women; however, so Mary hoped to resume her photography dream when the kids got older. She never did.

Rheumatic fever took her life when the kids were older and her dream stayed just that: a dream.

It had been a long time since Gwen had allowed herself to dwell on her mother's memory. Her eyes momentarily filled with tears, but she immediately brushed them away. She mustn't lose control when she thought of her mother, or she might never get it back.

Mom would want me to be strong. She summoned up a smile. *I know you'd want me to go where my writing takes me, even if it is far from home.*

With resolve she decided, *I'm putting in for a transfer. I'll continue to send the family part of my paycheck though they really do seem to be getting along just fine.* Quickly, she typed a memo to her boss requesting a move to the overseas desk of the sister newspaper. She felt much better once she'd put it in the envelope.

SHE STOOD in front of Mr. Hartley, trying to discern his expression as he read her request. The man was short and wiry with nerves of steel. No one—not even his wife— went against him once his mind was made up. Under his thick brows were intellectual eyes that caught everything. The wheels were always turning. She swallowed hard, feeling lucky to have his attention for this split second.

"Sir, I need to be where the real action is. When we go to war, and it will be *when,* not *if,* I want to be in the thick of things. I want to let people know what war looks, smells and tastes like. I can't do that sitting in El Paso, Texas, sir."

"Well, Miss Mackenzie, I hope you're wrong about war being imminent." Hartley furrowed his brow and chewed his lip. "If it is, you understand this isn't child's play, right? War is dangerous, ugly, and it's not the best place for a young woman with her whole future ahead of her. I'll need assurance that your family is alright with this." Gwen nodded at him enthusiastically. "On the other hand, we could use a fresh set of eyes over there. Your articles have been on-target and well-written. People want to read what you write. Not everybody has that special ability. I'll keep that in mind when I consider your transfer request."

Gruffly, he added, "And Miss Mackenzie, if I grant it, there will be no turning back— no running home to Mommy if things get too tough."

"My mother passed away some years ago," Gwen replied flatly. "And if you send me, I will stay until the job is done. You can count on that, sir."

He tapped his fingers nervously on the desk and she knew she had him. She was going overseas to be a war correspondent! As she exited the office, she whispered silently to the heavens, *No regrets, Mom.*

Chapter 8

CAMP LUNA, named after Hispanic soldier Maximiliano Luna, was in northern New Mexico, just above the small town of Las Vegas. The terrain of San Miguel county was transitional: grassy plains that met up with pine-dotted land. It was much cooler than Fort Bliss was in August, and for that alone, the men of the 200th Coastal Artillery were grateful.

The sergeant's voice broke into the morning routine. "Get on your new uniforms and get in formation, men. The colonel has an important announcement."

J.D. was happy to remove his helmet. First issued in WWI, it felt like a tin can on his head. He replaced it with a crisply pleated cap, then straightened his tie and buttoned his belted thigh length jacket. He checked his collar one more time, wondering what all the fuss was about. What kind of announcement was the colonel going to make?

Colonel Sage stepped in front of the regiment, hands behind his back, feet apart. He beamed at his soldiers. "Men—you have accomplished a lot over the past eight months. Whatever we've asked for, you've stepped up to the task. You've given one hundred per cent."

"There were 2300 new recruits to this regiment—all coming from different walks of life, but managing to come together for a common cause."

J.D. surveyed his neighbors. He recalled back when they had first arrived. The others had called the New Mexico boys "cowboys, Mexicans, and Indians." Now they simply felt like brothers.

"Men, it is my honor and privilege to announce that you have been named *the best anti-aircraft Regiment for use in areas of critical military importance!*" The common area erupted in hooting and clapping. The noise was deafening. The colonel waited for the celebration to wind down.

"As a reward for your hard work, you will be sent on a top-notch mission very soon." As the colonel expected, his men became quiet. "It will be overseas., of course." J.D. could've heard a pin drop. A little knot began forming in his stomach. "But for now, we'd like to send you back to several towns in your home states for some parades and the like. You'll get to show off your newly honed skills to family and friends. It will be one hell of a send-off, I promise you that!" The quiet changed once more into hoopla among the troops.

J.D. wondered if they'd get to Mountainview for a parade. It wasn't as big as Albuquerque or Santa Fe, or Las Cruces. A guy could still hope though. The chance to wave to his parents on a street crowded with on-lookers filled him with pride. Maybe the kids from high school would come. Maybe some of the pretty girls would admire his uniform and worry for his safety. Maybe his past teachers would realize that he, J.D. Sommers, had bigger fish to fry than merely solving arithmetic problems or diagraming sentences.

⁕⁖⁘ ⁙⁕⁖⁘ ⁙⁕⁖⁘ ⁙

SEPTEMBER SUN RAYS fell in a different slant across the kitchen as Lainey sat at the table shelling black-eyed peas. Her mind was at peace for a change. It was a gift she gladly accepted.

The screen door slammed and she looked up to see Jesse trudging in.

"Fresh milk for the cook!" he said while placing a bottle in the ice box.

"Glad the dairy business remembers me once in awhile," she said with a smile. "Maybe I'll bake some fresh apple breads for everyone. Freeze some to send to Mike and Margo. The others we can take directly to J.D."

"Now, hold on a minute. When exactly do you think we'll get a chance to do that? We just saw him in that parade up north a few weeks ago. And the unit has barely returned to Fort Bliss. I can't afford to be takin' off work all the time, Lainey."

"Oh, but Jesse, he looked so handsome in his uniform, didn't he?" she asked, ignoring her husband's question. "I only wish we could have moved in closer....so many people on the sidewalks in big cities," she added wistfully. No one spoke until a pod full of peas scattered on the floor. "Oh shoot, you're breakin' my concentration! Now get on out of my kitchen," she playfully shooed him away.

"So we'll wait awhile before taking J.D. those breads," he countered.

Lainey's features softened and her voice became beguiling. Jesse knew that look and recognized that tone. He tried to arm himself with verbal ammunition.

"Why don't we go over next weekend. Something tells me we should. I can feel it in my bones, Jesse." He began to put up a fake protest. "I know, I know. We don't have the money to stay in a fancy hotel like we did in Santa Fe. I don't care *where* we stay. We can pitch a tent in the foothills for all I care. Please dear, don't say no."

Jesse knew he'd lost the battle when she opened her mouth. He secretly wanted to see his youngest son face-to-face before he was shipped out. That measly visit in the spring when J.D. had finished boot camp wasn't satisfying. It left him wanting more time alone with his son. Lainey was probably right. They better make up their mind to go to El Paso while he was still in the vicinity.

"Okay, Lainey, you win. Next weekend it is. But you realize we'll have to stay out of the way of the military. Rules are rules. The visit will have to be on their terms."

"Thank-you, Jesse. She wiped her hands on her red-checked apron and stood to give him a big hug. "I better get started on those breads." The light in her eyes calmed any doubts her husband harbored.

Two days later, an envelope with J.D.'s casual, sprawling penmanship appeared in the mail.

14 September, 1941

Dear Mother and Daddy,

I am writing this on the fly, so I hope you can make out my handwriting.

I know this wasn't how I planned it, but in a few days we're going on a train to San Francisco! From there, we're shipping out, but we don't know where exactly. As you know, our award for being the best anti-aircraft regiment made this mission possible.

Wish I could have seen you before we left, but now there's no time. It's all happening real fast. Maybe this time next year it'll be over. For now, we've got some Japanese butts to kick. (Sorry, mother.)

Say bye to Elise for me, and Margo and Mike when you next talk to them. Please give Star the oats she likes so much. I'll pay you back later.

I wanted to see the world---looks like I will!

J..D.

P.S. Don't worry about me---I'll be fine.

Lainey folded and refolded the letter. She looked at Jesse. "Our sixteen year-old-son is on his way on a ship to God knows where as we speak. I never even got to tell him good-bye.... "

Jesse put his arm around his wife but she shrugged it off. "We've talked about this a hundred times. The boy wasn't happy in school. He was itching for his independence. If it wasn't this, it would have been something else, maybe something a lot more troublesome." He made her look at him. "This is honorable, Lainey. God, I'm proud of our son. Aren't you?"

"Of course I am. I'm proud of all four of our children. Where is it written that a mother can't be proud of her children and afraid for them at the same time?"

" Fathers feel that way too. Lainey. Hey, last time I checked, we weren't in a war. Our kids are doing a little peacekeeping --- remember Roosevelt is only *assisting* England and France. They're the countries under attack, not us. We've been lucky enough to stay out of it so far. Let's keep our fingers crossed." He hugged his wife and this time she begrudgingly let him. "Where's the atlas? I want to see where our son might be headed. Leave it to that lucky son-of-a-gun to get sent to some tropical island. Doesn't sound like a hardship to me." He turned away from Laney to head for the bookshelf, letting the smile plastered on his face fall away, leaving a worried frown in its place.

Chapter 9

J.D. AWOKE COVERED IN MOSQUITOES and perspiration. It was hot in October and he sweated even when it rained. The Philippine Islands had not proved to be the paradise he'd hoped for. If this was seeing the world, well--- he liked home better. The 200th (or "the Regiment" as they liked to be called) had landed several days before and he was still recovering from his experience at sea. Much to the amusement of his fellow soldiers, he'd never found his sea legs for the whole eighteen day voyage. Most of his time had been spent on the S.S. Coolidge's ship railing, nauseated and trying to hold down the smallest morsels of food. He couldn't even enjoy the five hour layover in Honolulu.

"Tough luck, J.D." joked his bunkmate, Jimmy Farley, a beefy guy who was never too seasick to miss a meal. "Just keep feeding those fish. They appreciate your generosity."

J.D. was too weak to take the slightest playful swing at Jimmy. *I'll get him once we dock.* The heck with overseas deployment, he thought miserably. *My next assignment will be stateside.*

Even after disembarkment, he had yet to find his land legs, as he thought of them. He wouldn't admit to a soul that his legs were rubbery and he was as weak as a baby. It didn't help that Sergeant Garrett was in foul spirits. "How are we supposed to shoot the damn Japs with barely any guns and ammo?" the sarge would loudly ask the air, "And where the hell are the K-Rations? At least they're edible. This slop they're giving us ain't."

The questions made J.D. uncomfortable. *Where was all the equipment, supplies, and ammo?* He was itching to get in some target practice, using the standard M/carbines in this overgrown terrain. Luckily, he'd been hunting with Daddy and Mike since he was big enough to hold a gun, but that didn't qualify him to be a sharpshooter in the U.S. Army. Yeah, he'd practiced some in the Ft. Bliss desert, but he needed to get his bearing *now,* in this jungle.

He thought again about why they were here. The unit was defending Fort Stotsenburg, the largest American base on the island, from possible attack by the enemy. *But who were the enemy anyway?* As far as he could tell, his worst enemy had so far been the "skeeters". *Where was this Japanese aggression they kept referring to?* He didn't really get it. He was supposed to be on the lookout for spies at all times. *We're not at war with the Japanese, or are we? Maybe it's an undeclared war or something,* he reasoned. *I'm just a private.*

Better shut up and do as I'm told. With that, he would rise at 5 a.m., shine his second hand boots, eat the pasty porridge they called breakfast, and march in the warm, humid island rains past the tall palm trees. He considered it a good day if he managed not to scratch his mounting insect bites till they were bloody.

The only respite J.D. got from the monotony came from card playing with the guys, looking at the bows and arrows the pygmies were trying to sell, and dreaming about the village women who stared at him boldly. J.D. was too modest to realize he was fast becoming a very handsome young man, a fact not lost on the local Filipino women who were curious about these newest American soldiers.

One girl in particular was on the same corner at the same time every day, as he passed by. She was old enough to have a recently developed bust and waistline. Her brown oval eyes seemed to melt as she looked up at him when he passed--- her dark, long curly hair, cascading over her newfound curves.

It was hard to keep his mind on the job with such distractions. How he wished he were free to talk to her. Unlike many of his fellow soldiers from New Mexico, he wasn't totally fluent in Spanish, but he was getting there. In any case, he'd figure out a way to communicate with her. He recognized *beautiful* in any language on earth.

Problem was his experience with the opposite sex was limited. He had only recently learned how to dance, thanks to his older sister; and he still felt like he had two left feet. He'd never had a serious girlfriend, never been with a woman. He was sixteen and stuck out in the middle of nowhere, with little or no prospect for romance. *Didn't a guy have a right to dream every now and then?* He pinned his hopes on the beautiful young girl who made eyes at him as he marched by. One day, he would summon up his courage to look straight into her eyes and maybe say something. Who knew what could happen next?

Chapter 10

IN EARLY DECEMBER OF 1941, J.D.'s unit was standing in formation at 5:30 a.m. sharp. Their officer had been especially tenacious that morning, throwing the late sleepers out of their dug-outs like they were rag dolls. *What was the man's problem anyway?* J. D wondered. Sarge had been acting very nervous as of late. *Why? It's just another march through the jungle, same as every day for the two and a half months they'd been here.* He automatically felt in his pocket for the gum and candy always had on hand for Marisol, the pretty Filipino girl. He hoped she'd have a flower for him later today.

"Attention! Men, this is it!" barked the commanding officer, bearing down on the troops with steely eyes. "Pearl Harbor, in Hawaii, was attacked thirty minutes ago by the Japanese. Battleships were destroyed with the men still inside." His words were met with stunned silence. No one looked at one another.

"Should it happen, we will be ready as possible for an attack on Philippine soil." Now the sideward glances began. "I know many of you haven't been issued your gun. As we speak, the anti-aircraft guns are being unpacked. A number of you will be sent to help with that. We need others to distribute the ammo. Every man will be armed ASAP. You will receive your position from your own commander. And men, all I ask is that you do your best under these circumstances. Remember your training. You are tough and brave Americans! We can beat these sons-of-bitches!" The man beamed at his troops. The last thing he needed was panic and hysteria. His men responded quietly, marching rapidly to their posts with purpose.

J.D.'s body was filled with competing emotions. Surges of adrenaline were running through his veins. Yes, he wanted to take a shot at those damn Japs. *Who did they think they were--- sneaking up on our country like that*? On the other hand, his sixteen-year-old hands were shaking as he loaded his gun with sweaty palms. This was the real thing---*war*--- and he'd never been in one before. What was he supposed to do next?

Just remember the war games at Fort Bliss, he told himself firmly, steadying his hands and his nerves. *My helmet*, he thought abruptly, *where is it?* His head suddenly felt naked and exposed, like it might get bombed to bits without warning. After tearing around the area, he finally found it.

With little time to spare, he arrived at his post. Around him, some looked wary, some looked excited, but all looked like soldiers on this warm Sunday morning in December. The waiting game began.

At 12:30, just as they broke out their lunch rations, a barely discernible drone became evident. J. D. thought the sound could be a swarm of mosquitoes. Gradually it got louder until it was a buzz-z-z-z. He looked up, but the foliage filled terrain blocked a good view of the sky. J.D. peered helplessly across the tall trees. "Can you see anything, George?" His stomach churned as he waited for an answer from the next man over. He was no longer hungry for lunch.

"Incoming planes!" yelled Kiki Chavez. The military installation abruptly resembled a bed of ants as the men scrambled for position on the anti-aircraft guns.

Maybe it's our guys showing some force , thought J.D. hopefully. The loud buzz was now directly overhead. J.D.'s hair stood on end right before the first bomb's explosion. His fellow soldiers automatically began shooting their guns at the overhead planes. He found himself doing the same thing. "Don't think----just react" had been his trainers' mantra at Ft. Bliss.

Corporal Murray, a munitions expert, was manning the nearest "ack-ack" gun, as he affectionately called it. Before long, he caught fire from a strafing plane and he fell to the ground, blood gushing from a bullet wound in the arm. "I'm okay" he cried, "Keep shooting, men! Step up, Vasquez!"

Joaquin Vasquez looked around blankly. "Who me?" he said tentatively stepping up to the gun stand. He had never practiced on a 37 mm, which was from the WWI era. He aimed directly at the planes in the sky and began shooting.

"No, no, you're doing it all wrong! Does anyone know what leading the target means?" Murray growled the question.

J.D. remembered that phrase well: Daddy had always told him to aim and shoot the gun well ahead of the deer, instead of aiming right at it. He called it, "leading the target".

"Sir, I've never manned one of these before, but I know what leading the target means," Vasquez moved aside and J.D. stepped into shooting position.

He took shot after shot, but the Japanese Zeroes seemed to hang in the sky, mocking the American soldiers. Why didn't they fall?

A bullet whizzed right by J.D.'s ear. The taste of fear began to choke the teenager. "Sir, I'm trying as hard as I can!" he screamed out.

"Dammit, Sommers, the powder fuse trains don't look to be goin' high enough. How old are those guns, anyhow? It's not your fault, son. Be patient. One of these hot dogs will come in too close to the party and then you get him…" Murray passed out.

"He needs a doctor! Someone take him!"

They carried Murray away and J.D. was left without guidance. The deafening blast of the big gun was all he heard, and the planes coming at him was all he saw. He gritted his teeth. *Someone come in closer,* he begged. He was running low on ammo, and he didn't know where more was. He had never even loaded one of these suckers before.

In answer to his prayer, one Zero boldly dove in closer. J.D. knew a bomb would soon follow. *Okay, now just remember what daddy said about the deer…..* POW! He missed him. Damn! He felt like running for cover. *Keep shooting, J.D.* Bam,Bam,Bam--- the Japanese aircraft was on fire---it'd been hit!! It made a few more weak loops in the air before smashing to the ground. Everyone cheered for J.D. and this small victory. He'd never killed anyone before, but then again, he'd never had anyone try to kill him. It was all confusing to his young brain and he didn't have time to *feel* anyhow. The planes kept coming.

The afternoon was endless and became a dull blur in J.D.'s mind. Gunfire... the smell of planes in the Army hangar burning... screams of pain and desperation... blood, and endless bomb blasts. He wanted to make it all stop. Just when he thought he could stand no more, it did stop. The Japanese left, the guns stopped shooting, and there was nothing in the air but deadly silence.

By early evening a group of men gathered at the mess tent. "We'll whip those Japs before they know what hit 'em," one man J.D. didn't know exclaimed.

"MacArthur's gonna surround this island with our country's best warships. We'll get back our superior air cover. And hell, we downed five of their planes today with those lousy guns; we'll get even more next time when we get better artillery!"

Someone slapped J.D. on the back. "Heard you were one of those who shot down a plane. Good job, Sommers." J.D. looked back to see KiKi beaming at him. Soon many in the group came up to shake his hand. They were treating him like a hero, but he didn't feel heroic. He felt tired, shaken, and somehow guilty for gloating over anyone's loss of life, even the damn Japs'.

"Come on, now, Sommers, look alive! Have a beer on me, buddy. You deserve it!" Someone handed J.D. one of many beers being passed around. *Where did they get beer? What would Daddy and Mother think?* Oh well, they were thousands of miles away and he was trapped here in the jungle with nothing but mosquitoes and guns.

His friend, Jimmy, was now addressing the crowd. "The Japs will pay for this. We'll kick their ass! We have Right on our side!!"

The other men cheered, but not J.D., who suddenly felt nauseous. The beer hadn't gone down so well. He stepped into the bushes and threw up. It was time to head back to the trenches. That kind of talk made him feel uneasy, anyway. He may have been sixteen, but he was learning fast that no one, not even the "good guys" were invincible. He lay on his bedroll and tried to rest, but he couldn't turn off the day's events that flashed in front of his eyes. His heart kept pounding all night long, while his ears half-listened for the Japanese planes to return once again.

BACK IN THE UNITED STATES, Josie Price, from next door, came running up the lane to the Sommers' house at midafternoon. She ferociously knocked on the back screen door.

"Anybody home?" She peered in the house. "Oh, Lainey, thank God you're here. Did you hear the news? We've been attacked by the Japanese--- first Hawaii and then the Philippines!"

Chapter 11

FRAGRANT BOUGHS OF HOLLY lined the table tops, fresh mistletoe hung over the doorway, and the crooked little juniper tree was strung with popcorn, cranberries, and Lainey's hope. It was a little early for Christmas to adorn the Sommers household, but no one seemed to notice. On this day, no one noticed the decorations at all.

Their expressions grim, Jesse, Lainey, and Elise huddled around the old Philco radio.

"Yesterday, Dec. 7, 1941, a date which will live in infamy," boomed FDR, "the United States of America was suddenly deliberately attacked by naval and air forces of the Empire of Japan."

No one spoke or even batted an eye. Lainey's mouth tightened in a line so small it could barely be seen. Jesse repeatedly clenched his jaw and Elise realized she'd never seen her parents look so unhappy.

"...I regret to tell you that over 3,000 American lives have been lost," the president's baritone continued. "....Because of this unprovoked, dastardly attack by Japan, I ask that the Congress declare a state of war!'"

Lainey's hands flew to cover her mouth and all the blood drained from her face. "I knew something like this would happen sooner or later," she whispered.

Elise helped her mother sit down on the worn flower-patterned sofa. She searched for words of comfort. "Mother, Margo and Mike were aware of what they were getting into when they joined the armed forces. Their eyes were wide open. They're probably cheering right now. They've both been ready to fight for a long time now. Though I sincerely doubt Margo will see the front line..."

Lainey had to smile momentarily. "If she has her way, she will. You're right, Elise, Hirohito and Hitler had better watch out for those two." She looked up at her husband. "But what about J.D.? The Philippines were just attacked. He's only a baby." *Our country is at war today and so are my children,* she thought, *And J.D. is right smack in the middle of it. He didn't have to be. It's my fault for signing those enlistment papers... We should have stood up to him and told him no...What kind of parents are we?*

Jesse tenderly brushed a lock of hair sprinkled with some grey he'd never seen before out of his wife's face. "Like it or not, Lainey, J.D. is a young man now. Let's all take a deep breath and calm down." Jesse poured a glass of whiskey and lit his pipe. Elise had never seen him do that midday.

Ignoring her husband, Lainey got up and went outside in the cold. Elise started to get up, but Jesse put up his brown calloused hand. "Best not to follow her, sis. She needs to be alone."

The father and daughter heard Lainey whistle and call for Star until J.D.'s filly knickered in response. For what seemed like forever, Elise leaned on the south window, watching her mother stroke Star's mane. The older woman spoke to the horse as if it were human.

When the daughter could watch no more, she turned around in time to see her father take one last swig of whiskey before leaving the room.

CHRISTMAS of '41 was a dismal affair for the Sommers family. No one remembered to play joyous carols on the phonograph. Peals of laughter were seldom heard. The only thing that hung in the air was anxiety. Rationing for the newly minted war was already underway in earnest, leaving store shelves half-empty and lacking in variety. The number and cost of the gifts under the Sommers' tree was considerably less than in years gone by. Lainey and Jesse decided to forego presents to each other, focusing instead on decent items for their sons and daughters. Lainey insisted on having all the gifts ready under the tree, "just in case" as she put it. Each one was wrapped with loving care.

Even Margo's unexpected arrival home didn't help much. Excited to be home from training on a lucky week's furlough, the younger Sommers daughter tried her best to inject a little frivolity into this hushed version of her childhood home. Still, it seemed that from the moment her long legs set foot at the old homestead, everything was amiss.

Entering the doorway, Margo stood tall and straight in her new uniform, and appeared as neat as a pin with her starched collar and tie. At five feet, eleven inches, she was now half a foot taller than her mother, and could almost look her father directly in the eye. What she saw in her parents' faces drained the holiday excitement right out of her.

"Come on now, it's *Christmas,* Mother and Daddy! I'm so glad just to be *home."* She reached hopefully in the biscuit tin, only to come up empty handed. "I know—why don't I make everyone a fruitcake for dessert tonight?" She gave her mother a giant bear hug.

"You relax, Margo. Elise and I will scrape something together, won't we?" Lainey gave Elise a sideways look, and Elise responded by rolling her eyes. Margo actually hated to cook and rarely even attempted to boil water. Elise, on the other hand, had been cooking with her mother since she was big enough to reach the stove on a stool.

"Face it, Mother, she just wants to get a head start on the rum!" With a laugh, Elise elbowed her younger sister, and finally a small smile escaped Lainey's lips.

The big old platter decorated with a colorful rooster was always hauled out on the holidays. It was just the right size for the succulent roast turkey prepared by Lainey every year. This year, the rooster stayed put on the shelf.

Mike and J.D.'s gifts remained untouched under the tree. On the morning after Christmas, they looked larger and more forlorn than ever. They were begging to be opened and there was clearly no one there to open them. Lainey hastily began packing her sons' presents away in the back closet. Once that job was done, the crooked little tree stood alone, so she asked the girls to help her dismantle it. Soon there was no hint of the Christmas that barely got noticed in 1941.

Chapter 12

THE U.S. TRANSPORT SHIP was leaving the waters of the Pacific Ocean and heading into the Indian Ocean that spring day of '42. On the far off coastline awaited India, Thailand, and Burma, which was right below China. Mike swabbed the aft deck, while mulling over his new destination.

"Look alive, friend! Put some elbow grease into that!" Charlie gave him a lazy smile.

"Cut the advice or you'll find yourself holding the mop." Mike looked up with his own likeable grin.

"So, what are you looking all serious about?"

Mike leaned pensively against the ship's railing. "Just tryin' to figure out what we're doing heading to this place called Burma. We just passed by the real action over in the Philippines. That's where my brother is being attacked. I wish I could turn this ship around." He stabbed the deck with the mop to emphasize his point.

"Captain says we gotta keep the Japs occupied in this direction." Charlie replied. "Gotta keep the Burma Road open so the Chinese can receive munitions to fight the Japs with. Weren't you listening when captain outlined it on the board the other day?"

"I want to fight the Japs head-on! Supplying other countries so they can do the fighting isn't why I signed up."

"I know what you mean. Just be patient. We'll get our turn, Mike. And when we do---" Charlie made a gun with his fingers, taking aim, "I can't wait to shoot one of those Nip bastards right between the eyes." He laughed raucously.

Mike suddenly felt like dropping the subject. "Are there any monsoon rains in the Indian Ocean in March? I hope not , cause the deck is clean and dry. I'm through for now." He headed for the supply closet with his mop and bucket. Charlie followed, all the while talking about how he was going to kick some Japanese butt. As Mike deposited the mop, he noticed two mournful brown eyes peering out beneath the rags on the lower shelf. It was a dog!

"What'cha doin' here, buddy?" Mike said softly. He pulled the dog out and gave it the once over. The animal was medium sized, but skinny and scruffy, with a brownish-grey coat and dull white chest and feet. One of his ears was quite frayed and his black nose was scraped. It was clear he had been neglected or forgotten for some time now. Mike scratched his ears and patted his back. The dog responded with a friendly wag of his ragged tail, his pink tongue panting to form a canine smile.

"How in the world did you get on board?" he asked. "I'll bet you're thirsty. Want some water, fella?"

"What do you know--- a dog!" Charlie loudly announced. "What are the chances?"

"Keep it down, Charlie. A dog is against regulations. We need to figure this out first."

For the rest of the day, Mike kept the dog under wraps. He fed and watered him, and cleaned his coat as best he could. He let him sleep behind his duffel bag where no one was the wiser.

The next day, the whole unit was up top for a drill.

"Attention! About face!"

Lines of men fell into sharp formation. Mike was trying to keep his mind on the repetitive movements when a small skirmish broke out. Apparently, the stowaway dog had chosen this moment to make his appearance known.

He was nervously whining, while running in circles until he settled on his haunches next to Charlie. All of the men stopped in their tracks to stare at the dog as though they'd never seen one in their lives.

"What's the meaning of this, private Murdoch? Do you know how this dog got on board?" grumbled the captain.

"Charlie grimly shook his head. "No, sir, I've never seen it in my life." He gave the dog a swift kick in the ribs, which sent it sprawling across the deck. Once he got his bearings, the dog's ears pricked up to attention, and he began to howl mournfully.

"Jeez, Charlie, look what you did. Made the poor thing cry!" teased one of the men.

"He never howled like that before—wonder what's wrong with him," Mike wondered aloud to the man next to him.

"Dogs will howl at noises that hurt their ears, " someone observed.

Reflexively, the men looked skyward. A bomb was falling in their direction! "Get below deck!" screamed the captain. "Gunners, take your positions and fire on the bombers!"

Everyone scrambled. Mike grabbed the howling dog. It was over in the blink of an eye. Miraculously, the giant transport tanker sustained very little damage and there were no reported casualties. Apparently, the enemy was doing a test run.

"Damn that was close," Steven Ramo said to Mike. "That dog of yours is a godsend. He hears the bombs before we do!" He ruffled the stowaway's fur affectionately.

A crowd gathered around the animal. A hero had been born. Everyone wanted to pet him until they were forced to make way for the captain.

"Private Sommers, is this your dog? And if it is, how in tarnation did he get on board this ship?"

Mike came to attention. "He's not mine, sir. I found him in the supply closet, but I don't know how he got there. Requesting permission to take care of him until we make land."

"Permission granted, Private Sommers. He's a useful addition to our unit, especially in the area of bomb detection." The captain patted the canine's head. "Just make sure he's obedient." A cheer erupted for the newly minted army mascot.

That evening, Mike fed the dog extra scraps that he'd saved from the mess hall. "You deserve a name." Mike squinted his eyes, sizing up his new friend. "Buddy. That's it. We'll call you Buddy. You were definitely everyone's buddy today."

Buddy crawled up on Mike's feet and sighed deeply. He was clearly enjoying his new celebrity status. Even more, he liked having a place to call home, even if it was in the middle of the Indian Ocean with a bunch of American soldiers who didn't know what the future held.

As Mike lay in his bunk, he couldn't get the picture of Charlie kicking the dog out of his head. *What was the guy's problem anyway? Was he that afraid of getting in trouble?* The irony was that Charlie had been assigned latrine duty for abusing the ship's new hero. *Poetic justice.* Mike smiled at the thought before he finally drifted off to sleep.

Chapter 13

VINES SWISHED ABOUT IN THE HUMID NIGHT and falling rocks broke the heavy silence. Someone or something was coming. J.D. listened hard, gripping his rifle and breathing unevenly. Drops of sweat stung his eyes. *Japs could be everywhere, coming up from all sides.*

A silhouette emerged from the brush. Everything inside told him to fire but he didn't.

"It's me J.D." whispered the figure. J.D.'s heart rate dropped back to normal, and he lowered his gun.

"Damn, man, you scared the hell out of me," J.D. mumbled, clapping his shaky hand on George Perry's shoulder. "See anything?"

"Naw, but they're out there. May as well try to rest a little while we can, before sun-up."

"Maybe tomorrow our back-up forces will arrive," J.D. said as he lay on the hard ground.

"Yeah, maybe…" murmured George as he dropped off to sleep. Neither soldier held out much hope, but just the thought of rescue kept them going.

Weak and tired as he was, sleep would not come to J.D. Instead, he ruminated about the past four months, trying to figure out how he'd gotten to this point in April of 1942: on the run and hiding in a rocky outcropping called Bataan, surrounded by Japanese, cut off from help.

It wasn't two weeks after the war began that the Japanese began to make landings on Luzon. Somehow, they had seized every advantage and opportunity. The American Navy had already pulled out because there was no air cover. Half the airplanes had been destroyed on December 8.

It made everyone wary, especially the Filipino citizens. The last time J.D. had seen Marisol, the lovely village girl, her big brown eyes had been filled with fear. He knew she'd been taken prisoner by now. He prayed every night that they hadn't violated her, hadn't taken her beautiful innocence. If only he could have done more to save her.

As it was, General Wainwright broke off part of the 200th, forming the 515th and ordering them to protect the bridges around Manila while the citizenry evacuated. J.D. was now a member of the 515th and a sergeant to boot! Most of the evacuation had been a blur--- beyond the grateful Filipino eyes and the C-rations on Christmas Eve. That and the unending noise from the sky. Always the noise.

After Christmas, Manila was declared "undefended" and the 515th was forced to retreat onto this peninsula--- on the outer reaches of Manila Bay. J.D. remembered when they'd first marched onto this mountainous terrain. An ominous feeling had overtaken him.

"Kiki, it looks like we've run out of ground here. Hope the Japs don't back us up all the way into the sea." He stared down the cliffs into the crashing ocean.

"The Japs can't get to us anymore. Didn't you hear? Wainwright ordered all the bridges at Calumpit demolished yesterday. We should be safe from the Nips till reinforcements arrive."

J.D.'s heart sank. "Yeah, except you're forgetting one thing. If the Japs are cut off--- so are we! None of our supplies can get through from Luzon. We're on our own, buddy."

And he was right. After that, the men subsisted on less than 1,000 calories daily, though they easily burned 4,000 calories in 24 hours. Red rice and monkey became the primary source of nutrition. J.D. remembered the first time he'd tried the dish. He'd spat it out in disgust, but soon learned to swallow it down just to keep the dreaded hunger pangs at bay.

Over the next months, J.D. watched his body literally consume itself--- his muscles wasting away while Beriberi settled in, due to vitamin deficiency. God, he was tired! Yet, in spite of it all, a man emerged in place of the sixteen-year-old child who'd entered the army in 1940. His body may have been skin and bones, but his mind was working overtime, developing a maturity and a steel-trap cunning necessary for survival.

A month ago, word had come that their leader, Gen. Douglas MacArthur, had been pulled away to assume command of the Australian theater. Is our situation so hopeless that the military no longer wants the General associated with it? J.D. wondered. After MacArthur's departure, morale plummeted to a new low. The general promised to return, but it was too much for the men to hope for, given the current state of things.

"It's every man for himself, J.D. They've done forgotten us. Do you remember the Alamo?" Pat, asked with a hollow laughter.

J.D. tried not to listen, but an awful feeling kicked him in the gut. "Yep," continued his best friend,. "Have you heard how the new saying goes? 'We're the battling bastards of Bataan----- No Momma, no Papa, and no Uncle Sam'."

NOW, lying here in the rocks, vines and bugs, J.D. was sure the 515th was alone and forgotten. He wanted to go home, but in some ways he didn't quite know where that was anymore. Home had become his comrades, his fighting brothers. If he had them, he had his security.

By April 7, the men of the 515th were scrambling for their lives. After continuous shelling and bombing from land, sea, and air, the enemy had broken through the Allied lines. The men had no food, ammo, energy, nor a place to escape. Many were fighting for their body's survival and had nothing left over to fight the enemy with. For many, apathy replaced anger.

Against all odds, J.D. had still not given up. He and his unit were still shooting continuous rounds at the low flying Japanese planes—spending more ammo in one day than they had in the previous month. When anyone on the Bataan Peninsula managed to bring down an enemy plane, somehow the word spread like wildfire over the whole area. That helped boost morale a little. Other times, J.D. and others like him tried to lay low---evading Japanese tanks and shells. For now it seemed to be working. He and his friend had found a quiet spot in the jungle in which to rest their heads. Precious sleep finally overtook them.

"J.D., wake up,"George whispered. "I'm starving. What are we gonna eat today?"

J.D. shook himself awake. His head hurt from using a rock as a pillow, but he knew his belly would hurt more once the hunger pangs returned. A measly grub worm appeared in the dirt. Both men went for it at the same time. They stopped and looked at one another. A feeble smile escaped J.D.'s dry, cracked lips.

"You'd think it was a beefsteak the way we both jumped for it. Go ahead and have it, friend. I'll get the next one." In one swift move, the other man ate the grub worm alive.

"J.D., you've always been there for me. When we get back to New Mexico, I'm gonna repay you for everything you've done. I don't think I coulda made it without you, brother."

"Now, don't you go getting' sentimental on me. We both help each other." J.D. picked up a leaf and expertly licked off any remaining morning dew. How he wished it would rain.

ZING!! The quiet of dawn was broken by bullets whizzing through the trees. All of J.D.'s senses were suddenly awake and on high alert. "Come on, George, we have to get a move on."

J.D. began to crawl away, but his friend did not move. J.D. furiously turned back to repeat his directions. That's when he saw his comrade, sitting against the tree, wet leaf in hand, with blood trickling right between his open eyes. In a panic, J.D. grabbed him and shook him. "What happened, George, what happened? Answer me, damn it, answer me!!"

George didn't answer him, and never would again. J.D. knew it even as he searched for his friend's pulse. Before he could even grieve, more bullets ricocheted off some nearby trees and rocks.

Tears streaming down his face, the young man put his head low and crawled into the thick brush for cover. Now he knew how all the animals he'd ever tracked and killed must have felt. He vowed to never hunt again if he got out of this mess.

The bullets soon stopped. J.D. continued to lie motionless, afraid to make a single noise. Barely breathing, he was hungry for air.

After what seemed like an eternity, he began crawling again. Nothing. He crawled some more. Still nothing. He spotted some fellow G.I.'s. in a clearing. Better warn them.

"Guys," he called in a hushed voice, "they just shot George Perry. They're right behind me somewhere." He crawled into their makeshift camp, dirty, battered and dazed from his hasty retreat.

"What's George's location, soldier? Walt here is a medic."

J.D. hung his head. "He doesn't need a medic. He's -----dead." He choked on the words.

"Let's get the hell out of here," said the an older man they called Chon. "And stay together. Maybe we can overtake one or two of the sonuvva bitches."

THROUGH THAT DAY AND NIGHT, the small band of men moved on hands and knees through the jungle foliage, not eating or drinking; just staying low; desperately praying; and trying to set up crude traps for the enemy.

The second day, hunger overtook them. "Don't tell me not to make noise. I gotta scrounge up some food." Against orders, one of the younger men abruptly left the group. J.D. wanted to follow him. He, too, no longer cared about anything but eating.

Chon recognized the wild look in J.D.'s eyes. "Don't follow him, son. Stay with the group. This is no time to fly solo."

All that was left was to wait and hope for a miracle.

On April 9th, another soldier joined their group. Tired and dazed from constant running, he shared more bad news, if that were possible.

"General King surrendered. We're finished fighting. Officially. And he sent out word that every one of us is to destroy our weapons." J.D.'s heart sunk to a new low.

"Nothing gets between me and this baby," one man staunchly announced, caressing his weapon like it *was* a baby. J.D. felt the same way.

Sometimes his gun had been the only friend he could rely on to get him through another day.

Chon looked directly into the eyes of each man. "You're attached to your guns, are ya? How ya gonna feel when the gun you love so much is turned on you by the Japs? How's it gonna feel to be shot by your own gun? Or worse, see one of your buddies killed by it? You gonna love it so much then?" Without further hesitation, Chon pulled out his carbine, removed the ammo, and did everything he could to disable the weapon.

One by one the other men followed suit, quietly cursing, and more than one crying. It was the final straw, the destruction of the last shred of their membership in the 515th. They were smashing their identity to smithereens. And their only defense.

No one said anything after that. It was like they were all thinking the same thing and were afraid to voice it.

Finally, Walt, the medic, broke the silence. "Heads up, men. If we can get out of this, just think of the stories we'll have for our grandkids…"

Unbidden smiles cracked a few dry lips. J.D. said, "Grandkids. Right, Walt."

They first heard them a few hours later, well before sundown. They spoke quickly and urgently in Japanese and they sounded near enough to touch. Branches broke, rocks were rolled over, and the crunch of boots on the hard ground were all around.

The first to be captured was Walt. J.D. heard them screaming something in harsh tones and him tersely responding. "Don't shoot, don't shoot, I'm on the ground. Look---see? No weapons. I'm clean."

J.D. wondered if the enemy understood English or even cared about what Walt had to say. He just hoped they wouldn't kill the good medic.

For what seemed an eternity, J.D. continued to lay in the brush, the humidity so thick you could cut it with a knife. He felt like he was smothering, yet he was barely sweating, due to dehydration. Then too, he couldn't think of the last time he'd relieved himself. He wanted to so badly, but he mustn't move a muscle. Sooner or later these Nips would move on. Then he would eat worms and look for sources of water to ease the cotton in his mouth. But for now he remained as motionless as a corpse.

Soon, two Japanese youths were patrolling within a few feet. J.D. hunkered down, trying to make himself small. He held his breath and closed his eyes. Unfortunately, at that very moment, a snake slithered out of the nearby underbrush. "Oh-h-h—," screamed the Japanese soldiers, beating the snake with the barrels of their guns. In all the commotion, the underbrush was exposed and J.D. with it.

He slowly opened his eyes. Staring back at him were the dark eyes of the enemy. Suddenly it was over. He was a cornered rabbit, waiting for the final blast of the hunter's shotgun. He raised his hands in surrender. He was surprised at the odd sense of peaceful relief that flooded his body. No more running. No more fear of the unknown. Tomorrow had arrived.

One soldier looked like he was aiming to kill, but the other stopped him. He gestured for J.D. to turn face first on the ground. Dirt filled J.D.'s mouth, and he struggled to turn his head and spit it out. Then the body search began. They roughly searched every inch of J.D.'s body for any kind of weapon or contraband. Now General King's last orders made perfect sense.

Satisfied he wasn't armed, the enemy soldiers began kicking him repeatedly. The earlier sense of relief was short-lived for the seventeen-year-old. He hoped they stopped before they damaged a major organ. It hurt so badly! Maybe it would be better if they just kicked his heart in two and were done with it.

His captors finally became bored with the kicking and produced a rope in which to tie him with. Soon his wrists were so tightly bound they began to bleed. Al least he got to stand.

"What your name?" one soldier asked in broken English.

J.D. did not answer. One thing his training had taught him was to give no information to the enemy.

"Who is your commander?" Their questions were met with more silence.

"Start talking now, or get this!" The man held the butt of his gun threateningly close to J.D.'s face. "Now where are the other men?"

No response. CRACK! The rifle butt slammed J.D.'s cheekbone. Things went black and his face met the ground. An eye socket began to swell shut and blood gushed from his nose. He knew now why

his mother called him stubborn. He'd never talk.
Screw them....

Chapter 14

J.D. STRUGGLED TO PUT ONE ACHING FOOT in front of the other. Ever since the American forces were surrendered to Col. Nakayama, they had been walking. It had been days now, though it felt more like years. On his shoulder was one end of a pole, with the man in front of him carrying the other end. Attached to the pole was a canvas sling holding a man too sick to comprehend the situation. Dead weight dug into J.D.'s bony shoulders.

They weren't their own men anymore. They belonged to the Japanese now. The enemy. The ones they'd come over to defeat now called the shots. Thousands and thousands of prisoners marched along this dusty road---devoid of even a sliver of shade---bound for God-knows-where.

J.D. could see the disgust in their eyes. He knew from his training that the Japanese did not believe in the concept of surrendering. For them, *death*--- even self-inflicted---, was preferable and more honorable than surrender.

The sun was so hot, so brutally powerful. It felt like it could burn him alive. If he could have some water, maybe he wouldn't feel so dizzy. Sometimes he fantasized about how nice it would be to just lie down for a few moments. A few moments to get a little shut-eye, that was all. Other times he swore he heard Mother and Daddy's voices nearby. He never could make out what they were saying.

THWUMP!! The man on the other end of the pole fell out of formation. Down he went, as did the litter carrying the ailing man. J.D. bent down to look at the man in the sling. He appeared grey and near death.

One of the Japanese guards immediately stepped over to the prisoner who'd quit marching. He harshly yelled in Japanese, and then motioned with his gun for the man to stand up. The man shook his head; staring up at the guard with pleading eyes and clasped hands. "I can't go on. I need to stop awhile. I need a drink of water and then I'll get back up. I promise."

The guard looked right through him with cold and disdainful eyes. He grabbed a water canteen and acted like he was walking toward the thirsty man. At the last moment he veered off his horse and gave it a drink. Once the horse was done, he dumped out the rest with a smile.

Next, he again motioned for the man to stand up. Again the man refused. The soldier began kicking him hard. The prisoner let out a few yelps followed by silence. The guard yelled angrily in Japanese and turned his bayonet on the American without a second thought. Blood gushed everywhere.

"Why waste a perfectly good bullet on these cowards?" he said to his fellow soldier, and they both laughed. He then motioned for J.D. to keep walking.

"What about him?" J.D. pointed to the dying man in the sling. The enemy shook his head and pointed forward to J.D. J.D. complied though he felt guilty about leaving the man behind. His guilt grew as he realized how much easier it was to walk without the sling's dead weight. How dare he be relieved!

He couldn't afford to get on the guard's bad side. His left eye was grotesquely swollen from the last beating. He needed his good eye to see out of. Grimly, he marched forward. Would this ever end? He wondered if this was what hell was like. Day blended into night until time became one big blur. Being constantly in motion in 100 percent heat and humidity without food or water was more than many of them could take. J.D. learned to step over the bodies that littered the road from Mariveles to San Fernando.

On the 65-mile Baatan Death March that took 10,000 American and Filipino lives, J.D. had but one mantra that he repeated to himself between gritted teeth: *I'll never belong to you---you bloody bastards! You may have my body for now, but you'll never have my soul!*

Chapter 15

ELISE SUNG TO HERSELF that bright April morning in southwest New Mexico. She glanced over at the wall calendar----mid-month----hmm.... Time to start reviewing her students for finals in May. She wondered why she felt so lighthearted this morning, with the never ending anxiety of the war and all.

Number one, she'd gotten a letter from Joe Howard in which he'd professed his love for her for the first time. She chuckled, thinking of her sensible self getting this giddy and tingly every time she read and reread her sailor's letter. Wouldn't her students be surprised to find out that prim Miss Sommers liked to flirt and dance? They'd be even more shocked to know she had a big, handsome beau who wrote her flowery love letters.

A second reason Elise felt carefree this morning was that her parents were in a better mood. There hadn't been any breaking news from the Pacific lately, nor from Margo or Mike. They had no cause to believe something might be terribly amiss. That spring, they'd gone to church and put their three military children in the hands of the Lord. For now, they were at peace with that. Daddy worked harder than ever on his dairy business, while Mother tended to her garden and some sewing projects. They were all managing to live with ambivalence quite well.

And… with her parents trying to live their lives again, maybe she would move out and marry Joe Howard, once this damn war was over, that is. After all, how much longer could this thing last?

Elise shook war thoughts out of her handsome auburn head and concentrated on the task at hand---dusting the hall table while carefully wiping the antique frames of family photos.

Ding-dong! Someone was ringing the front doorbell. Unsuspectingly, she swung open the door. Standing there was a young man, not much older than a boy really, with slicked back hair and a brown uniform bearing the Western Union logo. There should have been nothing particularly memorable about him, but Elise would remember his face the rest of her life.

His eyes met hers and furtively darted away. "Telegram for Mr. and Mrs. Sommers."

Sick. That's how she felt. Waves of nausea pounded her body like the ocean surf. She willed herself to accept the message from the youth's outstretched hand. She didn't remember closing the door in his face.

Something had happened to one of her siblings.

"Daddy," she croaked. No one heard her. She tried again to call his name, but her voice stuck in her throat. She numbly put one foot in front of the other. Out back. That's where he was---out back.

"Who was that dear?" Mother stuck her head out of the sewing nook, looking preoccupied with her work. Elise didn't want to tell her, but she knew she had to. Wordlessly, she held up the telegram. Lainey's eyes zeroed in on it and she immediately stepped back as if it were a poisonous snake.

"Oh God, no. Get Daddy, Elise. Now." She sunk to the floor and rocked on her knees--- still unable to open the message.

Elise found her voice and hollered as she ran out the back door. In response, Jesse came trudging in from the barn, looking concerned and a little annoyed at the interruption from his work.

"What's all the commotion? All of our neighbors can hear you Elise---" he broke off midsentence when he saw his wife crumpled on the ground. "Why, what is it, Lainey?" She handed him the telegram, lips white.

"Open it, Jesse. I can't."

Summoning every ounce of courage in his body, he opened the dreadful, small, beige envelope and read aloud:

```
Mr. and Mrs. Sommers,
    We regret to inform you that J.D.
Sommers has been taken as a prisoner
-of-war. Your son is being held
prisoner by the Japanese in the
Philippines. This is all the
information we have for now.

Respectfully,
Gen. Dwight D. Eisenhower
U.S. Army
```

The worst sound Elise had ever heard came from somewhere deep within her mother. She made a low primitive moan while shaking her head and saying no. Jesse crouched on the ground to put his arms around his wife, but she just pushed him away.

"I knew this day would come. I knew it. It's been hell---waiting for the other shoe to drop and now it has…"

"It's God's way of punishing us for sending our youngest off to war," she continued. "He was just a baby. Now he's in the hands of the Japanese. What will they do to him over there?"

Jesse's hands shook like a leaf. He could barely hold the telegram. Soon his lips trembled as well. He wouldn't let his oldest daughter see him cry.

"I thought maybe the telegram said he'd been killed, Lainey. At least he's still alive. We've got to hold onto that. And don't forget he's young and strong. If anyone can make it, J.D. can. I feel it in my bones."

"That's right, Mother, he's not dead." Elise mechanically repeated her father's words.

Lainey finally stood up, her face as hard as a rock. "I blame myself, Jesse, and I blame you."

She went into the kitchen. They heard the water run like when she was cleaning up. No one spoke. Suddenly the eerie silence was broken. Smash! They heard the sound of glass breaking. Elise peeked around the corner and saw her prudent mother who never wasted a penny, smashing every glass they owned, one by one, into tiny shards of hopelessness.

The eldest daughter turned back to her father and took his hand. Together they sat on the front couch. Daddy's shoulder didn't seem as big and strong as it had when she was little, but nonetheless, she put her head on it and cried.

Like a bubble bursting, the romance had just gone out of the war.

Chapter 16

THE JAPANESE GUARDS PUSHED J.D. roughly toward the train door. He concentrated on keeping his footing in order to avoid being trampled by the others. With one high step up, he was inside and shoved into the corner of the boxcar. Late April in San Fernando, on the Luzon Peninsula, made it feel like ninety degrees with ninety per cent humidity.

"At least we've stopped walking," J.D. said to the man next to him, motioning to his blistered feet. The man barely raised his head to look back at him with empty eyes.

When the boxcar was packed with men, an outside guard slammed the door shut. The heat was nearly unbearable. With a shudder, the train lurched forward. J.D. didn't try to imagine where they were headed. Every possibility was too horrific. Instead, he took a swipe at the trickle of sweat above his brow and attempted resting.

After twenty minutes or so, J.D. felt an urgent tug on his ragged sleeve. The man next to him had taken a turn for the worse. "Water..." he croaked.

"In the name of God----give me some water..." He sagged forward in the small space he had.

"Does anyone have any water?" J.D. called out. "This man needs some NOW!" The sick man remained motionless.

"J.D., is that you?" A familiar voice rang out from the other side of the boxcar.

J.D. twisted his neck to get a better view. "Pat, is that you, Pat?"

Patrick Hunter put up a dirty hand in J.D.'s direction. "How the hell did we get in this mess?"

I don't know, Pat, but I'm glad to know you're alive. Have you seen any of the others?" They could have been the only two on the train. No one reacted at all to their words.

"No, I don't know how many of us they caught. That was a helluva long line of prisoners marching though. Know what I mean?"

"Don't think like that, Pat. Some of them must have gotten away."

J.D. was spent from the effort it took to call out to his best buddy. He wanted to say a lot more, but his energy was sapped. It heartened him to know he wasn't alone in this, but nothing helped the thirst. He shut his stinging eyes and tried not to dream of water.

The boxcar began slowing, then came to a grinding halt. J.D.'s stomach churned; not knowing what was next. At least he could get out of this crowded inferno. When it was his turn to exit, he barely managed to stretch his cramped legs. The man who cried for water was dead. The Japanese would have to dispose of his body.

After stepping off the train, the men commenced marching another nine miles until they came upon a dirty old sign with crooked brown lettering that read: "Camp O'Donnell". The second thing he saw was a huge enclosed area with high, high barb-wire fences and several guard towers. Armed Japanese sentries manned the towers. It felt like their automatic weapons were aimed directly at him.

Previously, he'd been running on adrenaline, with a heartbeat so rapid he could feel it pounding out of his chest. The sight of Camp O'Donnell— barren and devoid of shade— was too much. It was like his heart took a nose dive and landed with a thud. It might as well have quit beating, so hopeless were his surroundings.

J.D. swallowed the aching lump in his throat. He was too dehydrated for tears. Biting his quivering lip, the seventeen-year-old stepped into the entrance of Camp O'Donnell, feeling as if he'd just entered the gates of hell. He wished he could transport himself back into time; back to Mountainview, back home where life was good.

Standing directly to the left of the entrance was a sight for sore eyes. Jimmy Farley, Chon, Sarge, Pat Hunter, and many more members of Battery G had assembled to wait for their men with open arms. Each of them gave J.D. a big bear hug. It felt like old times for a brief moment. J.D.'s heart resumed pounding.

"God, I'm glad to see you, Jimmy," J.D. said, barely recognizing his friend. His beefy biceps were now merely spindly sticks.

"I almost got away from the Nips—I almost made it," Jimmy uttered defiantly.

"We did the best we could, Jimmy. Everyone knows that," said Chon. He looked at J.D. "Get rid of anything of value. They're doing shakedowns and executing those with trinkets that look Japanese." All J.D. had was a family photo, and it was *all* he had. He wasn't throwing it.

"They haven't beaten us yet," declared Pat. "We have to make a choice—a choice to stay strong, use what little resources we have, until we get rescued. We can either choose to live, or choose to die."

Hesitantly, the band of men surveyed the prison grounds. Small, dank, concrete bunkers held cots devoid of covers. Bugs were clearly more at home than any humans would ever be. There were no latrines, only buckets off to the side that reeked of urine and feces. Flies swarmed everywhere. J.D. thought he might be sick.

He suddenly realized someone he looked up to was missing. "Where's Kiki? I haven't seen him yet. Don't tell me the lucky son-of-a-gun got away!"

Silence fell over the group. Finally, Jimmy spoke. "They got him all right. He-he couldn't keep up with the others on the march. He couldn't take the heat."

"What happened?" J.D. asked fearfully.

"Took his head off, that's what. Bastard didn't even bother to get off his horse. Just sliced him with his sword, like he thought he was one of those Samurais or something." Jimmy's voice lowered to a whisper. "All because Kiki couldn't walk."

A silent scream erupted in J.D.'s head. "I don't know about you guys, but I'm not waiting around to see who gets it next. First chance I get, I'm escaping. Who wants to help me draw up a plan?"

Pat looked behind his shoulder at the guard tower, and then back at the group. No one answered J.D.

J.D. took a deep breath, shoving his fists into what was left of his pockets. Turning away, he thought, Who knows how long we'll be here? A week, a month, a year, or maybe until the war is over? BULL!! They'll have to tie my arms and legs together 24 hours a day to keep me here.

Chapter 17

CLICK-CLACK, CLICK-CLACK. Eastward went the trusted locomotive filled with soldiers and a smattering of civilians. Another Sommers son was taking a train ride, but this soldier was traveling within the safe confines of American soil; riding free without fear of bodily harm.

The seats in the train were uncomfortable when a person was yearning for a bit of shut-eye. No matter which way Mike twisted or turned, he could not relax. His tight military budget didn't allow for a sleeper car. After his visit home, he was more than a little sleep deprived. He'd expected the lull of the track's rhythmic sound to put him out like a light. And usually, he enjoyed the lonesome whistle blowing, but now it only deepened his confused sense of melancholy.

In his heart, he knew it wasn't the cramped quarters that were to blame for his insomnia. It was the pinched look on Mother's face when she hugged him so tightly it almost hurt. It was the emptiness of the kitchen that had always smelled of good things until now. It was Daddy's lack of conversation and the way he kept stealing anxious looks at his older son when he thought no one was paying attention. It was the way his sister scurried around, making small talk to fill in the gaps; then waiting on him hand and foot like he was royalty; something she'd never done in the past. It was the paint horse, Star, that stood out in the pasture looking incomplete without her rider. But mostly, it was the telegram, the damn telegram with the black smudged ink and the words "prisoner" and "J.D." all in the same line.

Mike's head began to throb when he allowed himself to think about it. A little girl in the next seat clamored on her mother's lap, big blue eyes staring out from beneath her red curls and a sprinkling of freckles. In spite of himself, Mike smiled. Watching the girl eat a cookie, Mike heard his own stomach growl. How long had it been since he'd eaten? He jingled the few coins he had in his pocket and decided to get a cup of coffee in the diner car. It would do good to stretch his legs. Instead of noticing the food being served on the train, he would focus on the meals he would eat in the mess hall once he was back on duty.

The uniformed young man made his way through the crowded railcar, feeling slightly better with each step. Reaching the diner, he surveyed the small tables for a place to sit. He noted with disappointment that all the tables were full. *Wait a minute, the last table just had a young woman sitting by herself. I wonder if someone's joining her. If not, maybe I can grab the other seat.*

The woman's back was to Mike, so he marched past her and felt himself reverting to his old shyness with girls. His shoes suddenly became very interesting. "Ma'am, would it be asking too much if I could take this seat? I-----" He looked up and there staring him right in the face was Gwen Mackenzie. Her hair was pulled back in a gleaming French braid, her lips were fashionably red, and she had on a smart cream outfit outlined in black with pumps to match. How could she look so grown-up and so beautiful all at the same time? He swallowed hard and was at a loss for words.

"Well hi, Mike, how are you? Don't just stand there! Of course you can sit down. It's been ages, hasn't it?"

Gwen was as surprised as he was. To see someone from back home in this packed train was unexpected. She appraised her fellow traveler. The Army had been good to Mike. Gone was the small-town naïve look she remembered from her waitressing days. Still a little shy, but something was different. He was muscular now, every inch a lean soldier. His crew cut showed off the interesting angles of his face and his dark, thick eyebrows set off his almond shaped eyes. That's it, she decided. The look in his eyes was different now. More confident, yet harder too. *I guess that's what war does to you.* "What are you doing in the States, Mike? Aren't you supposed to be over in Burma, keeping the supply lines open for the Chinese?"

Wow, she's knows a lot about the war, that's for sure, Mike thought admiringly. "It's a long story, Gwen. You probably don't want to hear it."

"Hey, I'm a news reporter. I want to hear *everything.*"

"So you're still working for the newspaper. Where are you headed?" Mike tried to deflect her curiosity with his own questions.

"As a matter-of-fact, the paper is sending me overseas to cover the war. I finally got my transfer to the England bureau." It was on the tip of her tongue to ask about Charlie, who was in his Company. Charlie *was* her boyfriend, and she was curious, but something in Mike's face stopped her.

"So—tell me--- what are you doing in the States?" Gwen persisted. "Where are you bound?"

"Well, you're right, we did just pull out of Burma--- by the skin of our teeth. That Chinese "Generalissimo" couldn't decide what he wanted. As it turned out, I needed time off to visit my folks. Now I'm headed back to the base. They'll be shipping us out soon for God knows where. I'm ready to get back into the action. I can't wait to take down Japan." His expression took on a hard determination.

Suddenly remembering the plight of Mike's younger brother, Gwen asked, "I've been trying to follow the Japanese takeover of the Philippines, but I can't get my information confirmed. Your parents must be worried sick about J.D.'s whereabouts. Have they heard anything from him?"

Mike carefully replaced his coffee cup and fiddled with his napkin. A lump developed in his throat. "Things aren't going so well, Gwen. J.D.'s been taken prisoner by the Japanese. He's being held at an undisclosed location." Mike looked up at her, his eyes glittering brightly.

Gwen felt like someone had punched her in the gut. She should have somehow known about this latest development. *Why hadn't Elise written her?* She wanted to crawl under the table. "Oh Mike, I'm so sorry. I can't even fathom how hard it must be for your family. Let me know if there's anything I can do to help." When he didn't answer, she filled the silence lamely. "How are your parents holding up?"

"As you can imagine. My mother is a wreck and my dad doesn't talk at all. Poor Elise is stuck somewhere in the middle, trying to pretend everything's gonna be all right." Mike peered out the diner window, hoping the passing scenery would block out painful memories of home. Instead of the endless grassy plains, he just saw J.D.'s excited face the day he'd signed up for the army.

The waitress appeared carrying a mouth-watering hamburger with piping hot fries on the side. Gwen couldn't help but notice the hungry look on Mike's face. "Would you please help me eat this? I couldn't possibly eat it by myself. Could we please have another plate?" she asked the waitress. Mike started to protest but soon changed his mind when Gwen put her hand up firmly. She deftly cut the sandwich in two, giving him the bigger piece.. He graciously accepted his plate and tried not to gobble his share down in front of the lovely lady facing him. He recalled that he hadn't eaten since the day before, at his mother's table.

Gwen watched Mike eat; feeling somewhat like she was helping a stray puppy. He needs nurturing, she decided. He *is* Margo and Elises's brother and he's suffered a bad blow. The least I can do is make sure he's okay.

"There's an empty place next to me, Mike. We might as well sit together on this trip, both of us being from the same town and all. You're welcome to join me if you want to."

There was a long pause and Gwen feared she'd pushed him too hard. Maybe he wanted to be alone with his thoughts and misery.

"After I collect my stuff, I'll be right there." Mike tried not to sound too eager; though there was nothing better he wanted to do.

Once seated next to Gwen, an odd sense of security overtook Mike. He realized he needed someone to talk to. "I wish I'd joined the Navy. They *will* take back the Philippines someday. I want to be there when it happens, , but just watch---I'll most likely be somewhere else, fighting the damn Nazis. I want to help set my brother free, Gwen. But I don't get to…"

The young woman peeked over at Mike and her throat began to tighten. "We're all doing our part. You *are* helping your brother by taking down the Nazis. Think of the big picture." She tried to sound convincing.

Closing his eyes, Mike began to feel a little drowsy now. "It's hard to leave the folks behind," he murmured in the half-state between wakefulness and sleep. "I see my mother set J.D.'s place at the dinner table. Every meal. What's gonna happen if he doesn't make it? Our family will go all to hell...." His voice cracked a little and then he abruptly quit talking.

Gwen understood he'd dropped off to sleep. *Good, he really needs it, poor thing,* she thought, watching him breathe. His troubles seemed to evaporate with every heavy sigh. Stretching out, he unknowingly put his head on her shoulder. It didn't feel bad at all. She resisted an urge to touch his soft crew-cut. *What was wrong with her?* Quickly, she folded her hands in her lap, but allowed his head to remain on her shoulder. *I'm helping a soldier feel better,* she told herself, *and there's no harm in that.* Besides, he was Charlie's best friend. She was just being nice----trying to stop the hurt. It was the patriotic thing to do.

Night fell on the train bound for destinations still unfolding for its weary travelers and potential heroes. While the soldier slept soundly for the first time in days, the newspaper reporter made plans for covering an overseas war that had insidiously crept into the lives of everyday Americans.

Chapter 18

THE DAY'S ROUTINE WAS ALWAYS THE SAME: get up before sunrise, eat a small portion of rice and stand in an endless line to get a few sips of water from the one functional water faucet in the whole camp. Then do backbreaking work all day until sundown, when a prisoner got the same rations as in the morning. The only respite to be found was laying one's head down at night on the bug-infested cot for a few precious hours of sleep till the cycle repeated itself the next day. *It was getting harder and harder to keep track of what day it was.*

And the worst part was the death that loomed ever present. Men who had died from dysentery and disease. Men who were killed for not working hard enough, not "cooperating with the guards." It disturbed J.D. that he was becoming oblivious to the sight and stench of dead bodies. He decided it was time to go.

He gathered Pat, Jimmy and Andy Kennedy around him one evening. "Tomorrow night's the night, " he whispered urgently. "Do you guys know what to do? It's just like what we've always talked about, right?" Pat looked over at Jimmy and Andy. All three nodded simultaneously.

"You sure you don't want to run with me?" J.D. looked intently into each of his buddy's eyes. "I hate to leave you behind in this hell hole."

Jimmy shook his head emphatically. "I'm not sure about anything, "specially about you trying this. There's things worse than being a prisoner if you get caught," His tone took on a desperate edge. "Stay with us, J.D. This'll all be over someday."

"I *can't* , Jimmy," answered J.D. "I can barely stay here another day. I've gotta try something or I'll go insane." The look he shot his friends said he meant it. "So—we're on for tonight just like we planned. I'll never forget what you've done for me, guys. I'll try to bring back help." He hugged each of them somberly.

Later that night, as J.D. lay his head down, a sliver of hope pierced the fog of despair he'd been living with for so long.

FROM THE OUTSIDE, the following evening looked the same as all the others, but the close-knit group of insiders knew better. Time crept by ever so slowly, like a ticking bomb. Avoiding secret sideways glances, everyone tried to act normally as they waited for the sun to set.

After what seemed like an eternity it was finally lights out. Andy swallowed hard before plunging forward. "Those aren't yours," he yelled. Give me back my shoes!"

"Prove it," Pat yelled, dangling Andy's shoes in front of him.

"I'll do more than prove it." Andy spat on the floor before pummeling Pat to the ground. Someone called out through the darkness, "Cut it out, guys. The guards are coming."

"Give them back, I say," shouted Andy, still rolling in the dirt with Pat.

By then, Chon and Sarge had joined the ruckus, throwing a few well-placed punches. Soon the whole place was involved in a full-scale brawl. The guard tower shone the spotlight toward the madness.

One older guard looked up from his bowl of chicken and vegetables, taking another sip of saki. "I didn't know they had the energy to fight like that!"

"I'm going down and shooting the instigators," said another guard.

"In that case, we may have to shoot them all! Just let them kill each other instead and save us the work."

The guards hurried toward the fighting prisoners.

It was in that chaotic atmosphere that J.D. slipped away from the others. He stealthily crept outside to the far corner of the barbed-wire fence. Taking a deep breath, he began to climb, numbing his mind to the agonizing points that were impaling his hands and wrists.. Thank God his feet were covered by his battered Army-issue boots.

As J.D. put his foot over the top, he held his breath while expecting the Japanese to bathe him in their bright spotlight. As soon as he was over, he jumped straight to the ground, breaking his jump with a last ditch roll to avoid further injury. On the other side, he raced away with all his might, running so hard it felt like his legs would break away from his upper body.

He didn't know where he was going, just that he was getting as far away from Camp O' Donnell as he possibly could. With each step came a measure of hope—like a glimmer of light at the end of the longest, darkest tunnel imaginable.

Using a cap to push sweaty jet-black hair off his face, the guard shone a flashlight on the prisoners. He was tired of this duty, tired of these dishonorable men who had surrendered. He wished daily for a new assignment.

As soon as the prisoners saw the light, they quickly broke up the fighting and stood silently, waiting for a reaction.

"Go ahead and kill each other—this makes it easier for me," said the guard in Japanese.

"Lay down and be quiet unless you want THIS!" the other guard yelled in English, gesturing toward his bayonet.

The prisoners obeyed immediately. Filled with disdain, the guards circled the men where they lay, kicking them frequently. Keeping an eyes on his captors, Jimmy whispered, "I can't tell if they're suspicious, can you?"

Pat silently shook his head, then pretended to sleep. J.D.'s empty cot stuck out like a sore thumb, but there was nowhere to hide it within the barren camp. He prayed they wouldn't notice it. Pat heard the click-click-click of the guard's shoes approaching once more. He kept his eyes closed. The guard paused, looked awhile, and then kept going. Apparently he hadn't noticed anything amiss.

Abruptly the clicking noise returned, louder and faster than ever. There was one significant pause. *Please go back,* begged Pat's mind. Now the guards began screaming at each other in Japanese. Several of them hurriedly ran outside to fire up the jeep. Pat's heart sank. They must have seen J.D.'s cot after all.

"Get up everyone! NOW!" The men were ordered to get in formation outdoors.

What was coming next? Pat wondered. Would the Japanese blame them for J.D.'s escape? Were they about to be beaten within an inch of their lives?

Just let J.D. get away, prayed Pat silently as his neck, shoulders, and arms began to ache from standing in one place for so long. And let him bring back help—that's all I ask. Whatever sacrifice we make will be worth it.

J.D. WASN'T SURE how long he'd been running, but it was time to stop. The adrenaline couldn't go on forever and neither could his thin legs. The few calories he'd been ingesting daily were not enough to keep him going. It was a miracle he'd made it this far. He fell into the brush and took some deep breaths.

Looking around in the dark, he recognized nothing. The intoxicating feeling of freedom was the only thing bolstering his confidence. It was the first time in months he could make a move without staring down the barrel of a Japanese gun. .

I can't believe I made it out, he thought. He didn't really know what to do next. He had no plans beyond escaping. I wonder where I might find some others like me. Maybe some renegades who were never captured in the first place, hiding out in the jungle. There's got to be some. Maybe they would share some water and possibly food. I could survive with them until the military finds us.

The unthinkable crossed J.D.'s tired mind. *What if there are no renegades to join up with? What if I'm in this alone?* Would he make it with only the hurried survival training he'd received at Ft. Bliss? That seemed like another lifetime ago. And would he go out of his mind being so alone? He hadn't lost it yet, at least.

Stop it! He reprimanded himself sternly. You <u>will</u> find others. You <u>will</u> be rescued. You <u>will</u> get home again and live out your life in peace—free of fear. J.D. shook his head at the last thought; smiling bitterly at the holes in his hands. *After this, nothing will ever scare me again.* He decided to take another few minutes before resuming a full-blown sprint through the foliage.

Would those few minutes have helped him in the long-run? Probably not. It was near an obscure thicket where the guards chose to charge forward, accompanied by dogs and lots of guns. J.D. never stood a chance, though he tried his best to make a run for it when he heard their boots breaking the brush. Like a cornered rabbit, he dashed away. They got him in their sights and calmly fired. It was as easy as target practice. The bullet that hit him didn't hurt at first, though it threw him to the ground. Blood gushed from his shoulder and once again, he was staring down the barrel of a Japanese gun.

Go ahead and finish it, he thought with resignation. I'd rather die than be back in that place.

The guard cocked the gun and pointed it at J.D.'s head. The young American shut his eyes and waited. As if the guard could read J.D.'s thoughts, he suddenly laughed and put the gun aside. "Get up!" he yelled in broken English. "You go back!"

The other guard said in Japanese, "Why take him back? Hang him on the barbed-wire fence to die."

Hands tied tightly and head down, J.D. rode silently back to Camp O'Donnell with his captor. He felt so sick he thought he might puke all over the jeep, but somehow he managed to swallow it back for fear of being shot again. Without the use of his hands, he couldn't wipe away any tears that were threatening to form, so he tried desperately to choke back his disappointment.

To have to walk back into that awful place—to see his friends' faces—it was almost more than he could bear. In many ways, he wished he would quietly bleed to death from his shoulder wound, but the guard had tied it off and it looked to be fairly superficial.

The jeep pulled in front of the prison. J.D. didn't move a muscle. The guard kicked him hard out of the vehicle.

"Get to your feet! Now!" he shrieked roughly at the youth on the ground.

J.D. made himself get up, though it was a painful struggle. Through the entrance they went, where the men were preparing to begin their long day of labor. Chon and Jimmy were sitting on their cots, talking in low voices. That was when they saw him. The guards were triumphantly dragging him to the middle of the camp. J.D. was dirty, bloody, and broken. He kept his head down the whole time. Without realizing it, Jimmy bit his knuckles, drawing his own blood. In some twisted way, it felt right.

"This is what happens if you run," shouted the older guard. "You can not get away. Do not try it. We will find you." With that, he playfully put his gun to J.D.'s head for the second time that day. Jimmy bit his hand harder. Pat turned away, devastated.

The guard began laughing hysterically. Again, he put the gun away. "Take him to the commander," he ordered his younger counterpart. "I'm sure he has plans for our young man." He gave the guard a knowing look and laughed once more.

J.D.'s despair turned to outright fear. *What would they do to him next?* At Fort Bliss, he'd heard stories about torture techniques employed by the Japanese. He had it drilled into him not to give them information, no matter what. *What information do I have, anyway?* A voice from the past unexpectedly rang in his ear: *Granny always said you couldn't get blood from a turnip. Wonder what they would think if he told them that? The stupid animals wouldn't understand what he was talking about!*

The Japanese commander, Officer Sasaki sat up erect at his station, his back straight as a board. His hair was short and clean ; his uniform was crisply ironed. He strummed his fingers impatiently on the desktop. *When would they bring in the prisoner who'd tried to escape? How did this happen? If the guards thought he would suffer fools, they were wrong. After he dealt with the prisoner, he would also make the guards very sorry they were not doing their jobs.*

At that moment, J.D. was hauled in. Sasaki looked up at him with his dark, penetrating eyes. "Please sit down," he said quite genially in precise English.

J.D. sat down, though it wasn't easy with his hands tied behind him.

"Escape attempts are a punishable offense. We did warn you. We must follow through to set an example for the others." Sasaki circled J. D. like a vulture. "If you answer some questions, we will go easier on you." J.D. appeared to inspect the floor as though he hadn't heard.

"What is your name?"

J.D. answered him with silence.

"What is your rank?"

Silence once again.

The officer began to lose patience. "Who helped you escape?" he asked through gritted teeth.

This time, J.D. looked up and stared defiantly into his inquisitor's forbidding eyes.

"Answer!" the man backhanded J.D. in the left jaw. J.D. remained motionless and mute. He shot a look of pure hatred at the pacing commander.

Finally Sasaki quit circling, coming to an abrupt stop directly in front of his captive. "Your punishment will begin now. You have no one to blame but yourself." He gestured to the guards, giving harsh orders in Japanese.

J.D. was led to another room within the camp. He started shaking all over, though it was well over 100 degrees. He couldn't stop his teeth from chattering. Whatever was coming next—he hoped it would be over fast.

As soon as they told him to sit down in an ominous looking chair, J.D. reflexively began to fight back. Despite the bullet wound in his shoulder, he kicked back; he bit; he slammed his head against them; he rolled off the chair----in short, he did anything to stay out of their reach. He would not give them the satisfaction of going down without a fight.

At long last, they tied him to the chair, trussed his feet, and gagged his mouth. Only when he couldn't move did they untie his hands.

"Keep your hands still, or I'll cut them off," warned a guard called Kumatsu. He showed J.D. an axe. The others laughed.

J.D. steadied his hands on the table. They were no longer trembling. Holes from the barbed wire were hidden because his palms faced downwards. The guards examined his ragged, dirty fingernails while exchanging terse words in Japanese. The young prisoner wondered why they were doing this. He soon got his answer.

Kumatsu soon produced some bamboo shoots. "One more time----who helped you escape?"

J.D. bit his lip, refusing to respond. Never give the enemy information and never give up a friend. It was the code. Besides, if he did talk, they'd probably torture him anyway for the hell of it. Just please God, give me the courage to endure this.

J.D. forgot the bullet wound in his shoulder. He forgot everything. White hot pain filled his being when the bamboo was brutally shoved under his nails. He never knew anything could hurt this bad. Rational thoughts left his brain. His mind literally left him. Kumatsu removed his gag. J.D. could hear primordial screams filling the room, not realizing they were his own. It took way too long for the blessing of unconsciousness to totally envelop him.

On that hot day in July, the other prisoners were not assigned to their usual labor. Instead, everyone was kept within earshot of J.D.'s torture. Many of the men frantically covered their ears. Others cried like babies. J.D.'s own unit was especially sickened by the screams.

"I told him not to go," Jimmy uttered miserably.

"I wish I had a tenth of his courage," said Sarge.

J.D. CAME TO many hours later. He was alone in a hole in the ground; a place the American prisoners referred to as "the brig". "The brig" was a place in which the Japanese put uncooperative prisoners. He didn't know whether to be happy or sad that he was still alive.

The torture came creeping into his mind. If he was going to make it, he must try to forget about it. Involuntarily, he looked down at his poor hands. They were caked in blood, throbbing with pus, further infected by the dirt. He didn't know if he'd lose his fingers. At least he still had his left hand.

Days turned into weeks, and weeks turned into months. During that period, J.D. kept track of time by making marks in the dirt with a rock. He lived through the pain in his fingers, nursing them with his own saliva to keep them clean. One by one, his nails fell off and gradually returned as stubby remnants of their former selves. They never felt the same again. The bullet remained lodged in his shoulder, but he eventually forgot about it the way he had his fingers.

He created an alternate existence in his mind, sometimes pretending to be with Marisol, the lovely Filipino girl, and at other times pretending to be back home with his family and his friends from high school. His favorite fantasies involved riding his horse, Star, over the rugged New Mexico terrain. If he tried real hard, he could still smell the mesquite and creosote brush after a good rain. Sometimes he had to remind himself that none of it was real, yet it *was* something that no one could take away from him—not even the enemy.

By now, the Japanese did not have to worry about J.D. trying to escape again. He was through with all that. Somewhere along the way, he'd accepted the fact he was living in captivity and would be until only God knew when. He accepted this in order to survive. Now he set his sights on one thing: living to see the end of the war and living to see the Japanese pay for what they'd done here at Camp O'Donnell.

Chapter 19

"MOTHER, I'M OVER HERE!" Lainey could here J.D.'s voice but she couldn't find him. On a hot July morning in 1942, Lainey awoke in a cold sweat. Shaken, she sat up in her bed. She wanted to tell Jesse about her dream, but he was already out doing his chores.

Yes, it had only been a dream, but the reality was a nightmare. J.D. was being held captive half-way round the world. She saw the sun peeking up over the mountains and wondered if he could also appreciate the glorious sight of another sunrise. Or was he instead locked away somewhere in the shadows, where daylight couldn't find him?

Her existence was filled with questions that had no answers. She didn't want to get up, but made herself put one foot in front of the other. Sighing, she gazed at her reflection in the full-length mirror. Her barely greying dark hair had gone partially white---almost overnight it seemed. New worry lines creased her forehead and overall, she looked as gaunt as a scarecrow. She didn't have much appetite these days.

Without vigor, she fed the chickens, gathered eggs, and found some tomatoes in the garden. As usual, she worried about what J.D. was eating. At first she confided in her neighbor, Josie, that she worried about her son's extreme food allergies. "If he eats nuts or strawberries, his whole face will swell up with hives…"

She'd never forget Josie's incredulous expression. "Are you kidding, Lainey? They save the fresh vegetables and fruits for their own troops. He'll be lucky to get rice and water." Josie immediately regretted opening her mouth when she saw Lainey's face fall. "What do I know? Don't listen to a fool like me."

It was too late. The damage was done. Of course her friend was right. If J.D. couldn't have fresh food, neither would she. She pushed away fruit, vegetables, cheese, eggs, milk, and butter. The list kept growing. Her family had continued to give her worried looks, while begging her to eat.

After the chores were done that morning, she went inside and set the breakfast table. First were plates for Jesse, Elise, and herself. Next, as she usually did, she carefully set out plates for Margo, Mike and J.D., always with forks and napkins. Now, she could relax slightly. The table looked complete.

After breakfast, Jesse joined her in the kitchen before his workday at the dairy.

"I wonder what he's doing at this very moment," she mused.

"Who?"

She shot him a hard look. "J.D."

He took a step toward her and put his hand on her shoulder.

"Don't..."

"I miss you, Lainey."

"We shouldn't have signed the papers, Jesse."

"He would have gone anyway. He wanted to be grown up like his buddies....we can't go on like this---blaming ourselves at every turn..."

Crack—she slapped him without a second thought. She looked at her red palm and then back at his face with the matching red hand print. He remained motionless, his expression devoid of surprise. Maybe he'd been expecting it.

A new fear filled her heart. She was going to lose her husband too. Tears sprung up in her eyes. "I-I'm sorry, Jesse. I didn't mean it." She softly stroked her husband's face, as if trying to erase the mark.

"What do you want me to do, Lainey? Join the army and go rescue him? I think about doing just that every second of every day. If I didn't have to leave you behind, I'd already be signed up. It's damn hard to sit back and do nothing. You're not the only one hurting, you know. Try to remember that."

Again, she touched her husband. "You better not leave me and Elise behind. We need you more than ever. Besides," she laughed through her tears, "you're too old to join the army. They wouldn't take you anyway." She rested her head on his shoulder, deep in thought.

"I heard J.D. calling out to me in my dreams this morning. He's in trouble—bad trouble."

At first Jesse didn't respond, but finally he put his long arms around her. "Do you remember how stubborn our second son is?" His deep voice soothed her senses. He pulled back and looked at her fully in the face. "Good luck to *anyone* who tries to hold him against his will. They are the ones who need a prayer, not him."

She smiled again, in spite of herself. It felt good. "The only prayer they're getting from me is to either release my son or be crushed by our troops."

Jesse kissed her hand and went off to his work. The subject was once more closed. That's the way it had to be or they'd make themselves crazy....

That evening, after the sun went down and the stars lit up the New Mexico sky, Lainey whispered into her pillow, "Son, I hope you can see the same stars I'm looking at. Just know that your mother is making a wish on one of them for your freedom. Sleep well, J.D." She closed her eyes, knowing one of many long nights lay ahead.

Chapter 20

IN THE FALL OF 1942, the editor at the overseas desk of the *London Daily* stopped his work to listen in on Gwen Mackenzie's phone call. Peering over the top of his horn-rimmed glasses, he watched the young woman speak with animation into the receiver. She *was* a good reporter, that one, and not at all bad on the eyes either. He just wished she spent more time writing, and less time talking. He scratched his graying head in consternation.

"Yes, Katie, I'm sure. Ever since Eisenhower was made Commander of the European Theatre, he's been waiting for an important mission. Now, the scuttlebutt is that Roosevelt and Churchill have ordered him to open a second front to the war. They're calling it "Operation Torch," I think. Pulling Hitler away from Russia is the plan, I suppose." Emphatically, Gwen sat up in her second-hand chair, posture perfect in a red checked blazer, tossing back her sleek brunette pony tail.

"Where? How do I know? Somewhere in N. Africa, they say. Yes, sometime soon. God, I hope the newspaper doesn't send me there. I'm not ready,"she said, making a face at her editor. "I like it here in London, even if it does rain too much. I can't get anything to dry out! How do you do it?" Sighing, she peered out the window at the morning fog enveloping the city.

The editor gave Gwen a disparaging look and signaled for her to hang up.

"Stick to the facts, Miss Mackenzie. Have you set up that interview with one of our boys who joined the Royal Air Force? It's interesting to see how many Americans can't wait to jump into the fray. Get on it now and do a bang-up job."

"Yes, sir." Gwen nonchalantly rifled through her daily mail. Not even a letter from her family today, which was unusual since it had been awhile. Then it caught her eye. A small blue envelope with a military postmark and Mike Sommers scrawled in the corner. To her dismay, her heart did a little flip-flop. Why did she care if he wrote? she wondered. This was *only* Elise and Margo's brother. *I know what it is*, she told herself. *I haven't heard from Charlie in awhile, and I'm hoping he'll give me news about him.* Curiously, she opened the letter.

5 October, 1942
Dear Gwen,
    I'll bet you're surprised to be hearing from me instead of my sisters. Hope this letter finds you happy and healthy. It was great to share that train ride with you back in June. You raised my spirits, which were pretty low that day.

I'm writing this letter to ask you for a personal favor concerning my family. Elise tells me you have been covering the Red Cross and its missions in the war. I heard one thing the Red Cross does is obtain letters from American Prisoners of War and see that they get sent home to their families.

Gwen, my family hasn't received any word of J.D. Not about him, not from him. Is there any way you could get on the inside track of the Red Cross and find out if they can get a letter from J.D. released? I know he's being held captive in the Philippines either at Camp O'Donnell or Cabatuuan.

It would mean the world to my family, especially my mother. Do you remember what I told you on the train? About how badly she took the news of his capture? Well now Elise says she rarely eats or sleeps anymore. I honestly don't know how she'll face the upcoming holidays, in her current state of mind. We're about to ship out on a special mission that Eisenhower is commanding. God only knows what will happen next.

I can't stand to think of my mother suffering in these uncertain war times. If only she had a letter confirming J.D. was still alive. I know this is asking a lot of you. I just thought that maybe with your connections....

We would be grateful for anything
you could find out.

Take care of yourself, Gwen,
Mike

Mike. His name had a nice ring to it. Why shouldn't it? He was a nice guy after all. Not as exciting as Charlie, but nice. He hadn't mentioned Charlie, and surprisingly, she felt no disappointment. Instead, she found herself remembering Mike's little brother, the aw-shucks cowboy who had recently learned to be graceful on the dance floor. The young fellow armed with a duffel bag and an attitude-----grinning into her camera lens that day he'd hopped a bus to Ft. Bliss. The boy so anxious to become a man.

What could she, Gwen, possibly do to help? Who did she know at the Red Cross with that kind of clout? Was Mike asking the impossible of her? She *was* just a civilian. He saw something in her that she could barely see in herself.

Involuntarily her fingers began to twirl the card rolodex. With sudden vigor, she put aside the other mail and grabbed the office phone. "Operator, could you connect me with…"

Chapter 21

THIS PLACE WAS SO TOTALLY DIFFERENT from Mountainview! The November weather in Morocco wasn't cold, but the constant winds made it impossible to keep the Sahara Desert sand out of his knapsack, socks, hair and worst of all, his eyes. To top things off, since today was Thanksgiving in the States, he couldn't get the picture of Mother's juicy turkey and cornbread dressing out of his mind. The food served here was mighty bleak in comparison. His stomach growled in defiant response. He tried to think of something else--- *anything else.*

Charlie strode up to Mike, eyes lit up like fireworks. It was clear he was on a mission

"I can't take this strait-laced country much longer. Their so-called 'moral codes' are killing me. Every man has *needs* and I'm gonna meet mine." He raised his eyebrows, signaling his intentions.

"What are you talking about?" Mike asked while absently thumbing through his mail.

"One of the locals is gonna set us up with some underground women. Let's get it while the getting's good." He rubbed his palms together in eager anticipation.

"Whoa now boy, slow down. What happened to your big romance with Gwen? You planning to step out on your lady—just like that?"

"Get off your high horse, Mike She's probably done the thing herself. What am I supposed to do? Be a priest?"

"What you're supposed to do is *nothing*, Charlie. Wait for your girlfriend." Mike wasn't sure why, but he felt compelled to say something to Charlie on Gwen's behalf. "I think you've got it wrong about her being unfaithful."

"Okay, maybe she has been good. But dammit, this isn't cheating in the technical sense of the word. I have to pay *money* for the women, for Christ's sake! What do you think I've done this whole damn war?" He flicked Mike on the head with his finger. "Now are you in or are you out? I've got to let my source know how many women to bring."

"I'm out. Now get going and let me read my mail before I do something I'll regret." Mike shook his head while continuing to scan his mail. One letter jumped out at him. The handwriting on the envelope was definitely female. On second look, Gwen Mackenzie's name was in the corner. Mike was glad Charlie had left the room.

Hope sprung into his throat. *Please let her have news of his brother*! He tore into the letter with a vengeance.

7 November, 1942
Dear Mike,

It was good to hear from you. I worry about you boys in N. Africa. How is Charlie? Send him my best and both of you stay safe! We are so proud of the work you all are doing over there!

I think we both raised each other's spirits that day on the train. That seems so long ago and far away from London. Sorry I took this long to get back to you, but I've been waiting until I had something concrete to share.

About J.D.--- I've been working on the release of a letter for the past month and a half. It hasn't been easy, Mike! So much information is classified and since we are at war, communications even on a humanitarian level are difficult. The crux of it is, the Japanese don't want to play by the rules.

At this, Mike stopped reading the letter for a moment. He didn't know if he could handle bad news from Gwen. She had to help him. Finally, he made himself look at the rest of the letter:

After many frustrating phone calls, I discovered that I do indeed have "connections". More than I could've realized. The Red Cross agreed to do me this favor because I've written about their good works. They let me know that a lot of good publicity and fund raising is a result of my articles.

There are insiders who can obtain P.O.W. letters under the most dangerous of circumstances. Mike, they go through hell to get their hands on these letters. They are the unsung heroes of this war. And I can't tell you who they are, for fear of their safety. They tell me they are closing in on negotiations for a letter from J.D. and others in his camp. I don't know exactly when anything was written.

Mike, I can't even promise that he's alive at this point (I hate those words) ---- but I'm doing what I can. Hopefully, your mother will get a letter soon, and it will give her something to hold onto.

The Sommers are like a second family to me. I'm so glad I could help a little. Your concern for your mother is touching. It makes me want to be a better person.

Yours Truly,
Gwen

P.S. May I ask a favor in return? Please let Charlie know he's in my special thoughts and prayers. It's been awhile since I've heard from him, so I wasn't sure how he was doing.

Mike carefully folded Gwen's letter and put it in his small locker. The girl was a godsend! He closed his eyes and said a prayer of thanks for J.D.'s potential letter. Now, if he could just get Gwen's mind off Charlie, everything would be perfect!

Chapter 22

THE WEEK BEFORE THE CHRISTMAS OF '42, a vehicle from the Red Cross pulled up to the front gate without fanfare. A smiling middle-aged woman with plump red cheeks got out of the vehicle clutching an envelope. Lainey looked up from her laundry washboard, feeling oddly unafraid. *It must be good news from the look on her face,* she thought calmly. Though she wanted to run, she made herself walk over to open the door to her visitor.

"Hello, I'm here representing the Red Cross. I have a letter from J.D. Sommers, Prisoner of War. Are you his mother?"

The envelope looked ragged and the writing unsteady, but it was his unmistakable hand. As his parents read the letter with trembling hands, they held onto each word as though it were spun from gold.

Dear Mother and Daddy,
   Don't worry about me. I am fine.
The war will be over one day and I'll
be home. For now, I can't say where I
am, but it's not so bad here. I have
regular food and a comfortable bed. I
play cards with the other guys.
Overall, they treat us pretty well. I
can't complain.
   I look forward to being home,
riding Star, and doing my chores. I'll
never leave again.
   I love you and miss you.
   J.D.

Lainey held the letter against her heart. She felt
an ecstasy akin to the four times she'd given birth.
Her son was alive!! The letter confirmed it! The
mention of his horse had J.D. written all over it.

A big smile crossed her lips as she hugged her
husband. "I can breathe again," she whispered.

Jesse was relieved to see his wife happy, but he
still had his own secret worries. Was the letter
authentic? What kind of duress was his son really
under when he wrote it? How long ago was it
written and was J.D. really alive now? If he was
alive, would he be a whole person again after the
hell he'd been through? It's what the letter didn't
say that concerned Jesse. He tenderly stroked his
wife's hair, turning his head to brush away a single
tear that he judged too "unmanly" for others to
witness. I'll never leave again. J.D.'s words went
straight to his heart.

LAINEY sprang into action in the days to follow. It was the holidays and there suddenly seemed a lot to do. It felt like she was emerging from a fog; seeing the world clearly for the first time in over a year.

She had decorations to put out and baking to do, not to mention gifts to buy. She'd coax Elise into helping her. Margo was training anew for the newly formed Women's Army Corp. at Fort Des Moines, Iowa. Maybe they'd let her off for Christmas. Maybe the war would somehow be over and her sons would also come home. Lainey pictured them freeing J.D. She would wrap her arms around him and never let go. She forced herself back to reality.

Yeah, and maybe there is a Santa Claus, Lainey thought, dismissing her fantasy with a sigh. Still, she remembered the growing pile of Christmas presents in the back of the bedroom closet. Someday J.D. would be home to open them all. And that was no fantasy.

TWO DAYS before Christmas, the phone rang, interrupting Lainey's whirl of activities.

"Hello, Lainey? This is Emma, with the American Legion Auxiliary. "We are putting together a food and gift drive for some of our military families. Would it be all right with you if we bring a holiday basket by your house? We know how hard it's been for your family lately."

"Good heavens, Emma, we don't need it! We're perfectly fine! I would like to help others though. What can I do?"

"Y-you want to h-help? I just assumed---oh never mind," Emma sputtered, obviously thrown for a curve. "Okay, Lainey, we're assembling baskets tonight at Olive's house. You don't have to deliver them or anything like that."

"Oh, but I want to," Lainey countered. "I'll deliver them all night if need be. Now who are we talking about here?"

"Well, there's the Williams family who lost their boy in the Philippines last spring. Joan is a Gold Star Mother, of course."

' Go on---- who else?"

"There's the Ramos family whose son was wounded in action. He lost a leg and seems to have other battle scars---you know---the kind that don't show."

Lainey nodded to herself. She had seen some of the boys home from war---the way they walked around town like zombies. Mere shells of their former selves. Many times she'd prayed her kids wouldn't end up like that. *Let them find their way.*

"Who else, Emma?"

Emma hesitated. "Well, there's the McFadden's son, Christopher. He's a P.O.W., just like J.D. I don't have to tell you what they're going through."

"I'll contribute to all three of those baskets. I'll shop; I'll bake: I'll make things festive. And I bet Elise can get her students involved, if it's not too late."

Okay, Lainey," Emma responded uncertainly. "Let us know if you're taking on too much. We'll see you Thursday night."

With determination, Lainey hung up the phone and pushed back her sleeves. Looking around the room, her eyes came to rest on her sewing basket. *I would have crocheted them all a blanket if I'd gotten involved earlier. Well-- maybe next year.*

Lord, it was good to feel something, *anything.* And she knew J.D. would approve of what she was doing.

Chapter 23

GWEN COULDN'T BELIEVE SHE WAS REALLY HERE.
By May of 1943, it was learned that the Allies had
finally turned the corner on the fighting in Tunisia,
North Africa, so she'd begged her editor to let her
cover the story firsthand. He'd balked at first, being
afraid for her safety, as usual, and as usual, she
shrugged off the danger.

Tenacity was what made her a successful
reporter, and it didn't fail her in this case either.
Like a merciless lawyer, she argued her side until
her boss had no choice but to warily relent. She had
ulterior motives that went well beyond journalism:
she'd finally get to spend the time with Charlie that
she'd always dreamt of. She would be melted by
those eyes, soothed by his touch. She could hardly
contain herself.

Tunis was a bustling city off the coast of the
Mediterranean Sea; full of life, colorful markets,
exotic food, and interesting people. Since the
population was predominantly Muslim, the women
wore head scarves that looked alluring and

mysterious to Gwen, who still had much to learn about the world. The scars of war weren't apparent to an outsider, though she gathered that the minority Jewish population had been beaten down by German propaganda. Much of their property had already been seized. Hitler's influence spread far and wide.

Gwen paused at a street vendor in order to buy a lunch on the run. She was surprised at the variety of food, so soon after the strife there. There were delectable lamb kebabs called "safud", couscous (steamed grains with fish and vegetables), and scrumptios baklava, a honey glazed flaky pastry for dessert. She made a clumsy attempt at French-Arabic and finally ended up pointing to what she wanted.

"Biera?" the vendor asked hopefully.

"No," Gwen laughed. "No beer for me. I've got work to do. How about--- how do you say tea---shai?"

Armed with her delicacies, Gwen made a beeline for her hotel room to begin organizing her interviews and research. She wrote about the German commander Rommel, more commonly known as the "Desert Fox", and how his Afrika Corps had gotten bottlenecked and cut off in Tunisia, thanks to the escapades of brave men like George Patton, a newcomer on the scene. She explained how reinforcing North Africa was one of Hitler's biggest mistakes. By committing his Luftwaffe to fight a battle of attrition, he ended up with losses he simply could not afford. In the end,

Gwen continued, the Allies took at least 230,000 German and Italian Prisoners of War.

Half-satisfied with her news piece, Gwen pulled away from the typewriter to survey herself in the mirror. She was a mess, albeit a happy one. Grabbing a comb, lipstick and powder, she proceeded to undo the damage done by hard travel, sleepless nights and deadlines. Tonight she was joining Charlie and his crew at a local establishment for a little rest and relaxation.

Though it was after 9 pm, the sun was just now going down, with the sliver of a moon hanging in a deep violet sky quilted by twinkling stars. Gwen took a deep breath, stepping off the curb to hail a rare taxi-cab.

Muslim society officially frowned upon alcohol use, but unofficially served outsiders. Also, women weren't generally welcome in bars, but again, travelers were given more leeway. The particular dive Gwen found herself entering was no different.

Upon the American woman's entrance, every man in the place looked up with undisguised admiration, almost hunger. Disconcerted, Gwen looked hurriedly for someone she knew. She saw Charlie across the crowded floor, talking to Mike and his friend, Eddie. A fair-skinned blond with wide, blue eyes and pink cheeks was listening raptly to every word that left his mouth. Charlie must have said something extremely funny, based on how hard the woman was laughing. The evening had just begun, yet Gwen already felt the ugly monster of jealousy rearing its ugly head. *Some things never change,* she thought.

Charlie was about to say something more to the blond when he spotted Gwen. He jumped out of his chair, ran across the room, and with a grand gesture, swept Gwen off her feet. Rendering her speechless, he kissed her full on the lips in front of everyone.

"God, I'd forgotten how beautiful you are in person. I've been carrying your picture for two and a half years now." Grinning, Charlie produced a tattered semblance of Gwen.

In spite of herself, Gwen wrinkled her nose in disgust. "Don't show that to anyone, Charlie! I'll send you a new one. And you still haven't sent me a good, clear picture of yourself! I love getting your letters, though. They help me through a lot of things." *I wish there had been more of them,* she thought.

As though he could read her mind, Charlie replied, "Hey, I'm not nearly the writer you are. I can't begin to compete with your letters—I didn't even try." Sheepishly, he added, "Well, we're together now...... What can I get you to drink, M'lady?"

"What do they have? I didn't know we had much of a choice."

"There's beer on tap, local French wine, and some Boukha, which is brandy made from figs."

"Look at you, talking like you've lived here all your life. Think I'll stick to what I know: wine it will be!"

Charlie turned to the bar keeper, "That'll be wine for the lady and you can keep the beer flowing for me." Though not terribly fluent in English, the owner caught the gist of the order. He refilled

Charlie's glass again, and offered Gwen a bottle of wine with a well-worn glass.

"Sit down, Gwen," Charlie said pulling out a chair for Gwen "I just want to sit and look at you. I remember the first time I really noticed you at Skippy's Diner. You were running around taking orders while I was soaking wet from the rain. My heart hasn't been the same since." He stopped himself long enough to gaze deeply into her eyes. Never short on words, Gwen couldn't believe how tongue-tied she felt this night.

Across the room, the rest of Charlie's crew continued their party. "Mike? Did you hear a word I said?" The perky blond, who happened to be a unit nurse, poked Mike's shoulder impatiently. Mike's head was turned away from her and all the others. He, too, had only eyes for one person in the room, and that was Gwen. Earlier he'd waved at her when she arrived, and she'd smiled brightly, waving back. He couldn't stop looking long after she looked away toward Charlie.

He watched her every move; the way she smiled her dimpled smile at Charlie, her pretty hands folded in her lap, and her slim ankles crossed so gracefully. *Dammit,* thought the young man, *he doesn't deserve her. She is way too good for him.* Mike wished he could get her to see that, but he knew all too well he couldn't get her to see *anything,* especially himself. It was like he didn't exist when Charlie was around. *What did that guy have that he didn't?*

Sighing, he forced himself to unglue his eyes from the attractive brunette, forced himself to quit thinking about the time they danced together, or better yet, the time on the train when she'd allowed him to fall asleep on her shoulder. *I'm her best friend's brother. Nothing more, nothing less.*

He turned his attention to his nurse companion, saying, "Wonder if there is music in this joint." As it turned out, someone had smuggled in a phonograph and several popular but scratchy tunes were cranked out. No one seemed to care about the condition of the records.

"May I have this dance, Patty?" Mike asked the blond, taking her hand chivalrously. Obviously pleased, the young woman rose and joined him on the small dance area.

"I was beginning to think you'd never ask," she confided.

As the evening wore on, Charlie and Gwen came out on the dance floor. Charlie could barely walk, he was so impaired. Mike wondered how many beers his friend had downed so far.

Between songs, Charlie and Gwen joined the growing circle of American and British G.I.'s. Eddie was regaling the group with stories of how his friends would skinny-dip in the "wadis" much to the locals' chagrin.

"What's a 'wadi'?" Gwen asked curiously, digging for the notepad buried deeply in her purse. Even after a few drinks, she was ever the reporter.

"A wadi is a ravine that fills up during the rainy season," said Bill Welborn, one of the Brits. He gave Gwen a second lookover, then issued a loud wolf whistle. "Charlie, if I'd have known you were hiding this little treasure all this time, why I'd —"

"Shut your mouth, Limey! Don't talk like that in front of a lady!" Charlie fairly glowered at the Brit.

"Aw, face it Charlie, ol'boy. You're just ticked because we did more damage than the Yanks did. Kicked the Krauts arses, we did." Bill's words were becoming slurred as he polished off his latest beer with the utmost satisfaction.

The men began to laugh at Bill, slapping him on the back, and telling him he'd pay for it in the morning. Charlie continued to glare hard at him. His dazzling eyes had grown cold and steely. He pushed his sleeves back, proceeding to stand over Bill, who was still seated.

"Quit looking at her, Bill. You heard me."

Gwen was shocked at the turn of events. Shocked at Charlie's transformation. "Charlie, he's *not looking at me.* Sit down. "

Charlie ignored her pleas. "I know what you're thinking, you bastard. You can't have her. She's mine." Charlie pushed Bill out of his chair and began to kick him in the ribs, just as he had the stowaway dog.

"Charlie, stop it!" Gwen screamed. She ran over and tried to pull him off Bill.

Charlie turned around in a rage. "You came on to him," he hissed before pushing her out of the way. She fell back hard on the floor, more humiliated than hurt.

Mike had just emerged from the men's room when he saw the ensuing action. Filled with instinct, he overtook Charlie in the blink of an eye. He gave him a left jab, a right jab, and a final undercut to the chin. Charlie fell in a heap to the ground.

Mike turned to Gwen, who had managed to pick herself up off the stone floor.

"Are you okay, Gwen? He-he shouldn't have done that."

All the lights in the bar came on. Her pretty hair had come undone and her face was flushed with mortification. A lone tear trickled down her cheek. She bent down to pick up a broken high heel, before making a quick move for the exit.

"Gwen, wait!" Mike called. She didn't appear to hear as she kept walking.

"Don't bother Mike," said Patty. Can't you see she's embarrassed? Wants to be alone, I imagine. I know I would."

Mike almost knocked over more people trying to get to the door. The crowded conditions were worse than any army obstacle course.

He looked up and down the street. No sign of her. She'd probably hailed a cab, of course. He stood there in the warm night air trying to figure out what to do when he spotted her sitting on a stoop down the street a ways. She was still trying to fix her shoe.

She saw him looking. "I couldn't get a taxi. I'm tempted to walk back, barefoot and all." She made a half-hearted attempt at a tipsy smile, but her eyes looked sad and disappointed.

"I'm sorry about what happened, Gwen. You truly deserve better."

"I thought I knew him. I can't believe I wasted so much time on someone I didn't even know." Her head hung down. "I really need to go. I've got writing deadlines and all. I'm here on a story. That's the *only* reason....." she emphasized, putting her chin up defiantly.

Mike understood. She didn't want to talk about it anymore. Fine. He glanced at her feet anxiously. "So are you really going to walk? Barefoot and all?"

"Hey, this is nothing. I've walked barefoot with your sisters many times on roads rougher than this one."

"Okay, then I'll walk you back. You shouldn't be walking the streets of Tunisia alone at this time of night. It's still a war zone, remember?"

They walked the entire time without talking. In no time, they arrived in front of Gwen's hotel. Mike couldn't help but wish it had been farther away.

"You're always so good to me, Mike. I appreciate you looking out for me." She gave his hand a grateful squeeze.

Mike didn't know how to respond. His hand tingled where she'd touched it. The old shyness crept back in. "It's me who should be thankful. After everything you did to get J.D.'s letter released to the Red Cross—wow! I hear my mother is like a new person. You helped her a lot, Gwen."

The young woman looked at Mike with fresh eyes. How honest he was and how strong. He probably didn't have a deceptive bone in his body, unlike Charlie. Suddenly, she didn't want the evening to end. Maybe she should get to know him better, invite him in for coffee.

"Mike, I was wondering if------"

A horn blared abruptly and a taxi came flying around the corner filled with people. Eddie, Patty, and all the others were crowded together, practically hanging out the windows waving. "Mike, we've been looking for you. We've got to get back to the unit before curfew. Climb in, ol' buddy!"

Mike looked reluctantly at Gwen. *He didn't want to go.* Heck with the rules. "What were you wondering?" he asked softly, so the others couldn't hear.

"Oh, never mind. I can see that you need to go. Thanks again, friend." She stepped closer to him and gave him a tight hug. For a moment he was sent to the moon and back.

Friend. The word suddenly leapt out at him and stuck in his head like a recording. He crawled into the taxi, disappearing into the night.

Frozen, she stared at the distant taillights for a long time; then trudged up the long, rickety staircase to her room, not bothering to hide the cascade of tears on her face. When she got inside, she reached for the lucky penny that was always in her pocket—*Charlie's penny.* She flung it out the window into the street below. She would throw away the whole jar, once back in England. *His, indeed!* She belonged to no one. And she never wanted to set eyes on his wretched face, not ever again!

Chapter 24

London Daily
 MacArthur Praises Sacrifice, by Gwen Mackenzie

Nov.1943---Gen. MacArthur has recently written words of praise for those involved in the Battle of Bataan. "History, I am sure, will record the defense of the Philippines as one of the decisive battles of the world. Its protracted struggle enabled the United Nations to gather strength to resist in the Pacific. Had it not held out, Australia would have fallen with incalculable results."

He was sitting down at an old oak table in a modest farmhouse on the outskirts of Mountainview. "Go on and start, J.D. I made all your favorites," said his smiling mother. Mouth watering fried chicken, steaming mashed potatoes and gravy, homemade biscuits oozing with freshly churned butter, and hot, crunchy ears of corn were piled high in front of him. Mother straightened her apron and pulled an apple pie from the oven for dessert. J.D. took the first fork full of succulent food, careful not to drop a morsel as it headed for his lips…

POW!!---a sharp noise woke J.D. from his sleep. Someone nearby whimpered and begged for mercy. J.D. rolled into a ball and covered his ears, trying to escape the sound of cruelty that was never far away. He always wondered if he was next. When the shouts in Japanese--- followed by more crying and pleading finally stopped, J.D. uncovered his ears and tried to find respite in sleep. He could feel the lice traversing up and down his body, making him want to crawl out of his skin. His stomach rumbled loudly, begging for calories. His ribs and pelvic bones, elbows and knees all protruded from a wasted body, a body covered in old and new bruises and dirty open wounds. He remembered the time so long ago when he'd tried to escape at Camp O'Donnell. Since he'd been transferred to Cabanatuan, they watched him like a hawk, and he had no physical or mental energy to try it again. Besides, the hellacious punishment wasn't worth the effort.

As was his custom, he tried to find some flesh to measure, but on this night he couldn't pinch even a tenth of an inch. His tattered army fatigues hung on him like a scarecrow.

The young man from New Mexico rolled over and tried not to think about how hard the cold ground was. His cot had long since deteriorated. He double checked under a hidden stone to make sure his spoon was still there. Thank God no one had taken it. He caressed it obsessively, wanting to be ready in seven more hours when the Japanese would fill it two times with watery rice.

J.D. shut his eyes, but sleep would not come. What was he doing in this nightmare anyway? He had lost track of time, but he figured he was nearing nineteen by now. Nineteen!

He should have stayed in Mountainview to help Daddy with the dairy and the prospecting he always loved. He could just see him now--- Daddy with the somber brown eyes quietly soothing the cows as he milked them; Daddy mining for gold and silver in the hills beyond their home.

He wondered if Mike and Margo had survived the war so far. Hope no Japs or Krauts got their dirty hands on them, he thought numbly. If they did, I hope it was a quick death instead of this slow torture.

Unfortunately for prisoners of Bataan, death *was* only too common an occurrence. J.D.'s experiences were no exception. Long before, he'd lost his bunkmate, Patrick Hunt, to what was probably Malaria. He had gone into a tailspin when Pat left him--- a panic really. He'd felt so alone and scared; he'd wanted to die along with him. But that was a long time ago, how long he didn't know.

A time after Pat succumbed, his other buddy, Jimmy, weakened. The only name for his disease was starvation, and its ravishes were slower than Malaria, harder to witness. J. D. didn't know why some guys kept going and others fell down. It didn't make sense. In the beginning, Jimmy had been the huskiest among them.

Determined to save him, J.D. shared his meager ration with his friend. "Take it Jimmy, you need it more than I do," he'd whisper, shoving his spoon under the barbed wire that separated them.

"No, I can't. It wouldn't be right, " Jimmy had weakly protested. "I keep telling you to save yourself. Quit sharing with me, dammit."

"And I keep telling you---- there's a girl back home waiting to marry you. You've got a lot to live for. Now try to eat this. Do it!"

Jimmy eventually tried, but as usual, he was too sick to keep it down. No one got the rice, but J.D. was still glad he'd tried. Jimmy died two days later.

Once again, J.D. had been left alone in that dark place, alone to ponder the bleak possibilities awaiting him. This time, when he lost his second friend, he'd grown a little stronger mentally. *These bastards aren't going to beat me,* he'd vowed through clenched teeth. *I'm not some insect they can crush at will. I'll outlast them, and then let's see who gets crushed.*

Back in the present, J.D. tried desperately to think of something different, anything else. What about his older sister, Elise—wonder if she got her last teaching credentials? Hope so because she sure made a good teacher. Bet she's keeping Mother company so that's good. Feeling his spine pushing through to his stomach, J.D. rolled over once more. He closed his eyes and saw his rodeo horse, Star, clip-clopping across the brush and cactus. Who was taking care of her while he'd been away? His mind drifted. Maybe he'd better feed and water her himself. He knew where that special stash of grain was. Come on, Star! He whistled and clapped, but this time she did not even bother to turn around. He realized she'd probably forgotten him long ago.

In 1943, halfway around the world from Mountainview, New Mexico, a devastating thought occurred to the young soldier at 3 a.m. in Cabanatuan. Would he ever again know the feeling of freedom before his short life was over?

Chapter 25

"PRETTY GOOD, YANK, but you should be pushing a pram!"

Margo clenched the steering wheel, having just backed the truck out of a very narrow London alleyway. Being in charge of the motor pool meant doing tasks like this on a daily basis. It had become second nature to her. She looked in the rearview mirror at her British counterpart. He was still standing there. He knew his comment had rankled her and he was gleefully waiting for a reaction.

Pram. What the heck is a pram? she asked herself, desperately scanning her memory for a clue. Suddenly, a picture of a mother pushing a *baby carriage* came to mind. She squared her shoulders and straightened her cap. She wanted to punch that chauvinist in the nose.

"Listen, mister. I'm doing my part the same as everyone else. Keep the wisecracks to yourself."

The soldier crossed his arms across his beefy chest, laughing hard and loud. "This war is making you Yank women too cheeky. Go figure..."

Margo's face flushed bright red. She felt like pummeling the man on the spot. Unfortunately, she had work to do. She was scheduled for guard duty at the top of the hour. She gave the man one last glare before driving away with a resounding screech. Left in the dust, he gave a half-mocking, half-admiring salute.

ONCE ON DUTY, Margo paused to take in her surroundings. She stood guard on the rooftop of a bus station that had been converted into a motor pool for the troops. She gazed across the war torn London neighborhood, relishing the feeling of open air and rare sunshine. It felt like the dreary grey clouds had lifted just for her, giving life and color to a world gone crazy with violence. Even the sight of the bomb-scarred houses below couldn't dampen her mood. The afternoon's last rays of sunlight streamed through facades of ruined buildings, still standing bravely after years of attack--- *much like the British people*, Margo realized.

Her mind began to wander. It wasn't so long ago she was back at the dairy, helping Daddy feed and milk the cows. She could hear herself yelling at J.D. to get off his darned horse and help her. She bit her lip at the memory.

After J.D. was taken prisoner, she had no second thoughts about reenlisting as one of New Mexico's first members of the Women Army Corps. "WACs", they called themselves. She'd asked for something besides boring old secretarial work. Transportation seemed like the place for her.

She and 64 others were shipped overseas aboard the Queen Elizabeth. Though the luxury liner was stripped down, Margo still felt like she was in a big hotel. She smiled to herself as she remembered how they'd eaten their meals in a gigantic emptied swimming pool.

And now, here she was on this March evening—watching the sun set on London; knowing that pitch blackness would soon befall a city waiting for the next round of bombs. *How long can the Germans keep this up ?* Margo wondered. Though the English referred to it as a "mini blitz", Margo saw nothing small about it. Of course, the air raids in 1940 and '41 were fraught with more destruction and more lives lost, but the current blitz of '44 had its own particular brand of terror.

The new V-1 buzz bombs were a case in point. The V-1 made a loud stuttering sound followed by an eerie silence right before it whistled down toward its target carrying 2000 pounds of explosives.

Margo chose to put the bombs out of her mind this peaceful March evening. Being secretly claustrophobic, she'd take her chances on this rooftop any day of the week. It beat being squeezed into one of those small, dark crawlspaces they called bomb shelters.

She looked up in time to see private Annie Larson climbing onto the roof. "Sargeant Sommers, I'm here to relieve you. We've just received a new shipment of jeeps for you to inspect."

Back on the ground, Margo went to work. It was always nice to get a shipment but the inspection process was rigorous and time-consuming.

"I have a better idea," teased Jerry Jackson, a new recruit, who appeared more boy than man. "Throw out that bloody checklist. Let's take them for a spin instead." He kicked a tire for emphasis.

Margo tried to give him a forbidding look, but came up short. "So you don't believe in doing things by the book, Jackson." She continued with her checklist, pretending to look stern.

At that exact moment, she heard the terrible sound of a V-1 coming in. It was very close by. She felt her heart in her throat. Her eyes went to Jackson, who had frozen in his tracks. *I must not show fear,* she thought, swallowing hard. The god awful silence of the V-1's engine cutting off filled the air. It seemed like it was happening right above the motor pool. Danger signals screamed in their ears.

Instinctively, Margo's training kicked in. "Hit the dirt!" she yelled. She dropped to the ground, but the young private chose to run away.

The loudest noise on earth jolted Margo to the core. A burst of shockwaves entered the young woman's brain. Around her, the new fleet of jeeps was demolished. Something sharp hit her back and neck. That was all she remembered before the world exploded into darkness.

∗⊕ᵀᴸ ∮∗⊕ᵀᴸ ∮∗⊕ᵀᴸ ∮

THE WATER STAIN on the editing wall stared back at Gwen, begging to be identified, like some

Rorshach ink blot. She strummed the desktop, reaching aimlessly for her standard cup of cold black coffee. Her mind was a blank. She had to make copy for this section, and none was forthcoming. The phone rudely broke into her thought process.

"Gwen, do you want to take this story?" asked Jim Roberts, assistant editor. "One of the motorpools downtown was bombed--- one death, and lots of injuries. A female American was involved. What do you think?"

"I've got it," Gwen replied, eager to get away from her desk.

Driving down the road, Gwen's mind took off. She began to plot story angles as she drove. One headline jumped out : *Do Women Belong in War?* Of course, *she* believed they did, but those kind of questioning headlines made good copy all the same. Her editor liked controversial topics that got the readers talking.

After displaying her newspaper credentials at the front desk, Gwen immediately asked about the victims, especially the female one. A middle-aged nurse took her to the Intensive Care Unit. She looked at the motionless woman in the bed, head bloodied and bandaged. It was an upsetting sight, but Gwen knew how to remain professional.

"May I have her name and hometown, please? I assume her family has already been notified."

"Yes, they have. Let me see, here it is. Margo Sommers from Mountainview, New Mexico."

The nurse did a double-take at Gwen. "Miss, are you alright?"

Gwen felt like she needed to vomit. All the day's coffee rose up in her throat and she gulped it back down. The motherly nurse looked concerned. "Take a chair, Miss." The nurse motioned to an orange plastic chair in the hallway, and Gwen lowered into it before her knees buckled under her.

How could it be? That still figure lying in the bed was her Margo. Margo..... the vivacious best friend who never let anything stop her. Gwen hung her head down, shielded her eyes, and let the tears flow.

With worried eyes, the nurse brought her a glass of water. "Are you feeling better? People have strong reactions to the sight of blood.."

"Oh, it's more than that. The woman in the I.C.U. is my best friend. We grew up together."

The nurse clucked sympathetically. "Small world, Miss. Way too small *these* days."

"I want to talk to her doctor," Gwen said urgently.

"Well, I don't know—you not being family and all."

"I represent the family," Gwen said firmly. "I can give them the latest information."

"I-I don't know. You'll have to sign some forms, Miss – er I didn't catch your last name."

"Mackenzie."

Looking officious and preoccupied, Dr. Browning walked up to the two women. Apparently, he'd overheard much of their conversation. "How can I help you, Miss?"

"I need to know the extent of Margo Sommers' injuries. I'm a close friend of the family and I'd like to keep them informed."

"She's not out of the woods yet." He removed his glasses. "I wish I could say she was. She's had a sharp blow to the head, caused by shrapnel from the explosion."

Gwen jammed her sharp nails into her palm. This felt like a bad dream. The whole war was a bad dream.

"We've got her on a strong medication for the time being," Dr. Browning continued. "We're giving her brain a chance to rest. The first order of business is to get the swelling down. After that ---- well, we'll just have to wait and see."

"See what, doctor?"

Dr. Browning looked annoyed, like he wanted to be somewhere else. His bedside manner had a short expiration date.

"When she wakes up, *if* she wakes up, we'll have to see if there is any permanent brain damage. It's a dicey situation, Miss-uh---"

" Mackenzie. Thank-you, Dr. Browning, for being candid with me."

"Miss Mackenzie, there's no need to alarm the family with too much conjecture. They are across the pond and cannot help her right now. The fact is----she's alive and she's resting. We told them we're giving her the best care possible. Leave it at that for now."

Gwen nodded slowly, backing away. So Mr. And Mrs. Sommers knew the bare minimum. Anything more would stir them up unnecessarily.

Her job would be to stay nearby. She asked where she could find a phone.

"Jim, I can't do the story. A dear friend of mine is seriously injured. I'm not going anywhere."

"But-but who will cover the article?"

"I'm sure you'll find someone else. I'll be in touch. Sorry, Jim." She hung up, still dazed. They would have to understand. She needed her job at the *London Daily,* but she needed Margo more.

Gwen pressed her face up to the glass pane and watched them work on Margo. I.V. tubes and oxygen surrounded her friend. Her face was swollen and bruised beyond recognition. Only Margo's long, tapered fingers remained untouched.

What must her parents be thinking? They had suffered so much anxiety already because of J.D.'s imprisonment. This could push Lainey right over the edge. She, Gwen, must appear upbeat about Margo's condition, no matter how scared she felt.

Involuntary pictures of Mike entered her mind. He was her friend, too. First, his little brother, and now his little sister. She was surprised at how deeply she felt his pain. The Sommers were paying too dearly on account of this damnable war.

She tiptoed into the I.C.U., masked and sterile. The shift had changed and a different nurse was now tending to Margo. She looked up with disapproving eyes. Gwen put her hands together as if to beg.

Please, she thought. Without permission, she softly touched Margo's still hand. " It's Gwen, Margo. I'm here for you, I'm not going anywhere." There was no visible response; no squeeze of the hand nor flutter of the eyelid. Gwen sighed. She just hoped her friend was in there somewhere.

The nurse charting Margo's vitals noticed a slight uptick in her numbers. With skepticism, she studied the snazzy newspaper reporter, noting her red lips and nails along with the two-inch heels on her patent leather shoes.

Reluctantly, the nurse decided to let her stay.

Chapter 26

STRANGE VOICES. DISTANT BRIGHT LIGHTS. Pain and more pain. Darkness, most of all. She wanted to speak but she *couldn't*.

"I see your eyelashes fluttering, Margo. You always had the longest eyelashes and the most dramatic eyebrows. Everyone was jealous of you. Open up those eyes, Margo!"

That must be mother I hear. I'm coming to you, Mother. Opening her eyes was like pushing a steel door open. Gradually, she did it. The smiling figure above her was quite blurry. The pain in her head and back rushed forward. Finally she focused. Sitting in front of her was not Mother, but instead her best friend, Gwen.

Where was she? Why did everything look so white and sterile? Why was she lying in bed like this? And why, oh why, did she hurt all over?

Upon seeing her confused expression, Gwen told her soothingly, "You're in a London hospital, Margo. A bomb was dropped on your motorpool. Some of the shrapnel hit you, but the doctors believe you're going to be all right."

Margo found her voice. "I-I don't remember being hit," she said hoarsely. "I was checking off our new jeeps. I was talking to Jackson. Something about..." She closed her eyes trying to picture the scene. Suddenly she tried to raise up, her eyes flying wide open.

"Is he okay? I yelled at him to hit the ground, but he ran anyway."

"Margo—he's fine. Hardly a scratch, I'm told."

A little tear trickled down the side of Margo's nose. Sheepishly, she whisked it away. "Isn't that the way it goes? I follow the training manual to a tee and look where it gets me." She gave her friend a wry smile.

Waves of relief washed over Gwen. Margo was still Margo. She had a bandaged head and back, but her sarcasm was intact, and more importantly, so was her memory. Gwen sensed a few tears of her own beginning to form. She tried to suppress them. Too late since Margo caught on.

"Eh-eh. Come on Gwen. You know big girls aren't supposed to cry." Briskly, she tried to change the subject. "How long have I been in this place? Feels like I just came out of a long dream. I guess I thought you were my mother."

Gwen hesitated, not wanting to cry again. She squeezed Margo's long tapered fingers. The two young women locked eyes for a moment, their enduring friendship speaking for itself.

"You've been here a week."

"Oh God, my poor parents! They're already worried to death about J.D., and now this! How much more can they take?"

"I'm sure the Army has let them know you're receiving care at this hospital. I've got communication through the newspaper desk. I'll keep your mother posted on your progress. Starting today. You keep working on getting better."

"You are a jewel, Gwen." She grimaced in pain. "I wonder what Mike will think. His little sister already wounded in action. I can hear him now."

"I'll update him as well. We've become good friends—ever since he asked me to work with the Red Cross on releasing a prison letter from J.D. I was glad he asked me for help."

"I didn't know you were behind the release of that letter! I wish I could read it!" Margo looked away wistfully. "Anyway, I hear Mother is now doing something..." she squeezed her eyes shut to think, "oh yeah--- crocheting Christmas blankets for the wounded or returning troops. I'm glad she's trying again. She didn't for awhile. Thank-you, friend." Margo let a sigh escape her lips. "That's why I don't want my injury to set her back once more."

There was a pause in the conversation, and Gwen knew she needed to let her friend rest. As she began to gather her things, Margo groped for a way to keep her longer. "S-So—what do you hear about Caroline? What is she up to; do you know?"

"As far as I know, she is working in a ship yard in San Francisco. She is doing welding work, if you can believe that. I'd love to do an interview with her—it would make a great feature story!"

"Our Caroline, a regular Rosie the Riveter". Margo beamed, in spite of her pain. "Who knew she had it in her?"

"She wants to do her part for the war effort. Especially considering that Slade is right there in the middle of it. She's crazy in love with that guy,"

"Don't all of us want to do our part? I get sick of people saying women don't belong in wars. Equality is not something they can legislate."

"It's an *attitude*, right Margo?"

"Right. So--- just where is Slade, now?"

"Last I heard was a long time ago when he was back in Burma with Mike and... and Charlie." Gwen immediately wished she hadn't said his name. It left a bad taste in her mouth. She continued, "That was awhile back. Don't know where Slade is at this time. Caroline would know."

At the mention of Charlie's name, Margo perked up. "So, are you and Charlie still an item?" She got a sly glimmer in her eye.

Taking a deep breath, Gwen looked away. Even in her current state, Margo took notice. "O, I'm sorry; I must've said the wrong thing."

"Charlie and I are history. He wasn't the person I thought he was", Gwen responded quietly.

"Maybe you were focusing on the wrong guy all along. Excuse me for meddling, but why don't you give Mike a chance? I saw the way he looked at you at that dance right before he enlisted. He may be my brother, and I may be biased, but I think he's a darned good catch."

Gwen looked uncomfortable and shook her head. "Oh Margo, look at you playing matchmaker on your hospital bed. You should be trying to rest so you can recover and go home."

"Go home? Are you kidding? I've still got a job to do. As soon as I'm well enough, I'm going back to active duty."

"I should've known better. Admit it, you like working around those handsome British soldiers." It was Gwen's turn to needle her friend.

Margo rolled her eyes. "I'm a little too 'cheeky' for their taste. But that's okay. The American men suit me just fine." Gwen noticed her friend was getting rather riled up. It was definitely time to go. She had calls to make and letters to write. She gave her friend's hand one last squeeze. "You rest for the time being. I'm so glad that you're okay.... What would I do without my best friend? I'll be here every day until you're released. Count on it."

"But what about your job?"

"I have lunch hours, right? And if you don't watch out, I'll make *you* my front page story. I can see the headline now: *Woman Decorated for Wounds in Combat.*"

"You better not or so help me ..." Margo murmured to herself, her long eyelashes fluttering as she dropped off.

Chapter 27

April 2, 1944,
My dear daughter,

It was so good to hear your voice yesterday. I wanted to see you so badly, but this war makes it impossible. You gave us quite a scare, but now you sound healthy and strong. Please thank Gwen for setting up the overseas connection.

After we hung up, I realized I had something more to say. I want you to come home. I was disappointed when they didn't send you back to the States to recuperate.

I know you've said you'll stay in the army until the war is over, but enough is enough, Margo. You've nearly given your life for the military. That's a high price to pay.

I am so grateful your life was spared this time and I see it as a sign—a sign that it's time to pack your bags and begin the long life you have ahead of you. Think—there's college, marriage, babies, and yes, of course a career ahead for you—all of it yours for the taking.

Come home, my girl. Your Daddy feels like I do—he just won't put his feelings into words. J.D. is God knows where and that should be enough worry for one family. Please don't add to our burden, Margo. Think about it.

Love,
Mother

A hasty reply read as follows:

May 5, 1944
Dear Mother,

Yes, it was also good to hear your voice last month. It's true that I am now fully recovered, though loud thunder still sends me scurrying under the bed. I'm working on that one.

I was filled with consternation upon reading your request to come home. I will tell you straight away: I an NOT coming home. And—I don't want to be made to feel guilty for "adding to your burden." That's just not fair, Mother.

Yes, I was spared, unlike some of the unfortunate others whom I work with every day. I have a job to do over here and the fact that I am still alive sends me a strong signal that is very different from the one you are getting.

I am not done, Mother. I have a lot left to accomplish in this war and I intend to stay here until that dreadful beast Hitler surrenders, at the very least. We've heard so many rumors about the atrocities he is committing: transporting men, women and children to death camps where they are gassed in large numbers. He is trying to take over the world with his madness and he must be stopped.

And this war is personal, Mother, because they've got J.D. I feel even stronger than ever about doing my part to see him set free. I would feel like a coward and a failure if I went home now, tail between my legs, knowing my baby brother was out there somewhere and I hadn't tried my darndest to help him.

Please understand, Mother. Make Daddy understand as well. I promise to take care of myself from now on. No more injuries. I will come home one day, and when I do, it will be with my head held high.

Always, Your faithful daughter,
Margo

Sighing, Lainey folded the letter and bit her lip. *Why am I not surprised*, she said to herself. *That's what we all love about Margo.*

Chapter 28

Assessing Normandy: One Month Later by Gwen Mackenzie

London—Over the past four years, France has been overrun by the Germans. Recently, the Allies decided to change all that. It has been exactly one month since the largest amphibious operation in history took place, under the command of Gen. Eisenhower, Gen. Bradley, and Admiral Ramsey. At that time, the Allies; consisting of the USA, the UK, Canada, France, Australia, and many more countries, crossed the English Channel to open a second front against Adolph Hitler. If the past were any indicator, the odds were against the Allies.

Five beaches at Normandy were targeted for invasion. Brave men paved the way with overnight parachute and glider landings, followed by air attacks and naval assaults preceded by minesweepers. Lastly, special vehicles that function on both land and sea were employed.

On June 6, 130,000 Allied troops stormed the French beaches. Half were Americans. The obstacles looming ahead seemed daunting, if not impossible. Hitler had erected a giant wall all along the French coastline, complete with tank-top turrets and barbed wire. He laid one million mines. Still, the men persevered and overcame the enemy. Numbers were on the Allied side: the ratio was 7:2 in the Allies' favor.

Much has been accomplished in the last thirty days. Allied troops have transported the following into France: 148,000 vehicles, 570,000 tons of supplies, and one million men. This looks to be one of the largest defeats inflicted upon Germany during this war. It was unfortunately also one of the costliest. Over 110,000 casualties have been reported on both sides.

Gwen critically studied her copy of the paper. Front page and center! Though initially proud, she wondered why her piece on "Women in the Military" hadn't commanded this kind of attention. They'd buried that one on the back page in the right-hand corner. *Oh well, it figures,* she thought wryly.

She gave the article another half-hearted glance. Maybe I should cut out the whole thing and send it home. *Would anybody even care? Dad's so busy earning a living and taking care of his new wife. The kids have all moved on.* Gwen had always shared her pittance of a salary with her family, but had yet to be thanked. *Dad used to want me to stay home and take care of everyone,* she reflected.

He never understood why a woman would want to go to college. And he never approved of the newspaper business. She flipped her article in the trash.

The jangle of the desk phone interrupted her thoughts. "Gwen, how are you?" The rich sound of Captain Noble's voice soothed her mood.

"Why hello, Jake. I'm fine, thank-you. Better, now that you called. I've been so worried about you and your men. What are you doing in town?"

"War planning with the commanders. But I have other ideas. What do I have to do to get a pretty lady to have dinner with me tonight?"

Gwen threw back her shiny brunette waves and laughed. She had been dating Captain Noble on and off for the past few months. She liked his no-pressure style: flirting, drinks, dancing, and a polite kiss at the doorway.

"Tell me the time and place and I'm yours," she chirped happily.

"I'll pick you up at 7 o'clock. Let's keep the location a surprise. Hey, by the way: nice article about Normandy. Your information was on the mark."

"Thank-you, sir," Gwen answered, pleased. "See you tonight." She hung up wondering what she should wear.

HEADS TURNED when the couple entered the elegant restaurant. He was dashing in his army captain's uniform; tall, imposing, and oozing with charm. She wore a green velvet dress with faux diamond earrings shown off by upswept hair.

Though she couldn't afford real jewels, the effect was still breathtaking. When he first lay eyes on her that evening, he'd whistled appreciatively.

"How is the war going? Are you holding up alright?" She asked with genuine concern.

His face fell immediately. "I don't want to talk about the damn war——I want to forget about it for one night. Talk about anything else." After an uncomfortable pause, his smile returned. "Like *you,* for instance.—let's talk about you," he took her hand and squeezed it. Gwen squirmed nervously in her chair. "I know you're birthday is coming and I'm afraid I'll be on-duty—so-o-o I got you something a little early." He presented her with a small gilded box. "Are you just going to sit there? Open it, Gwen." he coaxed with a smile.

Inside was a gold-chained necklace—an exquisite heart set with rows of diamonds and emeralds, her favorite. How could he have known? And this one was *real*. It sparkled brilliantly at Gwen. She couldn't take her eyes off it. She had always coveted other people's gems and could never afford any for herself.

This must have cost him an arm and a leg, all on an army captain's modest salary.

"I-I don't know what to say," she uttered, still not moving nor touching it. "You-you really shouldn't have."

"Go ahead and put it on," he urged. "It will complement your dress perfectly." He took it out of the box and got out of his chair. Deftly, he put it around her neck.

The intimate gesture set off alarm bells in Gwen's head. *Why had he gotten her such an expensive gift? What did he want in return?* She didn't know if she was ready to give her heart to any man, especially after the Charlie debacle.

"There. Almost as beautiful as the lady wearing it. May I have a dance before dinner?" He bowed gallantly.

She nodded, still speechless, and soon they were dancing very slowly to a waltz. Captain Noble pulled her very close to him. "I've been thinking about you more and more lately," he whispered in her ear. "I like being with you, Gwen."

Gwen waited for that rush of adrenaline she got when she was beginning to fall in love. Nothing happened. This man was so nice and ever so handsome. Yet still she felt nothing. Tears welled up in her eyes as she came to the realization.

"Jake, I don't feel like dancing right now. I'd like to sit down." She pulled his hand off her waist as she headed for the table.

"Gwen, are you feeling okay? What's wrong?"

"I'm feeling Okay, Jake. It's just that I can't accept this." Regretfully, she unclasped the necklace and put it back in the box.

His dark eyes filled with disappointment. "What's wrong?" He asked once more. "Have I done something to offend you? If so—"

"No, no, it's nothing like that." She cut him off while shredding the napkin in her lap. "It's not you. You are wonderful. It's me. I-I'm not ready to settle into a serious relationship. I take life one day at a time because of my job. I never know where my next assignment will take me. I-I can't be tied down," she finished lamely, avoiding his probing eyes.

He straightened up in his chair and squared his shoulders. "This necklace is a birthday present—no strings attached." He said the words gruffly and she knew Capt. Noble was back in full military mode. "Really, Gwen, you read too much into things. I would never presume to push you faster than you want to go."

Gwen finally met his gaze. "I'm glad because I do enjoy our dates. We have fun. We don't got too serious. Now listen to that music!" She grabbed his arm, ready to swing.

The rest of the night was dominated by small talk interspersed with long bouts of silence. Over and over, Gwen caught Noble stealing pensive looks at her when he thought she wasn't paying attention. Finally, the evening was punctuated by the usual doorway goodnight. Only this time, Noble didn't lean in for a kiss. Instead, he formally took her hand and pressed it to his.

"Good-bye, Gwen. I hope you find what you're looking for. I realized tonight that it wasn't me."

Gwen opened her mouth to protest, but he was gone in an instant. She walked into her boarding room, slamming the door behind her. She didn't care if she woke the whole place up. Another fiasco!! She threw her dress off and took her hair down. *What's wrong with me? My life is a total disaster where men are concerned.*

"Keep calm and carry on." That's what the King had advised his subjects to do during these

uncertain times. It would behoove her to follow that advice as well. With incredible self-discipline, she sat down at her typewriter—her only real friend it sometimes seemed. Her mind raced forward to her next assignment and a comforting feeling of security began to envelope her. *This was what she was good at.*

She wondered how long it would be until the Allies marched on Paris and liberated the once beautiful city from the clutches of the Nazis. She hadn't talked to Margo in a long while. Was she still in London? Margo would be back in the middle of the fray regardless. That's how she is... That girl is so stubborn, she thought shaking her head. *I don't know how Mr. and Mrs. Sommers can stand it. Please God, keep her safe........that family is already on the verge of breaking.*

Her mind unwillingly skipped to Margo's brother, Mike. *What was he doing tonight? Was he in some trench dodging enemy bullets, while she sat here safe in her comfortable room?* Feeling shallow and ashamed, she said a little prayer for his safety as well. Somewhere along the way, he'd gone from being "Margo and Elise's brother" to her *friend*---- one of her best friends during these hard times. She realized a long time before, she'd mistakenly perceived Mike's strength as predictability. Tonight it was as if she was really seeing him for who he was. He had to make it through this war. For everyone.

Pulling her tousled hair off her face, Gwen began to peck out a letter to Mike. Halting at first, the letter soon began to pick up pace. Eventually, the words poured out and she was telling him everything about her life, her family, the war, Margo's recovery and more. At least with Mike, she could be herself.

She felt better once she'd sealed and addressed the envelope. *I only hope this reaches him, wherever he may go.* Not bothering to remove her lipstick, she lay her head on the pillow where sleep mercifully rescued her.

WORLDS AWAY, Mike was on the outskirts of a battlefield, scrunched up in a waterproof tent that wasn't; downing the last slug of some homemade whiskey. He was dirty, bloodied, scared, and homesick. In times like these, as was always the case, his mind went to Gwen. Thinking of her was like wrapping himself in a soft blanket.

Her birthday was the day after tomorrow. How he longed to celebrate with her. How he wished he had something to give her. He bit his cracked lips, imagining how lovely she would look—stepping out in the London evening dressed to kill. That stunning hair, those glittering eyes, and the legs that went on forever.

Without warning, a darker thought interrupted his desires. Of course she would already have a soldier on her arm, helping her enjoy the special occasion. Her companion would be tall, handsome, and charming enough to knock Gwen's socks off. That was Gwen's type. He, Mike Sommers, was not Gwen's type.

Who did he think he was kidding to ever believe that Gwen would want him in a serious way? I am a shoulder to cry on, he told himself tersely. Why can't I get that through my thick skull? I'll never be more than her friend.

Mike's drinking buddy noticed his fallen mood. "What's wrong, pal? You look like hell."

""Yeah, well, guess what? I feel like hell too," Mike responded morosely. "Got any more of this hooch?"

"We're damn lucky to get that. You better hit the sack—we've got a lot of ground to cover tomorrow.""

The tent flap suddenly popped open. Patty, the unit's nurse, looked in. "Oh, there you are, Mike. I wanted to go over a few things tonight..." her voice trailed off uncertainly as she surveyed the empty whiskey bottle. "I guess I'm a little too late."

"No, no, feel free to lay your problems on me. I'm all ears." Mike glanced appreciatively at the curvacious blue-eyed blond. Here was an all-American woman standing within arm's length. She wasn't Gwen, but she was *here* and she was real.

He struggled to his feet. "What's on your mind, Patty?" He took a few wobbly steps forward before clinging to her elbow. "I'll walk you to your tent."

Patty chuckled at his condition. "Um, No Mike, how 'bout if I walk you instead?"

Chapter 29

SHE WAS SCARED, BUT AT THE SAME TIME, exhilarated. The P-51D Mustang dipped and turned sideways. Margo's stomach followed suit. The cramped cockpit barely held the three people inside.

"Cut it out, Roger. You're not funny," she cried. Evelyn gave her a sharp elbow to the ribs. Margo returned the favor.

"Relax, ladies. Didn't I tell you? We're in for a little adventure."

Shivering in her off-duty beige rayon skirt, Margo once again asked herself how she'd gotten into this peculiar situation.

Even the smart new summer uniforms couldn't ward off August's heat and humidity earlier that day. Margo wiped the sweat from her brow as she motioned in two more trucks for engine inspection. Now a sergeant, her confidence was brimming over, as were her responsibilities in the motor pool.

"I think these babies will be in mint condition when they join the Red Ball Express," she said to her co-worker, Evelyn.

Studying the red circles painted on the sides of the vehicles, Evelyn gave Margo one of her "million-dollar smiles". "I think it's excitin' that we're playin' our part," she said in a thick Southern drawl. "These trucks will be ready to take medical supplies and ammo from Northern England to the coast, and on to France."

"It would be more exciting if we could actually *drive* in the convoys," Margo responded wryly. "The colonel doesn't want women near a combat zone, so here we sit in London."

"I suppose he doesn't want the WACs in harm's way," mused Evelyn.

"As far as I'm concerned, most of Europe is a potential battle zone," said Margo. "At least that's what the shrapnel in my back keeps saying."

Evelyn looked thoughtfully at her friend. "You are so right. I wish we could get half the respect that men do. I've heard there's a lot of naysayers who believe women join the army just to find a man. They don't think we're carryin' our weight."

Margo felt her blood rising. "That's not what General Eisenhower thinks. I read that he called us 'efficient, skilled, spirited, and determined.' I never forgot his words."

Evelyn nodded. "What about that contingent of WAC's who recently landed on Normandy? They're settin' up mobile switchboards in the French countryside. Tents and huts mostly. I heard they had to dig trenches for drainage and..... take the dreaded helmet baths." She laughed. "Must be a bitch to put on lipstick usin' a mirror hanging from a tree."

Margo tossed her hair scornfully. "We do what we have to—fight this war and still remain a woman. There's nothing wrong with looking good." She grew quiet. "I wish I could've gone to France. That's where the real action is. I thought about throwing in for it, but honestly—switchboard operator isn't my cup of tea. I couldn't leave motorpool. Maybe....the colonel will change his mind about women in the Red Ball convoy...."

"Dream on, Margo," she said checking her watch. "Well, I'm clocking out now. I'll call you tonight and we'll see what kind of hell we can raise."

Before she returned to work, a newly hung recruitment poster caught Margo's eye. It showed a woman in a WAC uniform sitting at a desk with a typewriter and phone. A man was in the background clutching boots and helmet. The caption read: "Release a Man for Combat."

"I wonder what would happen if I tore that down," Margo scoffed as she turned away.

After work that evening, Margo could barely believe her ears.

"He wants us to do what?" Margo asked incredulously. "I must've heard you wrong, Ev."

"No, honey, you heard me right. Roger has invited the two of us for a private flight in his new fighter airplane."

Goose bumps ran down Margo's spine. Going on a unauthorized flight in a plane that was property of the Royal Air Force? It was unheard of. Who was this Roger Dawson fellow and what was wrong with him? She shuddered to think of the consequences if they got caught.

Still, something about that evening spoke to her. She was young, she was bored, and yes, she was willing to throw caution to the wind.

"What the hell! I'll get ready right now. Do I need to bring anything extra— special garb or supplies?"

"For what, Margo? He's takin' us on a little spin is all. We'll be snug in bed by 11 p.m. Don't over think it. Let's enjoy bendin' the rules tonight "

"Breaking them is more like it. What time do I meet you two at the hangar?"

"Eight o'clock sharp."

"We must be nuts. See you later, Ev." Margo laughed as she hung up the phone. It was fun to be crazy. Made her feel seventeen again, instead of the wise old twenty-two that she actually was.

⋯⋯⋯⋯⋯

HOURS LATER, she was high in the air, going 370 miles per hour, wondering what was next.

"Roger, you've got to turn this thing around. I have a long day ahead of me. Ev said you'd have us home by bedcheck."

"Bed check?" Roger hooted. "I'll get you home all right, but it'll be more like morning roll call."

177

Margo stared furiously into the darkness, wishing she could make out the terrain below. "Evelyn, maybe you can knock some sense into your fly-boy. I'm afraid I might choke him if he doesn't turn this plane around right now!"

"Settle down, Margo." The young pilot inhaled deeply on the Lucky Strike cigarette he had balanced between his teeth. He pointed to the far horizon. "See those lights? That's Paris, my friends." He gave another infectious laugh.

Dumbstruck, Evelyn dug her fingernails into Margo's hand.

Paris, France? This guy had to be kidding. Paris was across the English Channel. It was occupied by Nazis. Everyone knew the Allies were about to march on the French capital and liberate it from its oppressors. She, Ev, and Roger couldn't simply fly to Paris on a whim. Or could they?

At first they were too stunned to speak. It was as if they'd had the wind knocked out of them. Both young women looked ahead in awe at the upcoming twinkling lights. It wasn't as dazzling as they'd imagined, being mostly a patchwork of darkness and light. *Must have been the Nazis who turned off the lights.* Still—what they could make out was spectacular. Margo was sure that was the Seine River shining up at them.

Roger broke the silence. "See over there? That's the Eiffel Tower. And over there is the Notre Dame Cathedral. Now I'm getting my bearings. And over here..." Roger zoomed in lower to give the his passengers a better look.

Suddenly there was a bright flash directly below them.

"What in heaven's name was that?" asked Evelyn.

"I'm afraid it was a bloody explosion. Probably a bomb," Roger wasn't laughing anymore.

"Get us the hell out of here!" shouted Margo.

Roger veered the plane around so fast that everyone's stomach did a flip-flop. His big hands had a death grip on the stick. The RAF pilot began pulling the plane up when he realized he wasn't alone in the sky. Too close for comfort, another plane's lights came into view. *Was it friend or foe?* Roger focused on getting away from it, just in case.

At that moment, a projectile was launched from the ground, making a certain whistling noise Margo recognized instantly. She reflexively ducked her head for cover. "Oh my God, we're about to be shot down!"

With a violent blast, the other plane was hit instead. It turned into a horrific red inferno before shattering into a million pieces.

"Dammit, Roger do something! You and your great ideas got us into this mess----- you can get us out!"

"I knew the Resistance and the Allies would be clashing in the future---- but hell, I didn't think it would be tonight!" Roger tried to keep his concentration as another projectile whizzed by. If only these American ladies could use the .50 caliber guns mounted on each wing!

Evelyn whimpered in the back seat, while Margo merely fumed to herself. Why had she let herself get talked into this pointless excursion? She'd made it through the London bombing only to find herself in the eye of the storm once again. And for what?

"I'm making an emergency landing, ladies! Make sure your seat belts are tightened and hold on. Let's see if the hype about this Mustang is true." Roger began to go into a nosedive. *Where would he land? Right in the middle of downtown Paris?*

Chapter 30

"Do you have another cigarette?" Margo held her hand out to Roger, glaring daggers. "I'd like to bust your chops."

"I shouldn't give you one after that remark." Roger said, confidence fully recovered.

Margo disagreed. He owed her that much after their treacherous landing on an avenue near some very old distinguished buildings. Next to her, Evelyn giggled hysterically with obvious relief.

Margo inched out of the cockpit and looked around. For all the chaos in the air, there wasn't a soul in sight on the wide street opposing what must be the university, the Sorbonne, as the French called it. Though it looked unchanged by war, the place was too eerily calm. Margo gazed at the stately, ornate buildings stretching up in front of her. Any other time; the domes, archways, pillars, and towering trees would have enchanted her. She had always wanted to gaze upon the university's murals by Chavannes.

Now, one thought overrode all the others: How the hell will we ever get out of this mess?

Slinking out of the shadows, three mysterious strangers emerged. The first was a solemn young man wearing a khaki beret over his dark, wavy hair. Beneath his furrowed brow were deep-set eyes teeming with determination. A trench coat partially covered both a black turtleneck and a gun that hung casually from his waist.

The second person was a woman who looked to be in her early thirties. She could've been anyone's sister or wife. She had nicely coiffed hair, a crisp white blouse, and a a mid-calf skirt with tan pumps. The thing that set her apart was the machine gun she jauntily aimed at the three Americans. The look on her face said she'd have no problem using it. Even Roger gulped when he saw her.

The third person was a uniformed policeman. Big, bald, and intimidating, he followed closely behind the other two. His gun was not drawn, but he slapped a billy club to his palm.

Margo's heart sank when she saw the police uniform. He had to be employed by the Germans government! She and her friends would be arrested for their unsanctioned landing, at the least. At the worst, the Nazis would have their way with them. They would rub their hands together gleefully, drooling at the sight of three wayward Americans.

Nauseous at the thought of it, Margo reluctantly raised both her hands in surrender. Evelyn tearfully followed suit. Roger did nothing but look expectantly at the newcomers.

The man in the beret spoke tersely. "*Que avez vous*?"

Roger surprised Margo and Evelyn by answering, "*Est-ce que vous conaissez quelques mots d'anglais?*"

"Yes, I speak English." The young man spoke with a heavy accent. "So again I ask, Who are you?"

"Please believe us---we didn't intend to land here. We were having a little fun and we got lost. We mean you no harm. Please."

The young French man's face began to relax as he looked over the airplane and its British insignias. "So you are Allies?" The policeman gave them a half-hearted nod, but the woman continued to eye the strangers suspiciously, keeping her gun trained directly on them. "How do we know you are not German spies?"

At the thought of it, Margo and Evelyn held back nervous smiles. "We are Americans," Margo announced rather staunchly. "We work on vehicles that send supplies to the Allied front line to further your cause. We are definitely *not* German spies.

The woman still did not lower her gun. Roger suddenly brightened. "You are part of the French Resistance, right? A good British friend of mine is in Special Operations. Over the past year he has been coordinating with the Resistance. His tales of intrigue made me want to see Paris for myself."

The newcomers conferred in French while continuing to glare at their captives.

"Oh really? What is the name of your friend?"

It was like a game of chicken. "What if you're not who you say you are and I get my friend shot? No thanks, no names."

"You better tell us *something* before you get yourselves shot."

"While I can't disclose his identity, I will tell you what I know about the top drawer work the Resistance is doing. I know for a fact that Paris is coming unraveled thanks to the Resistance. I understand the railroad workers are on strike, which is fouling things up royally. Also my friend is behind many anti-German rallies now taking place. He is also working to put guns directly in the hands of your people". With his hands up, Roger walked carefully to his plane. Dramatically, he gave all its 32 feet the once over. He stopped at the RAF insignia.

"Go ahead," he said motioning at it. " Examine my Mustang to your heart's content, long as you don't bloody well fly off in it. Needs fuel anyhow..."

Acceptance began to cross the French people's faces. Margo, Roger and Evelyn took the opportunity to properly introduced themselves. Begrudgingly, the woman slung her machine gun back on her waist. "I am Suzanne. I have been working with the Resistance since the Germans first invaded."

"At least the French allow women on the front line," Margo commented, impressed.

"They don't have much choice. The Resistance recruits anybody and everybody, even children. After how the Nazis ruined my life, I'd like to see someone stop me from joining the fight." Her face was a mask of hatred. Margo wondered what happened earlier in

Suzanne's life, but she could see the subject was firmly closed for the time being.

"How did a policeman join your ranks?" asked Evelyn timidly. Now it was her turn to eye the man suspiciously.

"That is Alex. He only knows French. Much of the police force has bowed out or joined our side. It makes it very----how do you say----*convenient.*" She gave Alex a conspiratorial pat on the shoulder.

The young man next to the policeman stepped forward, removing his beret courteously. "I am Gabriel—Gabe to my friends. I choose to view you as friends– hope I'm not mistaken. People who cross me are sorry."

"You aren't mistaken, Gabe. I truly want to know what is going on around here tonight. We saw a plane get shot out of the sky and we were almost next. Hence our hasty landing. It looks like all hell is breaking loose earlier than expected. So why isn't the Resistance waiting for the Allies?"

"We only have so much patience, Roger. Our intelligence informs us that Hitler is on the brink of destroying our beautiful city. How long are we supposed to wait? If no one will save us, then we will save ourselves. We will get that bastard Hitler by the *couilles* if it's the last thing we do." He paused and stroked his goatee. "Now, Roger-is it— please tell us what you know about the Allies' plans."

"The last scuttlebutt I heard was that Patton's troops were marching towards the Seine River."

Gabe removed his beret, rubbing his head thoughtfully. "Good –you passed the test, though your information is dated. Now I will tell you--- I have it on good authority that Haislip and his Corps *crossed* the Seine earlier today."

"Good God, things are coming to a head!" For confirmation, Roger looked at the two American women. All three of them seemed to be thinking the same thing.

"Our troops are almost here," said Margo, her eyes shining. "Even if we *could* get out, I don't want to. There's no place I'd rather be than Paris right now. I want to witness the liberation of Paris!"

"But what if it doesn't work out?" injected Evelyn. "What if-what if the Germans somehow manage to hold on and we're stuck here under their noses?"

"Whoa—one thing at a time, people. No one is positive about what will happen next. Live with ambivalence. We do every day." The Frenchman shrugged. "For instance, the Resistance is wondering about one vital question: Where is Leclerc? We want our French troops on the front line for the liberation. This has been *our* oppression and we want to lead the fight out of it." Heat was rising in Gabe's face.

"Cool down, Gabe. I heard Leclerc is holding things down in Argentan. The Allies know how to be diplomatic, oui? Leclerc won't be left behind. I'd bet my bottom dollar that he'll be front and center when the time is right here in Paris. Don't lose sleep over it."

"If you say so..." Gabe threw a furtive glance at Suzanne like he wasn't totally buying it.   "

"All we ask for is a place to hide out until things calm down a bit and soon we'll be out of your hair," Roger said. "As military personnel, we are Absent Without Leave and in a shitload of our own trouble. I must keep my plane out of the enemy's hands or I need not return home... And we three want to simply lay low awhile until the coast is clear..."

Gabe thought a moment before answering. "We will provide sanctuary for you and your plane. But you must do as we say. If you do anything foolish, you could get us all killed. Unlike your little joy ride, our work is not child's play. Comprehende?" He nodded at Suzanne. "We must go before the sun comes up."

Suzanne took each woman by the hand with Roger closely following and led them into a crumbling side street apartment. Toward the back of the shabby place was a narrow stairway leading to a small basement, approximately 20 feet by 15 feet in size. "It's not much, but it makes a nice place to hide."

Margo shivered involuntarily. "I've got a raging case of claustrophobia. Hope I don't end up climbing the walls. I may choose to be upstairs with the bombs."

"Oh no you won't," countered Suzanne. "Coffee, anyone?" She handed out steaming mugs.

Margo almost spit her coffee across the room. "Ugh, what is this stuff?"

"Coffee, also known as barley, mixed with chicory."

"No thanks," said Margo, pouring hers down the dingy little sink.

Suzanne laughed bitterly. "You won't be doing that if you stay long enough. We French have been living on rations since the Germans invaded. They've seized much of our meat and produce production for their country.... leaving our people hungry." She swore under her breath in French.

Sighing, Roger lowered his eyes and folded his arms across his chest. "Girls, I'm not usually one to apologize, but I know when I've done something foolish. I'm sorry I brought you into this hell hole. My timing was obviously way off the mark. I thought the Liberation wouldn't happen so soon. Please forgive my ignorance, ladies."

Neither young woman looked at him or spoke. They both seemed to be worlds away— contemplating their predicament. A tear rolled down Evelyn's cheek. Margo prayed for the inner patience not to shake her friend and tell her to straighten up. She tried to think of other things to keep herself from going batty.

At that moment, Gabe appeared, looking as preoccupied as ever. "Are you going to be alright down here? It's not exactly the Hotel de Ville, " he said ruefully.

Roger was relieved at the chance to move beyond his mea culpa. "So, exactly what kinds of things are you doing to slow down the Germans? I know some of the stuff, but I'm sure there's a lot I don't know..."

"Very true. We've been cutting their lines of communication, as well as destroying road signs for some time. It drives the enemy crazy because they do not know France—they will never know France.

We keep them confused—always. They are lost without their precious signs." Gabe spoke with pride. "Another easy way to stop them is to puncture the tires of all their vehicles. Small acts that add up, oui?" He shot a furtive glance in Suzanne's direction. "Are you ready, cherie?" Suzanne emerged from the tiny toilette with heavy pants and boots on.

"Where are y'all goin? Don't you ever sleep?" Asked Ev.

"Let's just say we have more chaos to make."

"Tires to puncture?" Margo asked with a smile.

"Something like that. Here, I've brought you water and baguettes."

"Thanks, but what about cigarettes?" Roger protested. "I'm getting low."

"Make them last and stay put. We'll talk about everything later. Now, *allons-y* , Suzanne!"

They silently checked their machine guns one last time and hurriedly climbed the stairs without looking back.

Chapter 31

ELISE PUTTERED AROUND IN THE KITCHEN, pouring Daddy a coffee refill, and pulling some freshly baked biscuits out of the oven. She'd better step it up if she was going to find time to eat before the first day of school began. She'd learned her lesson in the past when attempting to teach 25 sixth-graders on an empty stomach.

"How'd you sleep? Did you dream about your new students?" asked Lainey rounding the corner. Not waiting for a reply, she continued, "I saw you got another letter from that Joe Howard. I can't wait to get to know him better, seeing how serious the two of you seem to be."

"Oh, mother, stop..." Elise blushed in spite of herself. She and Joe had secretly pledged their love to one another; had spoken of an engagement, but she didn't want the world to know just yet. Not even Mother. Her feelings were buried deep inside, like a hidden treasure full of riches. Someday she would share her secret with others, but not on this day.

"Uh-huh," she deflected the question, handing Lainey the hot biscuits. "Mother, Joe's submarine is headed for the South Pacific. The Navy won't let him disclose the details of the mission, but..."

You mean the Philippines, thought Lainey. *J.D.* She tried not to get on the roller-coaster ride of hope. "I'll pray for Joe and his.... mission." She sat down at the kitchen table while trying to send Jesse a meaningful look.

Jesse stayed behind his newspaper, pretending not to hear. He hated to see Lainey get her hopes up, especially this early in the morning.

"What about the latest on the European front of the war?" He said to change the subject. "We've made terrific progress ever since the Normandy landing. Wish we'd hear from Mike. I have no doubt whatsoever that boy is going to be standing on German soil soon enough. We're not gonna know *how* he got there but he will get there. He's strong, Lainey." He beamed out from the paper at his wife.

The kitchen grew still as Elise gulped down her garden melons while planning last minute lesson ideas; and Lainey contemplated Joe's mission. Another article caught Jesse's eye. "Says right here the American troops under Patton are marching toward the Seine River outside of Paris. The 2nd French Armored Division is not far behind," Jesse reported, his reading glasses slipping defiantly down his nose. "Paris is coming apart at the seams. Radical citizens are literally taking back their city, before the troops actually arrive. And listen to this----it says here that Hitler wants to destroy Paris at the last moment."

"Oh, Lord, I hope not! It's the most beautiful city in the world—so many bridges, so much lovely architecture," Elise replied.

Lainey looked up from her biscuits and ruminations. "Now—I hate to ask this, but I can't help myself. Is there any way Margo could have been sent to France?"

"You're doing nothing more than borrowing trouble. Get it through your pretty head—she's stationed in London with the motor pool. You know that as well as I do."

Lainey smiled at her husband. Lately she'd come to appreciate what a comfort he was. "You're right. The English Channel is between her and the fighting. I don't know why I imagined such a silly thing." With relief she arose to begin her morning chores. *When it came to her children, she was learning that no news was good news.*

Chapter 32

SHE OPENED HER EYES AND LOOKED AROUND. For a moment she had forgotten where she was—she thought she was back in London. The hard mat and the scarred four walls helped her remember she was in Paris. She yawned and checked her watch. It was nine p.m. She'd been asleep all day. Roger and Ev were still asleep in the corner, curled up together. Idly she wondered where their French friends were. *When would they see them again?* She couldn't believe how dependent she was on them already.

She needed the toilet, but she dreaded using the filthy thing. *I guess I should be glad to have anything. Maybe I'll stand up the way men do.* After that she scrubbed her hands with homemade soap and attempted to rinse them in the water that trickled out of the old faucet into the rusty sink. It didn't help, because her hands felt like they'd never be clean again.

A sharp click-clack of shoes on the stairs interrupted her thoughts. *Oh Lord, I hope it's them and not the Germans,* she thought fearfully.

Her face was blackened; her pants were dirty and torn; yet her gun remained intact. Both she and Gabe were breathless and beaming. Margo unabashedly hugged them both. "God, I'm so glad to see you. I thought you were the Germans."

Suzanne lifted the sole of her worn boot. "See these? The French people have wooden soles now. We ran out of leather a long time ago. You will know it is us by the sound of the wood. No fear, Margo."

Margo took in the sight of the two people before her. "What happened to you, anyway?"

"What happened to us should not be discussed," Gabe replied. "The more you know, the more at risk you are."

"Oh, bull" Margo retorted. "I'm stuck down in this hole —the least you can do is let me know what's happening out there."

Gabe and Suzanne exchanged wary looks, until Gabe's eyes relented. "Fine," Suzanne said. "If you must know, we bombed a gas depot." She looked proudly at Gabe.

"Bombed a gas depot," Margo repeated back. Evelyn and Roger were sitting up now, their eyes wide open.

"This is revolution, friends. It isn't pretty, but we're wearing down the enemy slowly, but surely." Gabe rubbed his face with an old towel and pulled off his shirt. "This is the safest place for us to stay tonight. Sorry it is so hot and cramped, but I must sleep now. Tomorrow will be worse."

Margo turned off the light, though her mind was going a million miles a minute. "How did you get so involved?" she whispered to Suzanne, who was next to her. "The men accept you as one of them. You must be damn good at your job."

"Margo, as I told you before, I have my reasons for joining the Resistance. Maybe tomorrow I will tell you about it. Tonight I need to sleep..."

The pitch black room went quiet, save the heavy breathing of slumber. Margo lay listening, wondering. She'd slept all day; she knew she wouldn't sleep tonight. Instead, she felt like climbing the walls.

✧✦✧✦✧✦✧

THEY WERE TAKING TURNS eating at a rickety card table on one crummy folding chair. *How ironic*, thought Margo. *We're in the city most famous for its cuisine, and look what we're having for breakfast, lunch, and supper*. She took a gulp of water with which to wash down the stale bread.

The stairs were filled with the sound of heavy footsteps. Ev and Margo looked intently at one another. *Were the shoe soles wooden?* Their expressions remained frozen until Alex entered the basement, sweaty, and all wound up. He nodded in their direction before exclaiming in rapid-fire French to Gabe and Suzanne. The three outsiders looked on curiously—dying to know what was happening. The policeman left as suddenly as he came, leaving Gabe to face the others.

"There's no turning back now. This is the beginning of the end where the Germans are concerned. The Resistance is now occupying the police stations, the town halls, the national ministries, and the newspaper buildings. People will remember August 19, 1944."

"Isolated pockets of German soldiers are being attacked by our people," said Suzanne. She looked at Gabe urgently. "We must patrol the streets immediately."

"I'm going on ahead to Place de Catalogne. I'll meet you in front of the bistro. You know which one, oui?"

Suzanne said something in French to him as he disappeared up the stairs. Dropping her food, she began to throw on her soiled boots and pants from the day before.

"Are you two lovers?" Margo asked, smiling.

"Gabe? Oh no, we're friends; fighting for the same cause." She shook her head at the thought.

"Before you go, tell me how you got involved in all this. I realize I'm prying, but I want to understand everything."

"I'm not sure anybody else can really understand how I feel. I don't usually talk about it, but you are—shall we say— persistent."

"I was an average young woman, four years ago, innocent as the next," she continued. "I went to jazz clubs and museums with my boyfriend. I was helping my family run their shop downtown. I had no particular political views. Live and let live is how I saw things. That was before the Germans took over." She stared out into space. "They shot Papa and Mama right before my eyes."

"They took my younger brother and forced him to become one of their soldiers. *Service du Traail*

Obligatoire, they call it. I call it kidnapping. They conscripted hundreds of thousands of French against their will for the war effort."

"I escaped, but I never forgot and I never will. I decided to do what I could to avenge the loss of my family. The Resistance has been the only family I've known for the past four years. And my only real friend has been this right here," she said patting her gun. "I am lucky to have it. Many in the resistance are unarmed. Anyway, Margo, I will not breathe easy until we regain our freedom."

Dumbstruck, Margo eyed Suzanne with renewed admiration along with a deep sense of sorrow. Roger and Ev listened intently to every word.

"And now I know..." Margo uttered to more to herself than the others. "Take care, Cherie," said the French woman over her shoulder as she left.

"*You,* take care. I only wish I was going with you!" *Anything is better than this,* Margo thought miserably, trying not to let the four walls close around her once more.

⚜ ⚜ ⚜

"A BLOODY ROYAL FLUSH? I give up!" Roger folded his cards and raised his hands in mock protest.

Evelyn had to smile as she gathered the pot of shredded paper that stood in for poker chips. "This is a heist, Margo. You never told me she was so slick at cards."

"How 'bout another hand?" Evelyn asked.

"What time is it?" Margo inquired. "Jeez. It's after eight. I wish they would get back. I hate depending on other people for food." She rubbed her stomach to make it quit growling.

Loud voices could suddenly be heard shouting back and forth in French. Gabe and Alex arrived wild-eyed and disheveled. They immediately dropped to the floor, sitting with their backs against the wall. Gabe put his head in his hands.

"What happened?" Roger asked.

"Where is Suzanne?" Margo inquired repeatedly.

Alex acted like he didn't comprehend. When Gabe refused to look up, Margo got down on the floor and directly confronted him. "Tell me, Gabe! Where the hell is she?"

The big burly policeman shook his head, rivulets of tears streaking his face. Evelyn began to sob at the sight while Roger reflexively put his arm around her.

Stiffening with fear, Margo put her hand on Gabe's shoulder and forced herself to look into Gabe's distraught eyes. "What happened?" she murmured.

"It should have been so easy. Our patrol was almost over for the night when we noticed a group of young soldiers approaching us on the street. Violence broke out, but you could see they knew they were outnumbered. They surrendered quickly, and Suzanne took her own prisoner."

"The kid looked so young and naive," He choked on his own words. "She---she forgot to check his pockets. She *never* forgets—I don't know why she did this time. He got this strange look on his face and pulled a grenade out of his pocket. Before anyone could react, he pulled the pin. One minute they were there and the next minute they were both blown apart."

Margo's mouth dropped in horror. The little basement was filled with anguished wails of grief. Roger slammed the wall with his fist, and Margo bit her lip till it bled. Ev continued her steady sobbing. The two Frenchmen looked inconsolable, but soon regained control. A hard mask of determination began to disguise their pain.

"She's gone-with her parents where she belongs. She knew this could happen at any time. I guess we all know though we try not to dwell on it. The best thing we can do is *finish this*---- for her." He repeated this to Alex in French. The policeman nodded—punctuating Gabe's words with a soft, "Bon Jour, mon cherie." Everyone was silent.

Finally, Margo spoke up. "I want to help."

"No." Gabe answered firmly. "The best thing you can do is lay low until our troops arrive. You are too obvious with your American accent and American ways. Do you want to find yourself in the same position as Suzanne?" His voice cracked when he said her name. "Herr von Choltitz has called a truce for the time being. He admits the Resistance has taken control over parts of Paris. Too late for *her*. But not for you, Margo."

The young WAC became quiet. She didn't know how to respond. Of course she didn't want to die, but life in this basement felt like a slow death in itself. What if the troops didn't get here?

Somehow—with or without Gabe, she would get some fresh air and a new perspective.

For now, she mourned Suzanne. Though she had known her less than 48 hours, it felt like a lifetime.

Chapter 33

"SIR, THE ENVOYS INFORM US that the Resistance controls most of Paris and all of the bridges," the voice on the phone said to General Eisenhower. "We aren't sure if Choltitz will obey Hitler's orders to destroy the city. The next move is in our hands."

"Send a shipment of food and coal to the capital now. I'll tell Bradley to send Allied troop reinforcements there as well. We must repay them for their great assistance in the campaign. We wouldn't be where we are without them."

"Sir-you know what this means..."

"Yes, I realize we are superceding the French action. Don't worry," there was a pause, " Leclerc's men will lead the liberation. The history books will reflect that. It's the diplomatic thing to do," he concluded.

Soon General Bradley ordered Gerow's American V Corps as well as a British unit, to accompany Leclerc. A northern and southern column began to approach the city. On August 24. the armistice was scheduled to expire at noon , so it was imperative that the Allies enter Paris before it was destroyed by Choltitz. The troops continued to close in.

Directly before midnight, a small force under one of Leclerc's men rolled along back streets and side roads, crossing the river at the Pont d'Austerlitz, and driving on its right bank to the Hotel de Ville.

Margo pulled back her hot, sweaty hair impatiently. *I'd kill for a shower or even a damn hair clip. Now I wish we'd flown out of here that first night...* She listened to Roger snore, wondering how anyone could sleep so much. The truth was, she'd always been an insomniac and probably always would be. Turning her brain off for the last five days had been next to impossible. To preserve her sanity, she planned her next cigarette run— something Roger never condoned. She couldn't help but notice though; he never turned down one of her precious smokes....

The streets had grown eerily calm, and Margo wondered what it meant. She'd considered the rumors that fighting was to resume, but so far it was only rumors. She'd also heard that Patton was sending guns and ammunition to fortify the Resistance. She pictured the posters that had appeared spontaneously on the street: "Patriotic French, Join the Struggle against the Invaders!"

In quiet stretches--- which were many--- she'd thought about J.D. What must it have been like to have been in captivity worse than this for the past 2 1/2 years? How had he managed to survive mentally? Worse, she couldn't imagine the physical abuse–the thought made her shudder. Would he be the same person when he came home? *If* he came home?

Home was another sore subject. Margo was awash with guilt whenever she thought of it. Had the Women's Army Corps declared Margo AWOL, or worse yet, MIA? Had they contacted her parents? It made her sick to think her fanciful outing may have caused her parents undue stress and pain. Almost getting hit by a bomb last year in London was all the drama she was allowed. Let them concentrate on J.D. now.

If I can get out of this in one piece, I will never, ever worry Mother and Daddy again. she promised herself. I will be the perfect daughter, like Elise; and I'll learn to accept the small town life.

She felt someone shaking her. *Leave me alone,* she wanted to say, *can't you see I'm finally asleep?* But he wouldn't leave her alone, and when Margo awoke, Gabe was there —tugging frantically on her arms—trying to pull her up.

He was pent-up with energy, his hair tousled, and his beautiful dark-lashed eyes more penetrating than ever. His voice rang anew with a tenor of urgency she'd never heard before.

"Get up! You've got to get out of here! The Germans are going house to house—clearing last hold-outs before our troops arrive. Our men *are* on the way as we speak. This is it!"

Everyone jumped up and began collecting their belongings. Gabe shook his head. "There's no time for that—let's go! Follow me!"

"B-b-But what about my plane," Roger sputtered. "You told me it would be safe."

"It is, my friend. I promise you that. You will have it back soon. Just not at the moment."

"I hate leavin' my things," Evelyn said, giving the room one last look of dazed regret. The three of them stumbled up the stairs, still half-asleep.

I'm scared, but I'm glad we're out of that dungeon, thought Margo. She took a deep breath of fresh air upon reaching the street. The sun was just beginning to come up on a scene of total mayhem.

Buildings were going up in leaping red and yellow flames, loud explosions were all around, and people were stampeding like cattle. Adding to the confusion, church bells from all corners rang joyously in the background. It seemed as if she was in the middle of a bizarre dream.

Margo's heart stopped when she heard the sound of voices calling out orders in German, something she'd never been within earshot of until now. She turned fearfully just as the Wehrmacht troops drew close behind her. She saw several men in Nazi uniforms. The light from the fires flickered across the swastikas, making her feel like she was being chased by the devil incarnate.

Gulping, Margo turned and fled with all her might in the general direction of the others. In the distance, Roger was dragging Evelyn along, as he tried unsuccessfully to keep pace with Gabe. She wanted to cry out, "Wait for me," but she knew it would call attention to herself if she did.

She looked back again. They were gaining on her. She could hear the menacing click-clack of their boots, could hear their walking gait turn into a run. Well, she could run too. Her WAC issued pumps were holding her back, so she took them off, though she couldn't make herself drop them.

She ran barefoot down the sidewalks of Paris, keeping one eye on Roger, one eye on the Germans. The only place she forgot to look was down—and she never saw how the curb made a sheer drop-off to the cobblestone street. Her ankle twisted right before she hit the ground.

Her knee was a mass of bloody scraped skin, while her whole foot throbbed incessantly; but it was her pride that was damaged most. She struggled to stand up.

"Here, let me help you," a smooth voice offered in a thick German accent.

Margo thought she would vomit. Perhaps a primordial instinct filled her soul—the urge to survive against all odds. Perhaps it was rage against the enemy and all they represented. Whatever it was, Margo swung back her hand and clocked the soldier square in the eyes with her ladylike pumps.

His death grip loosened on her as he went to rub his aching face. "Ugh-you bitch!"

In that split-second, Margo took off running again. She heard gunfire, but felt no sting of a bullet. *Where were her people? Why the hell didn't they wait for her?* They were gaining on her again and she knew it. Her body felt so tired–soon she would have to stop and she would be at their mercy. Her lungs were burning as she tried to suck in some air.

For now, she kept running. She made an abrupt left turn down a side street. She didn't know where she was going, only that it was somewhere out of the enemy's grasp. When she thought she could no longer put one foot in front of the other, a splendid sight opened up before her eyes. Throngs of cheering French citizens filled the nearby tree-lined boulevard. What was this? She threw herself into the crush of humanity. Furtively, she looked over her shoulder. Nothing. The Germans themselves must have wisely disappeared into the crowd.

Though no longer threatened, she still felt lost and alone in the sea of people when a wonderful face, a handsome well-chiseled face, emerged from nowhere.

"Gabe," she whispered in relief. "Where were you? They've been following me. They nearly had me one time."

"Sorry, *tres-belle*, I thought you were there with us, and when I turned around—you were gone. We are safe now—all of us." He put his arm snugly through the crook of hers and pulled her forward. "Let's get back to the others. Evelyn's very worried about you." Margo did not resist, though her legs felt like rubber. She wondered numbly if he'd just called her "beautiful" in French.

As they pushed their way through the boisterous crowd, it soon became apparent what was happening. Rumor became reality. The Allies had made it! Tank after tank and truck after truck rolled by the masses, who greeted them with adulation. The street was strewn with colorful flowers,

" It is the 2nd French Armored Division! Leclerc got here—I knew he would!" Gabe yelled above the din.

Over the heads of the people, Margo began to recognize her surroundings. This was the famed Champs Elysees and in the distance was the historic Arc de Triomphe; presiding, in its glorious height, above the military homecoming. It was like a scene out of a movie, watching the troops passed under the famous landmark. Margo choked down a sob that threatened to rise up in her throat. She was going to make it through this war after all!

"Look, way over there! It's Roger and Evelyn. Hold on to me and don't let go!" Holding Margo in a death grip, Gabe plowed west through the sea of excited faces until he was reunited with the others. Margo hugged Evelyn for a long time.

"Remind me to *never* go with either of you on one of your adventures again!" she exclaimed above the noise. Roger looked appropriately chastised, but not for long. He gave her a mock salute, followed by loud whistles for the arriving French troops. Evelyn clapped and giggled at his antics. *Those two are hopeless,* thought Margo happily.

"Choltitz has capitulated!" cried someone in the crowd.

"He can rot in hell!" was the resounding reply.

"The Americans have taken the East side of the city," someone else roared.

The bells of Notre Dame seemed to ring louder than ever. In response a voice chimed in, "*Our Lady of Paris* is free!"

It's truly over, Margo thought. Momentary sadness unexpectedly engulfed her. *If only Suzanne could be here to see this.* She resumed smiling as men and women everywhere began dancing and exchanging passionate kisses of victory. Evelyn and Roger were still locked in a romantic embrace long after the others moved forward.

"We are *victorieux*! To the City of Lights," proclaimed Gabe, holding a wine glass up to hers. "May She never see darkness again!" Before Margo could respond, he pulled her to him, surprising them both with a long and delicious kiss. After she caught her breath, she looked straight into Gabe's milk-chocolate eyes and made a toast of her own. "To Suzanne."

Chapter 34

HUNDREDS OF DIRTY, EMACIATED MEN with rotten teeth and tattered clothing worked outdoors in the tropical Philippine heat of early fall, 1944. Collectively they dug trench after trench for reasons only their captors could fathom.

At Old Bilibid Prison, strength and energy had left the men long ago, making every heave of the dirt-filled shovel an agony all its own. Clay Anderson sneaked a look at the Japanese guard. The young sentry looked bored and hot, oblivious to his surroundings. He dug in his uniform pocket for a smoke.

Clay took the opportunity to rest on his shovel for a moment. The chance to not be in motion, even for a few seconds was too precious to pass up. With his eyes, Clay signaled down the line that the guard was not at attention.

Next to Anderson, Tony Romero mopped his brow with quivering hands. He couldn't stop thinking about the water break, which wouldn't come for over an hour. Suddenly a distant hum grew steadily louder.

"What's that noise, Clay?"

"Probably the Japs conducting a drill," he whispered, keeping one eye on the guard.

"I don't know—it sounds different this time."

The airplanes came into view. All eyes went upward. The counting began. One, two, five, ten, twenty, thirty, fifty...... Finally there were too many to count. The planes began to descend for a moment, dipping nearer the men.

Clay peered hard at the side of the nearest plane. The shovel slipped out of his hand. "Hey, those ain't no enemy insignias, boys! They're Americans! They're coming back for us! I knew they would!"

In his excitement, Clay forgot to whisper, his voice elevating with every word. The guard forgot to care, so shocked was he at the sight of the U.S. planes. A huge cheer began to erupt among the prisoners. Their elation couldn't be contained.

The Japanese guards scurried nervously in circles. They did not seem to know what to do. Some tried ineffectively to shoot at the far away planes.

"Boys, we're going home!" cried Romero jubilantly. "By God, we'll be having turkey in Albuquerque!"

Everyone took up the chant. "Turkey in Albuquerque", they shouted defiantly. Even the Japanese who knew a little English were puzzled by the words. Hundreds of fists went in the air. At least 200 planes were now overhead in a major show of force. The men began to hug and cry.

The captors regained their composure. "Shut-up !" Guns were pointed at the prisoners.

"Work or else!"

With renewed vigor and smiles plastered on their faces, the men grabbed their shovels like they were digging for buried treasure. Half an hour later, the planes were gone. All that was left were trails of smoke in the sky.

"What are they doing now?" wondered Clay.

"Just as long as they don't forget us, I can be patient," said Romero retying the rags covering his blistered feet.

Days passed and nothing happened. Nothing. The sky was empty and the silence was deafening. The enemy showed no visible signs that anything was awry. Only the prisoners' hopes and dreams remained intact. Their spirit had been relit and wasn't easily extinguished.

BY THE END of September, something different was about to transpire. It was in the air. The Japanese were talking faster and louder than ever before. Few Americans understood their words, but no one missed the frenzy that was overtaking Bilibad.

One morning, just before dawn, the guards hurriedly awakened the prisoners. "Get up! Now! Get outside and line up! Quickly!"

Among the hastily assembled throng of men was J.D. Sommers, who'd been transferred to Old Bilibid Prison not long before. He rubbed his eyes and wondered what was next. Maybe the Japs were going to shoot them where they stood. Maybe they'd be thrown in a mass grave, the way Adolf

Hitler had been rumored to do things. J.D. braced himself and said a small prayer.

"March!" ordered one Japanese guard who was taking up the lead.

"Where are we going now?" J.D. wondered dully. His bare feet couldn't take a march like the first one so long ago.

"I don't know, " responded the next man, "but they can't hide us forever. Not on this little island. There's too many of us. Can't you see the desperation on their damn faces? The U.S. forces will find us. They have to. I've waited too long to be rescued."

Trying to keep despair at bay, the American prisoners disappeared one-by- one down the fateful road to places unknown.

Chapter 35

ONE OF THE 27 SUBMARINES based out of Pearl Harbor was the Parche. It was approximately 1500 tons with a hull length of 300 feet and a cylindrical diameter of 16 feet. It could travel a top speed of 20 knots and it could stay submerged for up to 72 hours without recharging. Painted a pale grey because that was the best camouflage on or below the water's surface, the Parche could withstand up to 14 tons per square feet of the ocean's pressure.

Located in the forward and aft were torpedoes and launch rooms. The heart of the submarine was the control room, which held the systems for diving and surfacing. Located toward the middle of the submarine were the crew's bunks, the washroom, the mess, and the tiny 6' by 11" galley. Quarters were cramped to say the least. A submarine was not for the claustrophobic.

70 men were deemed psychologically sound enough to serve on the Parche, and Joe Howard happened to be one of them. He'd been assigned to it since 1943 after his stint at submarine school in New London, Connecticut. He worked mainly as an

electrician, but he doubled as a torpedo man when it was called for.

Nights on a submarine could get lonesome, at least they did for Joe, whose lovesick thoughts were never far from Mountainview, New Mexico and Elise. He tossed and turned in his limited space. When they were battened down, there was no air conditioning, so he resigned himself to the fact that sleep was not going to come in this heat. He listened to those around him, wondering why he couldn't let go like the others.

Now that they were patrolling the "killing fields" of the Luzon Strait in the South Pacific, Joe found himself being called on to load and reload the "tube" as was called the torpedo launcher. His adrenaline pumped when he thought of those times. He hoped the sonar equipment would give off the familiar "pings" that let them know of another ship's presence. God, how he loved to be in the hunt....

As usual, his mind soon drifted back to the end of July, and what would unquestionably be the most exciting incident in his life. On the day in question, they had been above water when a convoy and its escorts were spotted. Joe's commander, Ramage, ordered two torpedoes fired as they passed a freighter. Both missed. One last shot was fired at the stern and the freighter was history.

Next, they fired four torpedoes at two tankers they were passing. One tanker was destroyed and the other was severely crippled.

By now, every ship in the enemy convoy was firing at the racing Parche. Bursting shells splashed around the submarine. Joe never knew that fear and elation could be so closely tied together until that day. He'd never felt so alive, and probably never would again as long as he lived.

""Pour in all the oil you have!" barked Ramage with a ferocity the men had never heard before. The Parche was going at top speed, swerving all the while. Soon it was boxed in by escorts, with a big ship dead ahead.

"Fire one!" ordered Ramage. Two of the three torpedoes eventually fired caught the bow.

"Top speed ahead," shouted Ramage. The Parche swung around to the side of the big ship and fired one more fatal blow to her midsection.

After 46 minutes and 19 torpedoes launched, the action was over with the Parche retreating. The comparatively small submarine had taken down three major vessels in that short time; the biggest one weighing 8990 tons. Joe didn't know it then, but his skipper would become the first living submariner to receive the Medal of Honor for his actions that day, and the Parche would also go down in the history books for those courageous 46 minutes.

For the time being, it was enough for Joe to lie in his bunk and relive the drama once again. How he wished he could hold Elise in his arms and tell her all about it. Now that he was fully awake, Joe sat up on his cot and pulled on some pants. He didn't bother with a shirt; hadn't worn one for days like all the rest of the crew. Sweat shone off his well-muscled torso as he swung himself out of the tight bunk and padded over to the mess area, careful not to wake his bunkmate, Ryan Tucker.

Adjusting his flashlight, Joe did what he always did when he couldn't sleep: poured out his soul to his betrothed in a letter. At least writing her might chase away his loneliness.

5 October, 1944
Dear Elise,

I can't sleep tonight so I'll talk to you instead. How are you, my darling? I am counting the days till this blasted war is over and we can begin our new life together. It's been so long since I've laid eyes on you, but I keep your picture in my breast pocket, close to my heart.

By the time you get my letter, the action will probably be over, but I want to share the excitement of our mission with you tonight. On this ,our third patrol, we are finally returning to the Philippines, just like Mac Arthur promised. It's something I've been itching to do since your brother was captured. We are traveling in "wolf packs"; on the hunt for Japanese vessels carrying munitions, trying to capture or destroy them, and keep them from retreating to Japan.

If I only get to do one thing right this entire war, let it be the chance to free your brother. I want to do that for you. I'm headed for him right now, sweetheart, with everything I've

got. I can sense your prayers for both
of us.

All my love,
Joe

Chapter 36

TWO-HUNDRED-TWENTY-FIVE MILES EAST of Hong Kong, the South China Sea appeared fairly calm that cool evening of October 23, 1944. J.D. Sommers was taking a cruise, but not the kind any human being would sign on for. His was referred to as a "murder cruise" on a vessel known as a "Hell Ship", otherwise named the Arisan Maru by the Japanese.

They were hastily smuggled cargo; those eighteen-hundred men including J.D. who'd been stashed below deck in Hold Number One. Cattle going to slaughter were treated more humanely. There was no room to move, and very little room to breathe. Like a deck of cards, the prisoners were flesh to flesh. The smell of sweat, excrement, and death were putrid and inescapable.

Nausea was also constant, partnered incongruently with bouts of gnawing hunger. Who knew that starving to death could hurt so much? *Why couldn't the Japs even allow the prisoners more than a few measly spoonfuls of rice? The cooks reported their captors fed themselves meat, fruit, and vegetables.* J.D. could only imagine. He was too tired to hate at this point.

Worst by far was the thirst. The tiny daily canteen of dirty water never lasted beyond the morning hours, no matter how hard J.D. tried to limit himself. Everyone jealously guarded their canteens as if they were made of gold. Now, at night, the craving for something wet to slide across his swollen tongue and down his parched throat was ever present. He had seen other men licking their own blood and drinking their own urine. As much as it disgusted J.D., he was pretty certain he'd be there soon enough. *If only they'd send us more water… Why can't they?*

ABOVE BOARD, the Japanese sailors had their own concerns: barely escaping the American forces returning to the Philippines, they were fleeing for their own lives. They couldn't forget about the air raids over Luzon. They'd seen the report of the "Shinyo Maru", torpedoed by the Americans on September 7. They knew these waters were probably crawling with enemy submarines and it felt like they were walking on egg shells. Still, their mission was to transport these prisoners to Japanese labor camps. They'd dragged them out of Bilibid dungeon and thrown them on this ship bound for Japan. With any luck, the brash American Navy wouldn't rescue their precious Prisoners of War anytime soon!

"Captain, are you sure the Americans aren't going to target us?" a Japanese kid looking wet behind the ears bowed anxiously.

"Soldier, our sea and air blockade is so tight they cannot get through. And our radar will sink any submarines...." The captain stood even straighter. "Our radio intelligence confirms we are clear."

The youth continued looking skeptical. "Maybe we should give the prisoners more water at least...to be wise. They will report how we treated them to the world."

The older man laughed. "Who says they'll ever be free or even alive to talk? Relax, young man, --- you worry too much. We'll be on Japanese soil soon and the emperor will be proud of our accomplishments. We can let the commanders at home decide exactly what should happen to these disgraceful prisoners. For now we simply follow orders. Enough of this nervous talk. Get back to your post."

...THE WATER slowly enveloped his head and he couldn't breathe. He gasped for air, but there wasn't any. The pressure was immense; his lungs were burning...

Below deck, J.D. opened his eyes, the dream ending with a jolt. There was no water here, yet he still could not get air. He struggled and clawed his way from under the body of another man. He had to get an air pocket before he was smothered.

"Move!" he croaked. The person on top of him was totally unresponsive. Summoning every last ounce of energy, he shoved the man's body off his face. Air filled his lungs, ending the agony. He had never felt a more beautiful sensation in his life.

With a few more trembling pushes and pulls, J.D. shrank away from the man next to him, a man whose eyes would see no more hardship, a man who had recently heaved his last breath. He was a man who could take no more. Soon his body would be thrown overboard, leaving his dog tags as the only thing left of him.

J.D. murmured a prayer for his neighbor, just as he had for all the others who'd died in his presence. He didn't know this man's name, but he didn't really need to know. *At least he's at peace now,* he thought with some degree of envy. He immediately shook off the feeling. *Don't do this,* he warned himself.

I will be strong. They will not break me. I will be rescued. I will go home again. To Mother and Daddy. To Mike and the girls. To Star. I'll prove I can. He kept repeating the mantra until hunger reared its ugly head and began eating a hole in his belly. A lone tear trickled down his cheek. He angrily wrestled his right arm free, in order to brush the tear away. Men weren't supposed to cry. At nineteen years and counting, J.D. had left boyhood behind a long, long time ago.

IN LATE AFTERNOON of October 24, one inexperienced Japanese sailor ate rations without much appetite. Still worried about the Enemy, he was more than ready to be off this gruesome ship and back on friendly soil. He tried to swallow his food, but it stuck in his throat. It would be dishonorable to admit that a sailor such as himself was actually seasick. He hung his head in embarrassment.

THUD!!! A massive vibration rocked the freighter. J.D. and his fellow prisoners were thrown around like rag dolls. *What the hell was that? J.D. wondered.* An odd sense of foreboding spread through his body. *We must have been hit.*

An American submarine crawled along the ocean floor southeast of the Pratas Reef. They were stalking a Japanese convoy---picking them off one by one.

"Skipper, we've got another one within firing range," reported the Chief Petty Officer.

"Man the torpedoes! What's your location, Baker?"

"Location is N20degrees-- 41 feet, E118 degrees—18 feet."

"Fire One!" The hubbub in the submarine ceased as the men waited for the reverberation from the impending explosion.

Nothing.

The skipper looked annoyed. "Fire Two!"

Silence as the men again awaited the confirmation of a kill. Again nothing happened.

"What the hell is the problem?" the skipper shouted irritably. "Why hasn't the fish found the target? Confirm location."

"Location confirmed, sir. It's the same."

"Fire Three!"

Having become complacent, the crew was slightly unprepared for the massive vibrations that shook the sub. Everyone cheered and clapped in unison.

"That's four for four, sir."

"Good job, Baker. Now, let's get out of here before we're detected."

As usual, The skipper's high feelings of elation were soon followed by a punch in the gut called guilt. Please God, don't let any American Prisoners be on board the ship, he thought. Deep inside, he knew that it would be just like the enemy to pull a dirty stunt where they loaded their munitions ships with prisoners. That fact was hard for him to live with.

The jarring thud caused the Japanese youth to drop his food and look for his commanding officer. The Enemy had found them after all.

The commander got off the radio. "Prepare to evacuate!" He cried furiously. "The ship's been torpedoed. Mid-ship on the starboard side! Remain calm and proceed to the lifeboats!" He noticed the young Japanese soldier standing around in a daze. "What are you waiting for? Follow orders and evacuate!"

The young sailor hesitated. "Sir, what about the prisoners?"

"Cut the ladder on both holds. They will hamper our personal rescue efforts. They are on their own."

But, sir…"

"Do it now or risk court-martial!"

The young man went to Hold Number One and severed the rope ladder. It limply dropped far below. He tried to mentally shut out the massive screaming beneath him. With his knife, he turned toward Hold number Two, and began to cut that ladder. Men were already frantically scaling it, and he couldn't beat them off. The first one knocked the knife out of his hands and pushed him backwards with surprising force.

A Japanese sailor grabbed his arm, dragging him along at full speed.. "It's time to get on the lifeboat! Come on, let's go!" The youth watched over his shoulder as the Americans spilled out of the second hold like ants. He hoped his officer wouldn't court-martial him, yet he was secretly relieved he wouldn't have all those deaths on his conscience. Like a robot, he boarded the lifeboat.

In Hold One, J. D. felt as if he was doing a balancing act just to stay on his feet. Men were pushing, shoving and screaming to be let out of the death trap. Some were bleeding from small pieces of the ship's shrapnel that had pierced their bodies. J.D. joined the pleas for help, yelling until his throat was raw.

Above deck, an alert prisoner cocked his ear and asked another, "Do you hear that? Men are screaming. Where is it coming from?" He and others followed the sound until he came to the other hold's entrance.

"Bastards cut the ladder," the man mumbled. He looked around. The rope wasn't laying around here anywhere. *They probably took it with them.* Thinking quickly, he shouted, "Is the ladder down there?"

All he heard in response was chaos and hysterical yelling. He shouted down to them, "Shut-up and listen! Do you see the ladder?"

J.D. heard the question above the din. So did several others. Someone spotted it in the corner and lamely threw it above them. It missed and there came a collective sigh from Hold One.

"Who can throw around here?" shouted one badly wounded old man

A prisoner J.D. recognized from Bilibid stepped forward and grabbed the rope. "I pitched baseball last year for the high school." He threw it as hard as he could and the man above was leaning over so far he almost fell in, but he managed to catch it by the tips of his fingers. The anxious men started climbing it before it was secured.

"Wait, dammit, we haven't secured it yet!" someone yelled from above. J.D. helped beat off the desperate men who tried to climb the flailing ladder. After a few futile attempts, the Americans above deck finally fastened the ladder to the ship. Below, the prisoners nearly stampeded trying to climb the ladder and escape. J.D. somehow managed to wait his turn. He wanted no part of the hysteria. He wanted to keep his mind cool and collected. He'd need it to survive.

When he made it above board, the first thing that greeted him was fresh air. He was so unprepared for how good it felt, that at first he just stood there and took gulp after gulp of it. The second thing he noticed was that the Japanese had left the freighter. They were either in the water on the last of the lifeboats, or they were boarding nearby destroyers.

The Arisan Maru began to rock and tilt in a terrible fashion. J.D. knew they wouldn't last much longer if they stayed on board. Still, he couldn't help but hope the Americans would come along and rescue them all. *And there are a lot of us,* J.D. thought surveying the throngs of emaciated men, reduced to bare skin, with clothing deteriorated to tattered rags.

From the beginning, a certain number of men couldn't stand the pressure. Fear permeated the atmosphere. A man with a faded tatoo and desperation in his eyes was one of them. "I'm going with the Japs---they've got boats." He jumped in the ocean's uncertain waters and swam for the Japanese destroyers.

Everyone left on board the Arisan Maru watched as the Japanese beat him and others like him with poles. The prisoners desperately tried to grab and claw at the poles, but the Japs clubbed them every time they had the smallest grasp. They simply would not let them board.

"But you brought us--- out here---- as prisoners. You can't just leave us to die!"The man with the tatoo screamed hoarsely. "Look at me!!!!" He swam in circles for another twenty minutes before his bobbing head went underwater for the last time. The Japanese "kid" was no longer wet behind the ears. He bit his lip doubtfully and looked away, trying to erase an image that would haunt him for another fifty years.

A new understanding spread through the ranks of prisoners still aboard the broken ship. They had but two choices: go down with the sinking ship, or jump into the water to swim until they tired and drowned. J.D. saw his own shock reflected on the faces of those around him. Denial was slowly turning into a grim acceptance of the facts.

"Men, we can't give up. Not yet. Maybe we'll get picked up by an Allied vessel. We're not going down without a fight!" J.D. made himself look calm and strong.

A 16 year-old private nicknamed Corky clung to J.D.'s words. His eyes took on a small glint of hope. "That's right Sergeant Sommers. I'm not jumpin' till I have to. I'm stayin' right here with you boys."

Chapter 37

THEY ALWAYS SAY A MOTHER KNOWS when something is wrong with her child. Lainey Sommers was no different.

Sometime during that October evening, she began to experience a very bad feeling. She tried to shake it off, tried to distract herself with crocheting blankets and listening to the radio. Nothing helped. Even Jesse and Elise's voices became background noise.

In the foreground was this *thing*, this strong sense of foreboding she couldn't overcome. Her stomach was churning and she didn't know why. Finally she decided to turn in early.

"Good night, you two. I'm more tired than usual, so I think I'll go on to bed."

Elise glanced up from her school papers and shot Jesse a worried look. Mother never went to bed before Daddy. Perhaps she was coming down with something.

"You okay, Lainey? Want me to fix you a cup of tea or some warm milk?"

"You look a little pale, Mother."

"Don't be silly. I'm fine. Just a little tired is all." She kissed the top of her husband's head and gave her daughter a quick hug. Thankfully she shut the bedroom door and sank down into her covers. She squeezed her eyes shut and said her prayers, which usually helped. This time, the prayers did nothing to relieve her distress signals.

Something was definitely wrong. She just couldn't put her finger on what it was. She only wanted it to go away. She finally dropped off not long before Jesse came to bed. When he tenderly touched his wife's hair, he couldn't help but notice her pained expression as she slept. Maybe one of her darned migraines was taking hold.

Jesse turned off the night stand lamp, settling back and trying hard to relax. He needed his rest. Milking the cows meant rising in the early morning darkness.

He wasn't asleep long when he heard Lainey begin to whimper and moan. He heard her call out J.D.'s name.

"Wake up, Lainey!" He pulled her close to him. "Shh.....it was only a dream."

Lainey half-opened her eyes and stared ahead unseeing. "It's J.D. He's in trouble, Jesse. Our boy's in trouble. I felt something all evening, and now he's come to me in my dreams."

"Did he say anything in the dream?"

She looked away. "Not really. He mainly seemed scared, Jesse."

"You've probably been thinking about him extra hard; worried about how he's being treated. Remember, you've had bad dreams in the past. It's your imagination working overtime." He hugged her tightly. "You can't do this to yourself, Lainey, or you won't be well when the war is over and our kids come home."

"Of course, I'm being stupid," she murmured. "You go on back to sleep." She rolled away from him, clutching her pillow in fear. Every time she closed her eyes, the dream became fresh in her mind.

She hadn't been totally honest with Jesse—hadn't told him everything about the dream. The part she had withheld kept replaying itself over and over. J.D. was staring at her with his big brownish gold eyes, mouthing the word, "help". Try as she might, she couldn't reach him. Every time she got near, he disappeared into the mist.

"God let someone help him," she whispered into the air. Jesse's heavy breathing was the only response. Soon, the clock began to sound like a ticking bomb. It was killing her. Softly and slowly, she stole out of bed, creeping through the room, looking for her favorite picture of her younger son. When her eyes adjusted to the darkness, she found it—J.D. decked out in military splendor, handsome in his new uniform. She crawled back in bed, photo clutched to her breast--- drenching her pillow with a cascade of tears.

They always say a mother knows.

Chapter 38

MINUTES TURNED TO HOURS, light had turned to dark, and dark was turning light once again. Still no other ship approached. The Japanese were long gone, leaving many of the prisoners to perish in the depths of the ocean. Empty talk had ceased, with the only sound being prayers and good-byes. Everything and everyone was unraveling..

How much longer can we stay afloat? wondered J.D. He knew it was a matter of minutes till the Arisan Maru would flop over and sink. Resignation replaced fear, as the young G.I. accepted what he and everyone else had to do. Hastily, he turned to shake the hands of those around him. "Keep your head up. Look for debris to hold onto," someone uttered.

Corky, hunched over in the corner, tearfully exclaimed, "I'm not going anywhere." Taking a deep breath, J.D. shut his eyes and jumped off the sinking 6,886 ton vessel.

SPLASH! The water was much cooler than he'd expected. White cap after white cap slapped his gaunt body around. Salt water stung his eyes and nose, forcing him to swallow mouthfuls of the stuff. At first, the young man couldn't put his limbs in motion- they just refused to move. It was as if the ocean were trying to swallow him. Jesus, it would be so easy to quit fighting it—just let this monster have him. Only the face of his mother kept him going. "Swim, J.D., swim", she seemed to be urging him. So swim he did until a deep reserve of inner strength and energy emerged.

He realized the water was now full of bobbing bodies; some cursing, some moaning, most praying, many trying desperately to swim. Some were no longer moving at all. Those soon disappeared into the depths of the ocean. Making headway in that choppy water would have challenged the most experienced swimmers. Still J.D. persevered, approaching a wounded, drowning man in the water. He yelled, "Get on your back, get on your back!" Miraculously, the man calmed down, attempting to follow directions. J.D. assisted him by hooking one of his arms around the victim's, so as to tow the man toward a faraway piece of floating debris.

Take a deep slow breath, stroke hard, kick your feet--- J.D. could see his Daddy's face encouraging him to keep going---just as he had when he was six years old and learning to swim in the old cow tank. He knew he could make it now. Too bad the debris was only enough for one person to cling to. J.D. let the other man have it. Relief flooded his body as he released the bleeding young man he had in tow.

"Th-th-thank-you, man. You saved me. I'm not letting go until someone finds us. My name is Felix

Salvador. Who are you? As he applied pressure to his wound, the youth's dark eyes gratefully searched J.D.'s face.

"J.D. Sommers," he answered, still panting, "from Mountainview, New Mexico."

Felix was asking him something else, but J.D. wasn't listening. He was distracted by more screaming. He turned back to see more heads bobbing behind him; more men drowning and pleading for their lives. He didn't want to hear the sound. His limbs were begging him to rest. And yet he knew better. He had been taught better. He turned back toward the ocean----wondering how in God's creation he would continue.

"What are you doing?" called Felix. "Are you crazy? Don't go back, amigo. Don't do it! Stay here and hold on! Wait !!!"

Felix's frantic pleas grew distant as J.D. concentrated on the water. He had his sights set on one particular individual. The victim in question was screaming in fright and was now just swallowing water. Somehow, J.D. must swim to him and put him on his back, exactly like the other fellow. *I'm still strong*, J.D. reminded himself proudly.

The second fellow was bigger—much harder to restrain. In full blown panic, he repeatedly dunked J.D. With the last bit of strength he had left, J.D. fought the man off his head to come up for air. The man started at him again. J.D. finally had to move away.

I should help someone else, J.D. thought. Still, it feels good to rest here in the water. With a half-hearted dog paddle, J.D. came to a standstill.

STAB. *What was that?* Another one. *Oh, the pain.* J.D.'s body began to hurt all over. He tried to move his arms and legs, but nothing happened. Cramps were taking over his whole body. How utterly stupid to be paralyzed like this!

"Help." The words formed on his lips but were heard by nobody. He gasped a few times before being submerged completely underwater. The panic finally passed and his soul filled with a strange peace. *Mother, I made it past Bataan. I made it off the Hellship for you. They didn't break me, Daddy. I'm sorry...I tried...* were his last thoughts as his lungs burst.

On the outskirts of Mountainview, New Mexico, a young paint horse with a star on her forehead suddenly looked up from her feeding trough. A little shiver ran though the creature. Somehow she knew her cowboy wasn't coming home.

Pacific War Memorial:
"Sleep, my sons, your duty done,
for Freedom's light has come;
Sleep in the silent depths of the sea,
or in your bed of hallowed sod,
until you hear at dawn
the low clear reveille of God."

Unknown Author

Chapter 39

THE COW LOOKED AT JESSE with trusting brown eyes. She knew what was coming, but that didn't mean she had to like it. With a sassy swish of her tail, she took a few steps backwards in protest.

"That's right, Della. You know why I'm here." Jesse patted her bony old rear, and got to work on the business of milking his best heifer.

The sun had been up awhile on that brisk October morning, and an unusually cold shiver went up Jesse's spine. He pulled his jacket closer to him, while drawing his weathered hat down over his ears. *Another day in the dairy business,* he thought as he milked the cow. The work wasn't terribly exciting, but it was steady and it kept food on the table. After living through the Great Depression with six mouths to feed, he never took that fact for granted.

Now there was less need, fewer mouths to feed. His kids had grown up and gone to war. All except Elise, that is. His mind wandered further as he worked. He thanked God for his eldest daughter.

She was such a comfort to her mother. He didn't know what Lainey would do without her.

Unblinking, Della looked back at him. She knew the milking session was over and she was ready to move on. Jesse stood up and scratched the bovine's head affectionately. Secretly, he was glad he was not a rancher; one whom had to butcher his animals. Yes, the dairy cows *were* his business, yet they were also his pets. He took great pains to care for each one, even took their losses quite personally. Thankfully, there were few of those.

The roar of a motor came from the distance, growing steadily closer. Elise was at school, teaching her sixth grade class---- so it was probably Lainey, coming back from town. She'd gone out early that morning, intent on getting her errands done before mid-morning. She'd mentioned something about the bank, the post office, and the store. *Must've forgotten her grocery list,* thought Jesse as he watched for the beat up truck.

Kicking up a trail of dust was instead a government vehicle, a new Chevrolet. It drove quickly up to the house with a young man in a Western Union uniform emerging from it.

Jesse's mouth went dry. His legs kept walking, but his mind had turned off like a light switch. Wordlessly, he approached the Western Union man. The youth handed him the telegram, a look of pity in his eyes. Jesse began to tremble all over. He could barely hold the envelope, he was shaking so badly. It was going to be one of his children---*Oh God, no!!!*

The messenger did not move, transfixed by a scene he'd been privy to many times in the past. Finally Jesse managed to open the envelope.:

```
Dear Mr. and Mrs. Sommers,
    On Oct.24, 1944, the Arisan Maru
was sunk. The United States military
regrets to inform you that J.D.
Sommers (service number 20843927) was
a prisoner aboard that ship and is now
officially listed as Missing in
Action. More information will come to
you as it is known.
    We will be forever grateful for
your son's service to this country.

Yours Truly,
President Harry Truman
```

"Sir, sir---can I get you a glass of water?"

"No, no I'm f-fine." Jesse gave the anxious youth a bone-crushing handshake before stumbling to the porch. He wasn't fine.

Lainey finished her errands around 10:30a.m.--- with enough time to put the groceries away before getting a good hot lunch on the stove. She drove up the long driveway, wondering to herself who that was sitting on her front porch swing. Squinting hard, she tried to make out the still figure. Why, it was Jesse! What was he doing there, sitting idly in the middle of a work day? *That's so unlike him---- hope he's not coming down with something,* she thought worriedly.

Parking the truck, she grabbed a sack of groceries and headed up the walk. "Are you gonna help me or just sit there all day?" She turned to give him a playfully scathing look. That was when she saw everything. The grey pallor to his skin, the empty look in his eyes, and worst of all, the crumpled telegram next to him on the swing.

"What is it, Jesse?"

"Lainey, it's---it's J.D."

She dropped the groceries to the ground. The brown paper bag ripped open, spilling beans and rice everywhere. She tripped on the overgrown prickly pear crowding the walk and nearly fell to the ground herself.

"What happened?" Her voice sounded distant and cold, like it came from somewhere else. She lunged for the telegram as her husband tried unsuccessfully to grab it first.

Her fist went to her mouth and she bit it as she read.

"J.D.---Missing in Action." No one spoke. "At least he's not dead, Jesse. They don't know *where* he is. He's just missing is all. They don't have proof he's dead! He could still turn up, couldn't he? Don't you see, Jesse? We can't give up on him. He's NOT DEAD!!"

Dry-eyed, she scooped up the scattered food. An eerie calm descended on her as she carefully put things away. *The rice goes in the pantry. The flour goes in the bin. Where should I put the lard?* Why was it so damn hard to remember what to do?

ELISE appraised her reflection in the antique gilt-edged bathroom mirror. Pale skin, swollen red eyes, mussed up hair, and was that really a wrinkle forming on her forehead? She was only 26 and she felt like she'd lived a lifetime. Had it really only been a week since they'd received the news?

The little autograph book from her own school years stood open to the page where J.D. had signed when he was only ten. His boyish scrawl haunted her with his words:

```
Dear Elise,
    Always remember and never forget,
the brown-eyed brother who thinks of
you yet.

Your brother, J.D.
```

He was eleven when he wrote that. Eight years ago. He died when he was only nineteen years old... A big fat tear splashed across the writing. Elise blotted the page hastily and put it away. Enough, she told herself. I have to be presentable for my students. They deserve a teacher who is prepared to face the world. J.D. would want her to go forward. He certainly had in his short life. Tears were still right beneath the surface. She pinched her cheek, saying, "Stop that!!" Besides, it wouldn't help Mother to see her like this.

"Elise, dinner's about ready! Can you set the table, dear?" Lainey's voice rang out with an awful false cheerfulness.

Smoothing her hair, Elise fastened a half-smile on her face. then dashed into the dining room. Grabbing three plates from the hutch, she added silverware and napkins. Lainey rounded the kitchen corner.

"Why only three, Elise?" She opened the hutch and gathered three more plates. "We mustn't forget your brothers and sister." She put one at Margo's place, one at Mike's place, and one defiantly at J.D.,s place. "Our table will always be ready, should one of them come back from war."

"But, Mother…" Elise tried to catch her mother's eye, but it was to no avail. Lainey's mind was far away as she fixed her children's settings.

Elise exchanged hard glances with her father when he came in from the barn. Biting his lip, he greeted his wife with a warm hug.

Lainey brought in the chicken, biscuits, and turnip greens mixed with bacon bits, but only watched as the others tried to eat.

"Well----seems awful quiet in here---how about turning on some music?" Elise turned the knob of the grand Philco radio that presided over the room. It was just in time for the news. The booming voice of the anchor filled the air.

"Today the Commander-in-Chief confirms that on October 24, the Arisan Maru was hit off the coast of China."

One could have heard a pin drop as an icy silence descended on the Sommers' kitchen. Jesse lay down his fork. Elise stared down at her plate. Lainey twisted her napkin into knots.

"A huge number of American Prisoners were on-board the Japanese warship, all held captive since the Bataan Death March. It is reported nearly all the men drowned, making this the worst naval disaster in history. A handful of survivors were reported."

"Turn off that god-damned thing!" Jesse snapped at his daughter.

"He could've survived," Lainey said softly. "They said a handful---"

"Lainey, they would have notified us if he'd been saved."

"But, he could be out there---washed up on some island, or suffering from amnesia---not remembering what happened or who he is. We don't have proof he's…"

"Mother, we should have some kind of memorial." Elise reached over to put her hand on her mother's shoulder.

Lainey's head snapped up. Glaring at her daughter, she replied, "Why that is ridiculous and out of the question! They haven't brought him home---there's no body to bury."

"There probably never will be, Mother." Elise looked kindly into her mother's troubled eyes. "J.D. deserves to be remembered. A memorial ceremony will honor his life. We could order some sort of plaque or headstone. It's the least we can do."

"Are you deaf, Elise? I said no! Headstones are for the dead and we have no evidence that he's dead. What if he comes home after the war and sees his name on a headstone?" She briskly buttered her biscuit. "Now stop this foolish talk and finish supper." Abruptly she headed for her bedroom, sharply closing the door behind her.

"I'm warning you, Elise. Don't bring it up again. The time isn't right." Jesse sternly looked across the dinner table, jabbing the chicken harshly as he spoke.

"But, Daddy…"

Jesse shook his head. The subject was closed.

Elise thought to herself, When is the time ever going to be right?

Chapter 40

BIG, TAN JOE HOWARD STROLLED ALONG the pristine Hawaiian beach; breathing in the beautiful scenery, glad to be among the living on this early December day. He squared his broad shoulders, replaying in his mind the Leyte Gulf Battle—four Japanese carriers, three battleships, ten cruisers, and 510 aircraft were taken out; and the U.S. Navy was largely responsible. Those were statistics he'd never forget. The citation from Admiral Chester Nimitz was another reminder. He smiled in deep satisfaction. Now he could enjoy being back on land again after six grueling months at sea.

"Hey, Joe, how's your "R and R" going?" Shorty, a diminutive guy with red hair and freckles, walked up behind Joe. "How come we haven't seen you at the pub playing cards with the others? There's plenty of local ladies to go around, you know." Shorty arched his red brows suggestively.

"I've got other things to think about. For one thing, there's a girl I want to get home to." He threw a seashell in the waves. "I just wonder what our next assignment will be. I heard our submarines have about finished off all the Japanese ships and merchant fleets. Guess we've done ourselves out of work!" Joe could not disguise the pride in his voice.

"Yeah, I heard the same scuttlebutt and that's not all." The young man grew serious, pausing in his tracks. "There's a rumor going round that one of the ships taken out in the Leyte Gulf Battle was carrying 2,000 of our own men. Talk about a crapshoot! Damned if we do, and damned if we don't!"

Secretly, Joe's heart did a little flip-flop. Could it be true? Surely Shorty was blowing smoke. Joe was aware there could be collateral damage—just not on the magnitude his friend was suggesting. With more bravado than he felt, he responded, "Sounds like a rumor the Japanese started to make us feel guilty. Anyway, it wasn't news to us that some ships were mismarked. They were carrying munitions, pal. Some things have to be done." Like that, he dismissed Shorty's gossip as just that— gossip. He had more pressing personal problems to consider. He bid his friend good-bye and walked the rest of the way alone only to find a letter awaiting him, one postmarked Mountainview, New Mexico.

Dear Joe,
    I hope this letter finds you safe and well. Today, more than ever, I need your loving arms.
    Our family has suffered a terrible blow. With a heavy heart, I must tell you that J.D. has been killed. He was forced onto an unmarked Japanese

vessel headed away from the Philippines. Not knowing who was on-board, the rumor is that our navy sunk it. I don't know many of the details, but apparently all but a few of the prisoners drowned. A huge number of men were lost.

J.D. is gone. I don't know what to do. I'm so sad tonight as I write this letter—I feel so empty. I wish you were here. I know I would find comfort in that. Please take care of yourself and come home safely to me. I couldn't take it if anything happened to you. I don't think I have any tears left to cry.

Say a little prayer for him, Joe, and always remember: I too pray every day and every night—for you.

Love,
Elise

Joe's hands shook as he crumpled the letter in his hands. J.D. was dead. He had been on a ship hit by the U.S. A sick feeling began to invade his stomach. His insides churned like when he was at sea, yet here he stood, feet planted firmly on land.

He remembered the rumors Shorty had spoken of. So it was true. Nearly 2,000 prisoners had drowned. He could only imagine the Navy's shock over the loss.

No matter how hard he rubbed his temples, Joe couldn't banish the throbbing in his head. *His sub had been on the hunt during the time J.D.'s ship was sunk.* His crew had made a few kills during that time. They did not know for sure whom they had hit.

"Hey, Joe, wanna go into town for a beer? Martinez is buying." called out Ryan on the bunk below Joe. He stood up and roughly tousled Joe's wavy black hair. "What's wrong, buddy? You look like you've just seen a ghost!"

Joe mumbled something incoherent and climbed into his upper bunk. He needed to lie down; to make sense of Elise's letter. There had to be a way to put her news into perspective.

Awhile later, Chief Petty Officer Myers made the rounds in the barracks. He noticed one lone sailor, face down on his bunk.

"What's wrong with Ensign Howard?" he asked one of the other men.

"He said he was sick, sir." The man shook his head sympathetically. "He wasn't kidding either. Vomited his guts out just now in the latrine."

The officer frowned and kept walking. These men have to learn to curb their drinking binges, he thought.

Joe's mind swirled as he pulled the covers over his head. One moment he'd been filled with pride—sure he had completed a mission that would free Elise's brother. Now all he could think of was the fact that he had failed to save J.D. Far worse was the fact he may have been indirectly responsible for his death. *Friendly fire* was what they called it. There was nothing friendly about it.

Never in a thousand years would he have imagined himself in this position. What should he do now? Should he try to run down more information----pinpoint times and places----try to ease his conscience by learning exactly *who* had torpedoed J.D.'s ship that fateful day? Chances were pretty high it *wasn't* Joe's sub.

Joe rolled over in his bunk. What if his investigation led him too far—what if it *was* his sub? It wouldn't bring J.D. back and it would most certainly break Elise's heart. She would never look at him the same way again.

Finally, Joe came to a conclusion. He wouldn't ask questions and he wouldn't tell anyone about his suspicions. He would go on not knowing for sure what had happened in the Leyte Gulf that week. God rest the souls of the men that were lost there.

Joe sighed in resignation as he threw his legs over the side of the bunk. He opened his eyes to the world around him. He could still salvage his life, though guilt was going to be one more side effect of this atrocious war. He couldn't let it consume him. He had to find a way to live with the "not knowing". So the saying *was* true: War is hell.

For now, he had a woman to get home to. A woman to comfort and love. A woman to marry.

Chapter 41

ANOTHER SISTER SENT A SIMILAR LETTER to London that same week:

Dec. 12, 1944
My Dear Friend Gwen,

I guess I'm supposed to say "Happy Holidays", but they're anything but happy. I'm stuck here in Paris where everyone is smiling and celebrating; glad to be free. At least with you, I can be myself and tell the truth.

Frankly, this is the crappiest Christmas I've ever spent. I suppose you heard that J.D. died as a prisoner of war. I just found out a few days ago. News travels slow in war.

I can't believe I'll never see him again, never hear his voice or his goofy laugh when he tells one of his corny jokes. I can't accept that he's gone. I feel like I'm trapped in a bad dream. I only want to wake up.

I can only imagine what it was like for Mother and Daddy when they got the news. J.D. was Mother's baby and she spoiled him rotten. Only the best for him. Buttermilk biscuits and apple pie at a moment's notice. I honestly don't know how she'll go on.

Every fiber of my being wants to go home, Gwen, but I can't. It isn't possible. Through a crazy twist of fate, I ended up smack in the middle of the liberation of Paris. Thank God my parents never knew the danger I was in! I'll tell you every detail someday. In fact, I have a story for your paper about a remarkable French woman named Suzanne who touched the lives of many with her heroism.

Anyway, at this time, we're all working feverishly under General Eisenhower. We're setting up the new French government. Much to my chagrin, they found out about my typing and stenography background. So much for my adventurous days in motor pool!

And then there's Mike. He doesn't even know yet about J.D. He is incommunicado. Who knows when he'll be told? All I can do is pray I don't lose my remaining brother to this God-awful mess?

Have you ever heard such a pity party? Bet you're wondering what happened to the old rough-and-tumble Margo. She's lost for now, but it doesn't mean she won't be back.

Wish you could magically get over here for New Year's Eve. We could get

smashed out of our minds and pick up
a couple of handsome French soldiers.
Now that might bring a smile to my
face!

Forever Your Friend,
Margo

P.S. A few German soldiers can attest
to the fact that my high heels still
come in handy when there's nothing
else close by. More to this story
later.
 I have so much to tell you!

Tears spilled down Gwen's face, ruining her
careful makeup job. She tried to swallow the rock
hard lump in her throat. She'd heard the rumors—
holding out hope against hope that the younger
Sommers brother had somehow evaded tragedy.
Now there was no denying the truth.

Her mind zeroed in on that day eons ago when
Elise and she had first driven J.D. to the bus
station. The hastily snapped photo of the sixteen-
year-old leaning against his duffel bag. The
yearning for adventure written all over his face. If
only they could have had a crystal ball that day---if
only.....

Her mind abruptly switched over to Mike.
Margo said he still didn't know about J.D. *Where
are you, Mike?* Without knowing why, she had the
urge to wrap her arms around him. She offered up
a little prayer instead: Please God, keep him safe.
Let him make it through the war and give him the

strength to bear the loss of his brother. *Death sometimes kills the living.*

Approaching mid-December, the Allies were encountering major obstacles on their trek towards Hitler. The densely forested Ardennes Mountains made it difficult for the men to hold their ground. As winter set in, deep snow inhibited their progress even further. In a given 24 hour stretch, snow would fall a foot at a time, stubbornly refusing to melt. Bitterly cold winds slapped the soldiers' faces as they tried desperately to make forward progress. To top it off, thick fog and overcast skies made air attacks from the U.S. Air Force and R.A.F. next to impossible.

Adding to the Allies' woes was the fact that Adolph Hitler was obsessed with regaining nearby Antwerp, the Belgian port recently taken by the Allies for vital supplies. Though the move seemed absurd to his advisors, the Fuhrer had amassed 400,000 troops to march or drive Panzer tanks over the frozen terrain of the Ardennes. The newest troops were a hodge-podge of Germans earlier deemed too young or too old to fight, as well as much needed troops from the Eastern front whom Hitler had yanked away with little qualms.

In these dark cold woods, the Germans obtained the upper hand initially, taking approximately 15,000 Allied prisoners. Because these December attacks created a bulge in the Allied front line, the

Press dubbed the military action, "The Battle of the Bulge."

In the white early morning light, men emerged from their tents to gather around the campfires for something that passed as coffee. Any other place, the rations would have been awful, but out here, they tasted like a feast. Especially held in high esteem were the canned fruitcakes and powdered hot chocolate, which were both used for intensive bartering.

Mike's feet had lost feeling a long time ago. Time and space began to elude him as well, since his energy was now spent on staying alive and not being overtaken by the Germans, who were everywhere. *I've got to keep a cool mind and not panic,* he kept telling himself. It also helped when he remembered what he was fighting for. *We're going to win this war and free J.D.* He hadn't been in communication with the States for a few months now and he couldn't wait to get a letter from his family. He missed everyone terribly.

He tried not to think about the one he missed the most. Unfortunately, his mind stumbled across her often: her shiny hair, her sparkling eyes, her kind smile, and yes, the way she turned heads when she walked across a room in a tight skirt and high heeled pumps. His arms ached to hold her as he'd done for one brief second in Tunisia. She must never find out how much he cared. As quickly as it came, Mike forced himself to suppress the image of Gwen, because it hurt too much to think about something he couldn't have.

"Hey, where's Charlie this morning? I haven't seen him since last night." Mike quickly scanned his surroundings.

"Yeah, I saw him earlier," responded Andy, still looking sleepy, as he downed his coffee. "Said he was gonna get some firewood. Shoulda been back by now."

Ever since the barroom fight in Tunisia, Mike no longer counted Charlie as his best friend. The guy was a jerk when it came to women. One drunken night, Charlie had admitted that Gwen had called it quits with him, and Mike was more than relieved to hear it.

Up here in the wintry forest, trying to beat the enemy, it was a different story. Ambivalence ran high when it came to staying alive. He still had Charlie's back and he knew Charlie had his. That's what mattered for the time being. He'd deal with the other stuff when they got back to the States.

"Hey Gibson, let's make sure Charlie didn't get lost," Mike called, signaling the other man to join him in a search. The morning mist remained thick and unpredictable. At first, a person might not be able to see his hand in front of his face; while in the next moment the surroundings were revealed in perfect detail.

Mike and his buddy trudged through the fresh snow; marking the path, listening for snipers, and wondering where the hell Charlie was.

"Let's not get lost ourselves," Mike finally said. "Maybe we better turn around and retrace our steps, just to be sure. This visibility is insane. He's probably back at camp, roasting his boots on the fire!"

As the pair made a careful u-turn, a scuffle broke out nearby. Fog had made the world white again so it was impossible to see what was going on.

"Don't move or I'll shoot!"

Mike and Gibson heard the sound of labored breathing followed by, "Surrender! We surrender!" The words came out in a heavy German accent.

"Charlie, is that you? Tell us where you are and we'll help!"

There was no reply from the eastern brush.

"What's wrong, you sorry cowards! Afraid I might shoot you? Afraid to die today? Put your hands behind your back and get on the ground!" he screamed. "Do it!"

"Don't, Charlie!" cried Mike into the thick fog. "They said they were surrendering. Listen to me. Keep their hands up and make sure they're disarmed. We're coming over to help take them prisoner."

"Mike, don't lie! You want them dead as much as I do. They're the reason we're standing in this shithole; the reason your brother is where he is," he said in a flat voice. "I should give you the privilege of pulling the trigger."

"It won't solve anything, Charlie! We both know there are rules we have to follow about treatment of prisoners. I have to treat prisoners the way I want J.D. treated. So do you! Hold on, buddy, we're almost with you."

Whimpering pleas and prayers in German filled their ears, followed by a long silence. The atmosphere was palpable with fear. Mike signaled Gibson to follow the voices. *It's going to be alright*, he thought.

Two crisp shots rang out in the frozen air; then two more. Mike and Gibson had hit the ground, when the fog unexpectedly cleared. Hands steady, Charlie still pointed his gun at the two bloody bodies that lay in the reddened snow. They were about the age of J.D.----fair of hair and skin, weathered uniforms covering their lanky bodies. They looked like they should have been ice-skating instead of fighting. What was left of their faces registered surprise and fear.

Gibson began vomiting while Mike stared at Charlie in disgust. He gestured at the two German rifles that lay at Charlie's feet.

"Don't say it!" Charlie warned through gritted teeth. "You damned well know that's what we're here for. To eliminate Nazis. Well, now there's two less to worry about." He picked up his things and strode calmly past Mike; whistling as though nothing had happened.

"You're wrong, man," Mike intoned, not moving a muscle. Gibson remained speechless; shaking his head and looking away.

Charlie did an abrupt bout face. "And just in case you two get any bright ideas—remember---- it was self-defense. They came at me first. If you say different, I'll take you down with me. Don't think I won't." He turned on his heels and headed back for camp.

Chapter 42

WITH THREE DAYS TO GO UNTIL CHRISTMAS, an unnatural silence hung over the Sommers' house. No wreath hung on the front door, no advent candles were lit on the hallway table, and the scrawny tree hauled in by Jesse still stood in the corner, bereft of ornamentation. The rooster platter continued to gather dust in the back of the cabinet, and there would be no turkey to serve on it anyway.

Lainey's eyes stared out the front window, unseeing. She knew she should get caught up on the chores, but she couldn't seem to get moving. She couldn't concentrate on much anymore. Elise walked through the living room, stopping to turn on the radio. Kate Smith was singing "I threw a Kiss in the Ocean".

"Shut that stupid song off this instant! If I hear it one more time..." Lainey glared accusingly at the radio.

"Okay, okay Mother." Click went the Philco. In her most patient teacher's voice, Elise continued, "Listen, don't you think we better dress up the tree Daddy so kindly got us?" Elise appraised her mother worriedly. "I'll get the ornaments from the attic."

"Whatever you want," Lainey's return to calm did no good in reassuring her daughter.

Just then, there was a crisp knock at the front door. Lainey stirred herself to get it. "Well, hello, Emma. How are you today?" Lainey reluctantly let the silver-haired elderly woman inside.

"Lainey, we've been missing you at our Auxiliary meetings. We could sure use a hand assembling those Christmas baskets. Your homemade blankets have been a godsend. We need you." She looked hopefully at Lainey.

"You know, Emma, I'm just not up to it this time," Lainey said, remembering her half-finished crocheted blankets. "I guess you could say I'm not in the Christmas spirit," She gave Emma a blank shrug.

The elderly woman took a step toward Lainey. She touched her shoulder. "I can only imagine how terrible it's been for you and your family. Don't think the Legion isn't aware of your sacrifice. We're ever so proud of J.D. And we pray for Mike and Margo."

At the sound of J.D.'s name, Lainey took a step back. She could no longer bear the woman's kind touch. "Please. I don't need pity."

"Lainey, you're a Gold Star Mother now. No one pities you. You have given *everything* for your country. I'm actually surprised your Gold Star isn't in the window, where it belongs. It displays your pride and sacrifice."

"I-I-'m not sure where it is…" Lainey mumbled. Besides, she thought, I don't want to think about any sacrifice. I just want him back home.

After once again declining the invitation to join the Auxilliary's activities, Lainey politely showed Emma out, leaning against the closed door in relief.

Quiet as a mouse, she tiptoed across the room to the hutch drawer. Cautiously, she opened the second drawer. *Where was it?* Digging beneath some recipes and old photos, at last she found it. She pulled it out carefully---holding it at arm's length like she was afraid of it. Slowly, she let her fingertips rub across the top of it.

Why did everyone want to say she was a Gold Star Mother? She had no proof he was dead. She allowed her eyes to rest on it awhile longer. Enough!

Just like that, the Gold Star was flung back in the drawer, where it was closed with a resounding crack.

"Elise, did you find the decorations?"

Elise was already in the corner, hanging stars, birds, and glittery balls on the tree. "That's more like it." Lainey said, clasping her hands over her heart. "We'll make this place look festive after all---we still have time. We have to be prepared---just in case…"

"In case what, Mother?" Elise refrained from decorating to stare up into her mother's determined eyes.

"Oh, never mind, Elise. You keep doing what you're doing. I'll go get some packages from the closet."

Soon Lainey returned with the three scruffy presents which she'd wrapped back in 1941. The handwriting on the tags still plainly spelled out J.D.'s name.

Elise's heart sunk and tears sprung to her eyes. "Mother, stop this! He's not coming back. You saw the telegram. He went down with the ship, just like the others!" She couldn't stop herself once she started. "You're hurting all of us with your game. At least think of how Daddy feels. And you still have three other kids. Do you ever once think of us? Think of Mike trying to stop Hitler as we speak, or– or Margo in Paris, or what about me? It's not fair, Mother!" Elise dropped the ornament in her hand and fled to her room weeping.

Ignoring her daughter, Lainey dusted off the gifts and placed them just so under the tree. How nice they looked there! If only she could make everyone understand. There was no proof that J.D. was dead. What if, somehow, some way, he found his way home by Christmas? How would he feel if they hadn't remembered his presents under the tree? She had to be ready. Just in case.

Chapter 43

THE ALLIES RALLIED AFTER the Battle of the Bulge and never looked back. By April, the American army had sealed off the Ruhr region, the heart of Germany's steel and coal production. The troops, led by Omar Bradley, encircled the area, trapping 350,000 German troops inside. By April 14, the German pocket was divided in two and by April 16, the Eastern half had succumbed to pressure and surrendered. Two days later, the western half did the same. 325,000 Germans were taken prisoner and the U.S. Army entered Dusseldorf.

Other things were happening fast. At the end of April, Hitler killed himself in his bunker. The Russians were marching on Berlin and by May 7th, 1945, the high command of Gen. Jodl and Admiral Friedeberg had signed their official surrender in Eisenhower's presence.

Mike was consumed by a fatigue that cancelled out the exhilaration he should have felt about the war's end in Europe. Moreover, he couldn't forget about the battles still raging in the Pacific. His brother's fate was never far from his thoughts.

When he did manage to catch any shut-eye, it was fitful. His dreams quickly morphed into full-blown nightmares. He spent too many nights reliving the deaths of his fellow unit members----one in particular who'd died in his arms. Every night in his sleep, he worked in vain to save his friend and every morning, he woke up to the same depressing outcome.

Other nights, young German faces, a lot like his own, popped up before him. Sometimes they were coldly aiming guns at him, and other times they were already dead. Their grotesque faces reflected the shock and pain of being shot to death. Blood was everywhere—on the Germans' uniforms, on their boots, but mostly coming out of their mouths, nose, and ears. He dreamt often of the Germans Charlie had executed.

The worst dreams by far portrayed the Jewish death camps he and his unit had come across. At Wobbelin near Ludwigslust, mountains of naked skeletal bodies stared at the sky with open eyes and gaping mouths. *If only you'd gotten here earlier,* they seemed to be saying. Perhaps even more disturbing to Mike were the haunting images he could not shut out, even in his waking hours: the *survivors.* The emaciated mothers and children whose faces were filled with hunger and despair. The men whose cheekbones jutted out of their hollowed faces, their legs spindly sticks, and their hands mere claws reaching toward Mike for help.

There were too many for Mike to help all at once. It was too much. Too much.

Ever since they'd arrived on German soil, Mike began to incorporate Adolph Hitler's face into his dreams. Out of nowhere, his face would flash before Mike. Unremarkable in stature and appearance, the "Fuhrer" might have gone unnoticed in a crowd, had he been out of uniform. His choppy haircut with the extreme side part along with the squared off push-broom mustache made him appear almost comical. It was Hitler's eyes that had given away his maniacal fanaticism. Behind those eyes had resided the soul of a monster. Mike didn't get why the average German citizen had found him charismatic, but in his dreams, *he* knew exactly why the man had been so feared.

Mike was worried he wouldn't be able to discern his dreams from reality someday. For the moment, he focused on putting one foot in front of the other, and appreciating the lives saved by the arrival of the Allies.

On the morning of May 10, he was extremely relieved to wake up out of his dreams, though he remained distracted throughout breakfast and mail call. His heart leapt at the sight of the Red Cross insignia on the envelope delivered to his hand.. Here was the reason he'd fought with such ferocity---the news he'd prayed for the whole time he'd marched determinedly toward Germany. Last fall, MacArthur had returned to the Philippines. *Surely they'd found J.D. and freed him from captivity.* Now that he, Mike, was back in the lines of communication, the Red Cross must be confirming J.D.'s release.

Who knew—maybe he was already back home helping Daddy with the dairy, riding Star through the desert brush. Mother would finally be resting easy, and they could all be together soon as a family. His fingers trembled with anticipation as he ripped open the letter.

GWEN PUSHED HER CHAIR back on two legs, leaning precariously against the office wall, all the while studying the letter with Mike's return address. The postmark was recent: May 11. He had survived the war! Her exuberant smile faded when she remembered Margo's last correspondence. Mike still didn't know about J.D. As if it had eyes of its own, the letter burned a hole right through her. With every ounce of courage she possessed, the young woman opened the letter.

Dear Gwen,

I guess you already know we lost J.D.

The words look so strange on paper. None of it seems real or true. Worse yet, the only feeling I can conjure up is anger. And I don't have anywhere to put it now that the fighting is over.

I've requested an extended leave, due to my family's circumstances. I dread seeing Mother and Daddy's faces. I can't believe they've known all this time--- since last fall. How terrible they must have felt when they got the news. I wish I'd have known sooner---

I can't stop thinking about what an idiot I was to believe that if I came across the world and rescued other people, someone would return the favor, and rescue my kid brother.

I don't want to be this bitter.

I'd better go, Gwen. I'm just rambling. Thanks for listening to me and my self-pity.

I'll be home soon.

Your friend,
Mike

Gwen slowly folded the letter, and put her head on the desk. Her throat and eyes ached simultaneously. *The last thing you are is an idiot, Mike*. After what seemed like forever, she forced herself upright. With leaden fingers, she dialed her boss.

"Yes, Mr. Roberts, I need time off immediately. I need to go back to the States. It's a family emergency of sorts."

Chapter 44

IN NEW MEXICO, a spring day is something to behold, especially one in mid-May. Warm sunshine and brilliant blue skies showcase the new leaves. It was the kind of day Gwen normally rejoiced in, but on this day---there was no rejoicing. The war was over, leaving heartache in its path. Mike had gone home to comfort his parents; however she wasn't quite sure why she felt needed. She'd felt a strange magnetic pull, and she'd followed it. Thank God she'd made her editor realize that work would just have to wait.

The hand-built house still looked the same, though perhaps a bit more weather beaten. Colorful snap-dragons grew rampant in the front yard, and the west windows were overgrown with honeysuckle to block out the sun. The screened front porch still held an assortment of potted plants, though many looked neglected. She tapped on the door, preparing herself for whatever look might be on Mrs. Sommers' face. She was relieved when it was Mr. Sommers who answered the door. The man looked a lot older, but he hadn't lost his unyielding ability to command respect.

"Well, hello, Gwen. It's been awhile since we've seen you in this neck of this woods." He opened the door to let her in.

Gwen wanted to hug him, but she held back---he always had seemed rather reserved. She opted for a firm handshake instead. "I am so sorry for your loss, Mr. Sommers."

Jesse turned his head, cleared his throat, and quickly changed the subject. "Thank-you, Gwen. So---where has the paper assigned you now?"

As the two exchanged pleasantries, Gwen noticed that the house was quiet as a tomb. She remembered how noisy and active it had been growing up. She always played dolls with the two Sommers sisters, while the brothers played cowboys and Indians outdoors. Mike would be hiding in the brush, a toy pistol ready in its holster, while J.D. sought him out in a red felt cowboy hat tied with a cord under his little chin. Gwen swallowed hard.

As if he could read her mind, Jesse explained away the silence. "Lainey's resting right now---she doesn't feel so well. And Elise---well you know her. Forever the trooper, she'd be teaching school if the world were coming to an end."

"And Margo?"

"She'll be back real soon, after she finishes in Paris. Might be on her way as we speak. Can't wait to see her. And we can't thank-you enough for all you did when she was hospitalized in London. Her mother and I wanted her to come home right after that, but do you think she'd listen for one minute? That girl's a stubborn mule. Must've gotten it from me, I suppose." He looked at her with curiosity. "So how can I help you today?"

"Oh, um– will Mike be coming as well?"

"Mike's here. He's been a comfort to his mother, but this afternoon he took off for the river. Think he wanted to fish a little---like he used to with---with--- his brother."

"He goes to the West Fork of the Gila River , doesn't he?" Gwen tried to keep the question casual.

"Yep, you remember well. He tries not to show it, but I think the boy is taking things real hard. I'm worried about him."

Gwen got up and headed for the door. "Well, thank-you, Mr. Sommers, for your time. You take good care of yourself and your wife. Tell her I'm thinking of her." This time Gwen hugged him hard.

Jesse watched the young woman climb into her newer model Ford. He vaguely wondered how those high heels would fare in the river sand.

SHE ALMOST STUMBLED as she descended the steep side of the river bank. The bright spring sunshine provided rays that slanted through the fresh new foliage at intriguing angles. Green river willows and rushes lined both river banks. Making soothing sounds, the Gila coursed over a stone dam. Any other time, it would have been a perfect day in New Mexico.

His fishing equipment was left untouched. He sat in a clearing, slumped against the trunk of a low branched oak tree. Head down, he was someplace else, oblivious to his surroundings. She hated to admit it, but he looked utterly defeated.

"Do you plan on catching anything today?"

The familiar voice startled Mike, bringing him back to the present. He quickly looked behind him, though he already knew who it was.

"Your dad said I'd find you here." She looked back at him uncertainly.

He still had the same hazel eyes and heavy, dark brows, but the eager smile was gone. Pain was clearly etched all over his face. Try as he might, he couldn't hide it. Strangely, his eyes were dry.

"Gwen," he uttered her name as though in a daze.

Before he could stand up to properly greet her, she'd sat down right beside him on the bank of the river, her high heels mired in mud.

"I'm so sorry, Mike. So sorry about----about---*everything.*"

"Me too, Gwen. Me too."

A grey squirrel ran up a nearby tree, and two white butterflies chased each other. The rushing water was the only sound.

Mike finally broke the silence, seeming to talk more to himself than to her. "You know, he always copied me. If I hadn't been in such a big damn rush to join the army, he wouldn't have dropped out of school to do the same thing." Mike scooped up some river sand, letting it sift through his fingers.

"One thing led to another, and before any of us knew it, he ended up in the center of the bull's eye."

Gwen nodded quietly, not knowing how to respond.

"My mother always felt it. She knew it was all wrong from the beginning." Mike looked straight ahead, stone faced.

"Hey Mike, why don't we take a walk. It'll do you good to get up from here; maybe clear your mind."

Mike started to protest, but Gwen was already on her feet. "I haven't been out here for years. Was almost afraid I'd forget the way. Let's look around."

They walked quietly under the spring's new leaf canopy, side by side, fingers accidentally brushing at times. Startled birds emerged from bushes and newly hatched dragon flies whooshed by the wild flowers. Mike paused at a lazy spot in the river where the water lay in a deep pool. He studied the rocks with care until he found a flat one in the shape of a coin. Deftly, he skipped it across the water. It took four bounces before sinking. Gwen whistled in appreciation.

"Let me try."

He picked up another flat rock, saying, "This should do the trick."

Clumsily, she cast the stone into the river, where it immediately sank. "Where did you learn to skip rocks like that?" she asked.

"Daddy taught us years ago. J.D. could make one skip across the whole river, six bounces or more." His face darkened. "I was so jealous of my kid brother—my only brother."

Gwen squeezed his hand, looking for a distraction. "Hey, I wonder if I could cross that log without getting wet?" She pulled off her pumps and nylons so as to teeter across the narrow log. She hoped she wouldn't get wet mud on her good clothes. Mike couldn't help but watch her walk like she was on a tightrope. She appeared to be doing reasonably well when she suddenly lost her balance and fell smack into the water. She let out a loud shriek as the cold water enveloped her.

Mike jumped on the log and extended his hand. "Now you're not going to pull me in if I help, are you?" he asked with mock suspicion. Something close to a smile threatened to cross his face.

"I wouldn't dream of it—just please pull me out!"

The thought of pulling him in *had* crossed Gwen's mind, but he looked too vulnerable, like he might break.

After he'd pulled her ashore, she tried to wring out her clothes and hair. Gone was the spiffy Gwen who looked as if she'd just stepped out of a hatbox.

"I honestly thought I could make it across," she said sheepishly.

As they walked back, Mike took off his shirt and offered it to her. Surprisingly, he felt no embarrassment, probably thanks to his time in the military. His shyness was a thing of the past.

She stepped behind a tree and emerged in his shirt, which was nearly to her knees. She knew she

271

looked like a drowned rat. "I better go, Mike," she said.

"No, don't go," he said, blocking her forward motion, by putting his strong arms between the two trees ahead of them. "I feel better when you're here."

"I don't know, Mike. I look like a wreck and all..."

Mike touched her face and wet hair. "You look beautiful to me."

Gwen felt herself blushing deeply red. "I guess I could stay a little longer." She knelt down in the clearing, afraid of her feelings. He went to his truck and put an army blanket around her. She rested her head on his shoulder. They sat that way for a long time, watching the sun go behind the lava rock and limestone hills.

Finally Mike broke the silence. "There's one thing I can't forget. One thing that stays stuck in my mind."

"What?".

"If only I'd talked him out of it. I wish I could go back and do it over again. He might be sitting right here beside me today, instead of lying at the bottom of some ocean halfway around the world..." She didn't answer.

"My head is hurting. I want to cry, Gwen, but I can't..."

Without meaning to, Gwen put her arms around him. Mike began to cry uncontrollably. He pressed his face against her shoulder, muffling his grief.

"Shh-Shh-let it out. It's going to be alright." Gwen patted his back, speaking as if he were a baby. She felt like she might break down at any second.

After what seemed like an eternity, the young man finally gained control of his emotions. He pulled back sheepishly. "I shouldn't have done that." He touched her shoulder. "Look, I got you wet all over again. I'm sorry I'm such a mess. Guess that's why you went for Charlie from the beginning."

"Forget Charlie! There *is* no Charlie. ...." She traced her fingertips over his mouth and looked into his eyes. Softly, she began kissing his neck. Sighing, he closed his eyes and involuntarily touched her brunette hair.

"Gwen, I don't know if---are you sure you want..."

"Shh---You talk too much, Mike."

The two old friends lay back on the riverbank, banishing the world and all its strife. For one fleeting moment on a late spring evening in 1945, tender love was made and peace was found.

Chapter 45

MIKE LAY ON THE TWIN BED he'd grown up sleeping on, looking around the room he'd once shared with his brother. Everything was pretty much the way they'd left it four years earlier. The picture of J. D. smiling on the back of his horse, Star, still stood on the night stand. His chaps still hung in the closet, ready to be worn by their owner. It felt like his little brother had merely gone on an out-of-town trip. When would it ever sink in that he was gone for good? Mike's eyes began to smart and his head threatened to throb.

Time to think of something else----anything else. When he closed his eyes, *she* appeared. Gwen. Gwendolyn Mackenzie. The girl of his dreams. He replayed the scene at the river as he had done many times in the past. The aching sorrow, the unexpected comfort, and the ensuing pleasure. Before he knew it, they'd fallen asleep in each other's arms. If he tried real hard, he could still smell her hair, could feel her soft skin against his.

Though he tried to block it---the next memory came flooding back vividly---the way the sound of her car motor had awakened him; how he'd found himself lying on that riverbank, alone and desolate.

Why had she left without a word? He believed he knew the answer. She could never think of him as more than a brother. That's what it always came down to. She had only meant to comfort him--- never meant for it to go that far. One thing led to another; that was all. She'd used him to distract herself from her own demons. Her mind was probably on someone else, maybe even Charlie. Well, damn her! Guiltily, he remembered Patty, though he couldn't seem to picture her face. At least he knew where he stood with her. Sitting up on the edge of the bed, Mike made a decision. It was time to go. He'd stayed in Mountainview long enough, wallowing in grief and a healthy dose of self-pity. He knew his mother could barely stand the sight of him leaving again, but he *had* to. He'd helped his parents as best he could; now it was time to help his country clean up the lingering remains of war. Mentally, he thanked Sarge once more for this brief reprieve, and for watching over his dog, Buddy, while he was gone. He wished he would now assign him to the Pacific to finish off the Japanese, though he knew that was doubtful.

Snapping open his suitcase, he commenced packing. Again, Gwen's face popped up in his mind. *That's right, Mike,* he told himself, *we used each other in a moment of weakness. Nothing more, nothing less.*

THE BUS rumbled along the rural highway, dodging tumbleweeds and giving off diesel fumes that made Gwen nauseous. She wished she could slide a window open, but was afraid of burning up the other passengers. The first day of June had finally turned the world hot and dry.

Stealing a glance at the elderly woman perched in the seat next to her, Gwen decided against her bid for fresh air. Best not to wake up her seat mate, who clearly enjoyed long-winded visits. She tried to pretend she was sitting by herself so she could think her thoughts, and yes, sulk, most of all.

Why had she done it? she thought, for the hundredth time. S*ex was something you waited for marriage to engage in.* She didn't know Mike particularly well---not as a man that is. He wasn't her boyfriend--- more like a really good friend in recent times. She wasn't supposed to have feelings for him. She had never even kissed him before that day at the river. Try as she might, she couldn't shrug off the memory of him kissing her and how good it felt. She should have made him stop. She should have stopped *herself.*

Why did I go to the river? Why did I even come back to Mountainview in the first place? She asked herself, as though seeking the first piece to a difficult puzzle. I felt bad for the family, felt sad for him. I wanted to sit with him, just let him know someone was there for him if he wanted to talk. We were both two lonely people, she rationalized.

She tried not to remember the warmth of his breath and his broad bare shoulders encircling hers. Hot blood rushed to her face. Guiltily she looked around to see if other passengers had noticed. *What kind of a woman would they think I am if they could read my thoughts? I'm embarrassed and ashamed of myself. That's why I left him alone at the river.*

Now came the real kicker. Gwen scribbled nervously on her notepad, thinking of how Margo had sought her out later in the week, filled with her own pain and loss.

"Hello, friend---where have you been? Daddy said you came by earlier this week looking for me." Margo appeared a little hurt. Gwen noticed she was thin and pale; not nearly as tall and confident as she usually seemed.

"Margo, I-I didn't know you were back," she had responded lamely. "I'm so sorry about J.D." She hugged her friend tightly. She added, "I hate what this war is doing to families."

She had excused herself from going to the Sommers' house---insisting that Margo stay over at her home instead. There was no memorial to attend anyway. The two young women caught up on everything under the sun---Margo's adventure in Paris, her overall military career and subsequent romances; Gwen's own trials and tribulations with the newspaper. Charlie was a sore subject she didn't care to pursue, no matter how much Margo poked and prodded.

Not being able to stand it any longer, Gwen had innocently asked about Mike. "I never hear about his personal life---does he have anyone to help him through this awful time?"

"Well---yeah---there's Patty."

Patty. The name stabbed her like a knife. "So he's got a girlfriend named Patty?"

"She's some nurse attached to his unit over there. He's been mentioning her a lot recently. I don't know if it's serious or not." Margo smiled for the first time in a long time. "I suspect it might be. We could use some good news in our family. I'm rooting for wedding bells." With teasing eyes, she added, "Gwen, you should have nabbed him when you had the chance."

Gwen swallowed hard, trying to appear nonchalant. The muscles in her face ached from an artificial smile. She'd entertained Margo the rest of the hour, counting the seconds till she could usher her friend out the door and throw herself on the bed, hot tears of shame drenching her pillow.

How could she have been so stupid? She made her decision then and there to get back to work---to leave Mountainview---maybe for good. She had to forget his face, his eyes, his arms; had to put him and his precious Patty deep into the past.

Chapter 46

BY MID-OCTOBER, THE WAR MOP-UP was winding down with some of the troops being sent back to the States. The prospect of discharge was imminent and despite the trauma of war; Mike would miss the camaraderie of the military service immensely. Like many of the other young men, he had the rest of his life lying before him like a great, blank page.

Mike sat at a table, studying college catalogs with some others, thinking about his future. Maybe I could go to school and make something of myself. I could get a degree in business or maybe become a teacher like Elise. I always wanted to be a high school coach. His mind kept going round in circles till it landed squarely on the one subject he'd been avoiding: Patty. He was filled with ambivalence whenever he thought of her.

How had he gotten himself into this entanglement with Patty? Yes, they had briefly dated on and off during the war. Recently, she'd come to him distraught. Her pretty yellow hair was in disarray and her eyes were puffy from crying.

"What's wrong?" he'd asked.

"I-I'm scared I may be pregnant. I'm sorry, Mike."

It couldn't have been his, because he'd never been with her in that way. Something had always stopped him. Shouldn't he have felt betrayed or at least jealous? He was surprised he felt nothing more than curiosity at her words.

"What will people say? My family will probably disown me if I am. How can I hold my head up high ever again?"

"Have you told the father?"

"I don't want him to know. He doesn't mean anything to me. Not the way you do."

Making no comment, Mike had squirmed uncomfortably in his seat.

"I made a mistake, Mike. Now my life is over." She had looked so sad. Not knowing how to respond, he'd awkwardly put his arm around her.

"You always make me feel better. I need help, Mike. Could you help me?"

"What do you mean?" he'd asked, feigning innocence.

"I need someone to give this baby a name. I'm scared to face the future alone." She'd pressed her face into his shoulder.

How he'd wanted to run! He'd never felt so cornered, not even as a soldier. He had mumbled some lame excuse and strode off for the barracks. He had a lot to think about before he could get back to her. She did look miserable and defeated, of that he was sure.

Now here he was, far from Patty, but her not-so-subtle proposal was never far from his mind.

There was still a chance she wasn't really pregnant. That would solve the problem for everyone. But if she was----should he step up and marry her, knowing he might not be able to love her the way she deserved to be loved? *What was the right thing to do, the most moral thing? Was this the only cure for the loneliness he sometimes felt?*

"You gonna sit there all day looking at school catalogs like some kind of egghead," called out his friend, Rudy. "Let's join the poker game in the other room. I'm feeling lucky, *vato*!"

"Well, good for you, but I'm not feeling it," Mike responded genially. "I need every penny of my paycheck." He also knew Charlie was leading the card game, and Charlie was someone he tried to avoid.

"Live a little, brother. Life's too short..." Rudy was cut off by the entry of the Military Police through the barracks front door.

"We are looking for Private Charlie Murdoch." They held up a photo. "Does anyone know where he is?"

The room went silent. After a long pause, a couple of soldiers pointed to the adjoining room. "He's at the poker table."

"Are you Charlie Murdoch?" the M.P.'s asked him as he nonchalantly dealt cards.

"So what if I am?" Charlie scowled, swinging himself around to face the officers. "I haven't done anything illegal, unless you call an honest game of cards a crime."

"Private Charlie Murdoch, under the authority of the United States Army, you are hereby being charged with the murders of two German soldiers in the Ardennes Forest on December 20, 1944."

"Wait a minute." Charlie stood up and began backing away as he shook his head in disbelief. "You've got the wrong man. I've done nothing wrong."

One of the M.P.'s grabbed Charlie's arm and twisted it behind his back. The other one snapped the handcuffs shut.

"Murdoch, we have eye witness accounts and hard evidence that you shot those men in cold blood *after* they surrendered. We have strict statutes regarding the treatment of prisoners in wartime and you violated them. Those men were in your custody while you were in this country's uniform. You committed heinous acts while representing the United States of America."

Charlie bared his teeth in an unnatural smile. "You! It's you who trained me to kill the enemy. Now I'm in trouble for following orders? Make up your mind! Prisoners of War--- bull! Those Nazis would have been freed to turn around and kill more of our own. I did you a favor, you hypocrites! You should be treating me like a hero, not a criminal!"

"Shut your trap, Charlie!" someone called out. "You're incriminating yourself with every word!"

"Private Murdoch, you have the right to an attorney, who will be appointed to you by the U.S. Army. You are being court martialed for the charges as stated, and you will be placed in the brig-- pending trial. Is that understood?"

As he was hustled out, Charlie fixed his eyes ahead, seeing nothing. Nothing that is, until he passed Mike. Coldly he paused to survey his old friend.

"It was you," he said in a flat voice. Mike's expression remained dispassionate.

"Keep moving, Murdoch,"said the M.P.

The room got deathly quiet as everyone turned to focus on Mike. He got up and left the compound in order to escape their questioning faces.

Did war bring out the worst in some people, or were they going to be like that anyway, he wondered sadly. Unbidden memories of high school flooded Mike's brain. He and Charlie in football uniforms under the Friday night lights. Charlie throwing him a perfect pass that sailed right into his waiting hands. The crowd going wild. The crazy after-game rides down Main street. Going into Skippy's Diner with all their friends. The burgers, shakes and good-natured jokes. Watching Charlie work the girls like he never could. Mike couldn't believe he'd ever looked up to him----ever wanted to be like him.

Mike's mind zeroed in on that rainy autumn night back in '41. Gwen was there talking and smiling. So was J.D. He remembered the silly thing he'd done on impulse that night. *Why did I ever think I could keep the attention of a girl like her?*

As fast as it lit up, Mike's mind shut down. Those days were gone and so were those people. Luckily, he still had his faithful dog, Buddy, who looked up at him as if he could read his thoughts. He whined pitifully and pawed his leg. "That's right, Buddy. The only thing left to do is to move on."

Chapter 47

THE SIXTH GRADERS OBEDIENTLY COPIED "September 2, 1945" in the corner of their papers. With her back to the class, Elise pounded out steps to a division problem on the blackboard. Without skipping a beat, she said, "Heads up, Will. You may be called up here to explain what I just did."

The class tittered. Apparently, their teacher had been correct. Will looked up in surprise. *How did she do that anyway?*

Elise turned around to face the whole class when she noticed a figure in the doorway. "Mr. Moore, how are you today? Class, can you say good morning to Mr. Moore?"

As the class greeted the principal, Elise waited with secret impatience. What interruption could take precedence over these children learning their arithmetic skills? She didn't want it said that she had graduated a class of fools.

Beaming, Mr. Moore answered the class with an extraordinarily friendly response. "And now, Miss Sommers, I know you were in the middle of a lesson, so I'll be brief. I have an important announcement to make." He paused for effect before continuing. Elise tried not to fiddle with her chalk. "Japan just surrendered to the Allies. The war is finally over!!"

He was met with stunned silence, followed by thirty 12-year-olds jumping up and down, cheering joyously. Mr. Moore noticed Elise had turned away in the corner. It was very unlike the young, no-nonsense teacher.

"Why, Miss Sommers, are you feeling alright?"

She turned toward him, her nose red, wiping her eyes with a dainty lace handkerchief. "I'm fine, Mr. Moore. Absolutely fine." Joe Howard was coming home; coming home to start a new life with her. Then there was Mike and Margo. She wondered if they'd come back and settle down in Mountainview. Both of them appeared to be on the path to marriage as well.

If only…if only… She tried to push his name out of her mind. She shouldn't think about him right now. *J.D.* There, she'd done it anyway. *He should have been coming home, too.* She inhaled deeply, hoping her voice wouldn't quaver. "Thank-you for that announcement, Mr. Moore." Neatly folding away her kerchief, she continued, "Now children, return to your seats immediately. Will, please demonstrate how the problem is divided…"

THREE WEEKS LATER, Lainey drove downtown to do some shopping. The chickens had been laying like crazy, and she had a little extra money to spend. Ever since the war ended, she'd felt more energetic, like something special was in the air. It wasn't something she could put into words around her family.

Her eyes darted up and down the street. Where was there a blasted parking place downtown on a crowded Saturday morning? Suddenly, her heart began to palpitate. Going the opposite direction, a group of servicemen were making their way toward the sidewalk in front of the Silco Theater. She saw a familiar thatch of dark hair. Screech! She hit the brakes to avoid hitting the car in front of her.

"Hey lady, watch where you're going!" the driver yelled.

Lainey paid no attention. She'd lost the group of soldiers. How could she possibly drive and look for them at the same time? In vain, she searched for a parking place, but there wasn't one anywhere. She spotted the men, who were pausing in front of a shop window further up the street.

Lainey squinted. The height was right, the posture so familiar. She rolled her window down. "J.D.! Over here, J.D.!"

None of the servicemen looked up. However, a lot of other people turned around to see who she was calling to.

He must not be able to hear me. As if on a mission, she parked her car in front of a bright red fire hydrant, leaving the keys in the ignition, and her bag on the seat. She scraped her ankle as she mounted the high concrete curb, jostling shoppers as she half-ran down the stidewalk.

"J.D.!" she called to the young men, who were well in front of her. Pow!! She slammed directly into an older man, scattering his packages everywhere.

"Sorry, Sir! Hold on and I'll help you in a minute!"

The man stared in bewilderment as Lainey continued her trek up Main Street. Just when she thought she'd run out of oxygen, she spied him up the block going into the drugstore. With one final push of energy, she propelled herself through the entrance and up towards the display he was examining.

So tired she could barely breathe, she uttered, "J.D., where have you been?" She couldn't stop herself from giving him a familiar tap on the shoulder.

He spun around in surprise, facing Lainey full on.

It was not J.D.'s face that looked at her with confusion.

Lainey's heart filled with disappointment. "Oh my goodness---I'm sorry. I-I- thought you were someone else."

Red faced, Lainey slowly turned away, as if in a trance. The young man's surprise quickly turned to concern. "Ma'am, are you okay? Can I get you anything?"

Lainey stumbled out of the drugstore and walked aimlessly for a few blocks, not even bothering to retrieve her car. Where was he? Where was her J.D.? Mightn't he be coming home, now that the war was over? They say he never made it off the sinking ship. But what if he had? How would she ever know for sure? Was this what they meant by "being in limbo"?

Half-crazed, she pictured boarding a plane for the Philippines. She and Jesse could scour every island in the Pacific and Japan too if necessary. They needed to find J.D., dead or alive. As soon as she considered it, she knew the idea was insane- for one thing, they didn't have the resources. But oh, how she desperately wanted to with every fiber of her being....

Back on the street, parking tickets were attached to her car, and her purse was gone. She didn't care about losing the purse, but how would she explain away the lost egg money to Jesse? None of it really mattered anymore.

I'd rather know and feel like hell, than be in this purgatory of not knowing. Every ring of the phone, every knock at the door, every car coming up the drive… It's too much. Will I ever be at peace again?

Chapter 48

THANKSGIVING OF '45 WAS CLOSING IN on Mountainview, New Mexico. The skies were a threatening slate grey, and the air was cold to the bone. The wind forced dead leaves back to life again, making them dance and twirl across the bleak late November landscape.

Lainey sat in the living room, doing nothing in particular. Another year where she hadn't made plans for the holidays. What kind of a mother was she? How would she face her other three children with her failures?

"Lainey, where are you?" called Jesse, stomping mud off his boots from the barn. "That Wilson kid wanted to stop by today. Said something about thanking you for a homemade quilt. He oughta be here soon."

Lainey jumped up in surprise, automatically responding, "You didn't eat all my apple bread, did you? I'll slice some of that and put on some hot tea. Make sure there's enough wood on the fire." Somehow, she transformed herself into the picture of hospitality. She straightened her worn cotton house dress and ran her fingers through her shock of white hair. Why did Jesse always wait until the last minute to tell her company was on the way? She didn't even have time to shake out the throw rugs.

"What's his first name, Jesse? Wasn't he one of those who made it back from the Philippine's?" Lainey tried to keep her voice casual as it dawned on her just who this houseguest was. Her thoughts were soon interrupted by a couple of tentative raps on the front door.

"Make regular talk," Lainey whispered tersely, steering her husband forward. "You know I don't want to talk war."

When they opened the door, a hollow-eyed man-boy was standing there, clothes hanging off him as if several sizes too big, his feet shuffling nervously. He stuck out a thin hand that was prematurely aged by scars and too much sun.

"Hello, Mr. And Mrs. Sommers. I'm Ben Wilson."

"Ben, we're pleased to meet you. Come on in out of the cold.. I see it's starting to snow." Jesse showed him the chair nearest the fire, while Lainey offered him hot tea.

"I-I got one of the blankets that you made," he dove in, looking up shyly at Lainey. " I use it every night and it's real warm. It helps sometimes, you know, to chase off the bad thoughts, the fear. I don't know why, but it helps, Mrs. Sommers." He shrugged and looked away, embarrassed.

"Why thank-you. I appreciate you coming all the way out here to tell me that. I don't know if this makes sense, but when I crochet blankets for servicemen like you, it chases off my bad thoughts and fears too. So we're not all that different, Ben." She smiled encouragingly at him while Jesse gave her hand a proud squeeze.

"Actually, that's not the only reason I came out today." The young man fell silent, searching for something in the dancing flames of the fireplace. Finally he focused on the middle-aged couple who were waiting for him to continue. "I-I knew a little about your son." Hesitantly he added, "Do you want to hear what I remember?"

"Of course, son, go ahead and tell us what you know," Jesse responded steadily.

Lainey jumped up, white as a ghost, grabbing the tea kettle with trembling hands. "I'll get more tea," she murmured, exiting the room as she always did when overcome by emotion. Safely in the refuge of her kitchen, she let down her guard. Her head began to pound in unison to the drumbeat of her heart. She'd warned Jesse, hadn't she? She didn't want any war talk, and yet here was this boy threatening to shatter her last remnants of sanity. *How dare he?* She wouldn't listen any further. Nothing he could say would make it better.

She stood in the center of the yellow and white tiled floor, arms folded across her chest; an island stuck in a sea of misery. She didn't know what to do with herself. Her own skin was foreign and uncomfortable.

She could hear the low hum of the men's voices back and forth. Maybe she should cover her ears just in case. *In case what?* She asked herself. *In case a word about J.D. penetrated her brain and made her cry? What kind of a coward are you, Lainey?* She didn't want to hear, but in a strange way, that's all she wanted. She didn't understand her feelings.

Ever so tentatively, the conflicted mother crept forward. First she peeked out the kitchen door into the backroom. Next, she moved like a frightened rabbit, nearly frozen in its tracks. They couldn't see her in there, but she could hear every syllable they said.

"I didn't really know J.D. personally, but I heard what the others said about him. The way he stood up to the prison guards. He hated being held against his will." There was a long pause. "We all did. But at least he tried to escape. It didn't work, but everyone knew he had guts. He did what we couldn't." Lainey bit her lip, digging her nails into her palm. Tears began to trickle down her face. She should go to Jesse, but she couldn't move.

"He spent his time being strong for others. I always heard he shared his food with guys weaker than he was." There was no response from Jesse. "Someone told me how he would recite Bible scriptures through the wall. It kept some of them going. Made them feel like they weren't alone." Another long pause. "The enemy never truly had him, Mr. Sommers."

Still there was no audible response from Jesse. "Well, I best be on my way. I just wanted you to know what kind of person your son was. Tell your wife it was nice to meet her and thanks again for everything."

Lainey swiped away her tears and bolted forward. "Wait, Ben. I want to thank you again for coming by. And I heard your words. They meant more to me than I can say."

Ben looked awkwardly at her once more before turning to go. His eyes were a reflection of isolation and pain. Lainey realized he was an island as much as she was.

"Would you mind horribly if I gave you a hug?" she asked surprising even herself. He smiled and shook his head self-consciously. She carefully embraced him. Stiffening at first, he then relaxed to accept the comfort.

She stepped back, attempting a smile. "Now enough of this, or we'll both be blubbering like babies. You go on about your day. Live your life well, son. Do you want more apple bread to take with you?"

"No, ma'am, I'm fine. Good-bye, Mr. and Mrs. Sommers."

Without further ceremony, he left the snug house; walking down the lane to the highway, making footprints in the new-fallen snow. Jesse and Lainey stared after him, long after he was gone.

Chapter 49

THE CHILDREN KEPT CHECKING THE CLOCK and even Elise tried not to look up at the school calendar posted on her bulletin board. Snowflakes, children in mittens sledding, and red-cheeked people caroling. It all signaled December and with that came Christmas. An involuntary sigh escaped the young teacher's lips.

"What are you looking so glum about?" Lulu Johnson, the fifth grade teacher next door, stuck in her head. "In case you forgot, Christmas break starts at the end of the week. I can't wait. My soldier's taking me to every dance for miles around. And just think, Elise! No rationing this Christmas! I can buy all the silk stockings I want. The war is really over!"

Elise had to smile at her friend's frivolity. "I'll be glad to be with Joe this year. I've never spent a Christmas with him before." Thoughtfully, she played with her modest engagement ring. "I wish I could concentrate on him alone."

"Why don't you? Chin up, kiddo; you think too hard. Don't take home any lesson books. Forget the students for two weeks. Believe me, they'll still be here when you get back."

"No, it's not school that's bothering me. It's the way Mother always gets around Christmas." She made eye contact with Lulu. Now her friend was on the same wavelength.

"It must be very hard for her, Elise," she said sympathetically. "Hard for the whole family, I'm sure."

"You have no idea, Lulu." She wanted to say more, but stopped herself. "Enough about my problems. We still have to finish out the week and the kids are as wild as March hares, aren't they?"

TRYING NOT TO LOOK as anxious as she felt, Gwen peeked around the back gate of the Sommers' home. No one had answered the front door, but there were cars in the driveway. Surely someone would be around on Christmas break.

"Yoo-hoo----is anyone home?" She smoothed her hair nervously, wondering if she should have adorned it with a poinsettia. Then again, that might have seen too dressed up for a simple visit to a friend's house. She pressed her lips together, taking care not to smudge her red lipstick. Her hands shook a little as she refolded the aluminum foil covering the plate of cookies that had been rolled, cut, baked and iced with the utmost of care. *Why couldn't she get rid of the butterflies in her stomach?*

"Hey, Gwen, how are you?" Margo bolted across the yard toward her best friend, looking stunning as ever in a red gingham checked Western shirt tucked smartly into a long-legged pair of denims finished off with red cowboy boots.

After a tight embrace, Gwen thought, She looks good, considering what she's been through. A little thinner, a little wiser, but she hasn't lost that twinkle in her eye.

"I had to come over and see my oldest friend--- how are *you*?"

"Oh you know me, no worse for the wear." A quick shadow passed over Margo's face and then it was gone as suddenly as it had come. "I hadn't heard from you in so long, I was afraid you'd dropped off the planet."

"I wanted to give you some private time with your family. Besides, I haven't been back that long myself."

Footsteps crunching in the new-fallen snow could be heard rounding the corner of the house. Gwen looked down at her feet, hoping to hide the blush that was creeping up her face. She felt like she couldn't breathe. She wasn't sure she could face *him*, but after the passage of time, she'd decided to try.

"Gwen, just look at you! What a city slicker you've become!" Elise rounded the corner with open arms. "This seems like old times. The gangs all here!" Her brown eyes sparkled, though not quite as brightly.

"Elise, I hear you won't be gadding about with us single gals much longer. When will you and Joe be hearing wedding bells?"

"We're setting the date, Gwen, and you'll be the first one invited. I can't wait, though I'll miss the fun times we had riding around Mountainview, singing at the top of our lungs, waving to the boys." She giggled in a way that was very unlike Elise.

She's happy and I'm happy for her, thought Gwen.

Looking like the cat who swallowed the canary, Elise continued, "And the way it's going, I won't be alone. Maybe we should be planning a *triple* wedding! We could get our family married off at once."

"Triple wedding, what do you mean?" Gwen tried to keep her voice from squeaking. Her heart was pounding so hard she was sure the two sisters could hear it.

"Miss Margo over there is not so secretly engaged to Rob, and the last I heard, Mike was making his promise to that nurse, Patty something or other. So there you go! Three for three!"

"Wow, I never thought Mike would take the plunge. Are you sure about it, Elise?" Gwen asked evenly.

""He should be here shortly. He can tell you all about it himself."

Once more, Gwen found herself smiling until the muscles in her face smarted. If only she could swallow the growing lump in her throat. "You're all a bunch of lovebirds---you Sommers!" She abruptly changed the subject. "I have an idea. I heard Caroline is back in Mountainview. Why don't we meet her downtown at the drugstore for a cherry coke. For old times sake and all that! I'm actually not sure how long I'll be in Mountainview, so I want to get together with everyone."

Disappointed, Elise countered, "I knew this town didn't have a hold on you. I wish you'd stay….."

"I'd like to, but I've got my career to think of. As it is, I'm waiting for my transfer back to El Paso. That's where the action is for me, not to mention all the handsome military men to choose from at Fort Bliss."

"You never change, Gwen! Always playing the field! Well come on then, let's round up Caroline and have a gab fest. We can't be gone too long, or we'll miss Mike's homecoming."

Gwen lay her plate of cookies on the hall table. Before joining the others, she turned and ripped the tag off the plate. The three young women piled into Gwen's car and drove down the old road like teenagers once again.

"HELLO! Where is everybody?" Mike came breezing in the front door, still in uniform, looking handsome as the dickens. His deployment was winding down, and he was back in the States to stay. The clean-up after the war hadn't been easy, and he was glad to have it all behind him.

Lainey stepped out of the back room. "Mike! It's so good to have you home! Tell me you're here for awhile." She hugged her son's neck, and stepped back to give him the once over. "You're growing up into quite the man. So tall and debonair! And is that your army dog in the back pen? I don't mind if he comes inside sometimes, long as he's had a bath."

" Yep, that's Buddy. Thanks, mother, you're a good sport. He's clean and pretty well behaved." Mike noticed the plate of cookies on the nearby table. "I see you've been baking again. They smell delicious—mind if I have one?"

"You never change! Always thinking about your stomach!" Lainey laughed and gave him another hug. "You know, I don't know who brought those cookies. They didn't leave a card. But go ahead and dig in."

"Where are the girls?"

"I don't know. I just got in myself. Probably off gift shopping with old friends. Don't worry, son, they've been anxiously awaiting your arrival. I'm sure they'll be back soon." Lainey was a little amused at Mike's interest in his sisters' whereabouts.

"Which old friends were they with?" An unbidden picture of Gwen passed through his mind. Pain pierced his heart like an arrow.

"I don't know. The usual. Now enough about *them*. What about you? How are you? You look wonderful." Lainey did not disguise how grateful she was to still have him..

"Mom," he began uncertainly, "I'm thinking about settling down, maybe getting married…"

"I've heard the rumors from your sisters. But, slow down a minute. We haven't even met this girl. We want you to bring her home to meet us. Patty, right?" Lainey studied her son carefully. *He doesn't look very happy or enthusiastic about being engaged.*

"So what is she like, son?"

"Oh, she's a nurse. Nice enough and all that. You'd like her, I'm sure."

Mike suddenly wanted to escape the barrage of questions. He grabbed a couple of more cookies and headed for the barn. "Gonna check on Star," he called back to his mother.

He didn't feel like confiding in Mother. Maybe he could talk to Daddy about things. He seemed wise in the ways of love and marriage. Maybe he could advise him. Mike needed perspective. It turned out Patty wasn't really pregnant. He didn't have to help her out of a jam anymore, but she still wanted to get married. He took another bite of the delectable cookie. If only….his mind went to another time, another place, another girl.

In no time, he had brushed Star's coat till it shone brilliantly. He patted the mare's neck. Everything will work out the way it's supposed to. I've learned that the hard way. We all have.

Chapter 50

THE ENVELOPE LOOKED LIKE ANY OTHER Christmas card. The only difference was there was no return address. Lainey scrutinized the handwriting, but it was unfamiliar. The post script was from Washington, D.C. She realized this was no ordinary greeting card:

Dec. 20, 1945
Dear Mr. and Mrs. Sommers,
   With much respect, I feel compelled to share new information about your son, J.D.
   Eye witness accounts of the events that transpired on October 24, 1944 are beginning to surface. We are piecing together what happened that day based on the few American survivors' testimonies, as well as some accounts given by the Japanese.
   It has come to our attention that your son was undoubtedly a hero. More than once, he gave aid to his fellow prisoners. He selflessly kept others afloat, swimming tirelessly in the

open ocean without regard to his own safety. Ultimately, he sacrificed his own life.

We are proud to honor men like him who have served in the United States Army and we wanted to share that pride with you.

Let the records show that J.D. Sommers has earned a Purple Heart and a Bronze Star for distinguished service to his country. A ceremony will be held in the near future to bestow these honors. We will be in contact.

Yours Truly,
Douglas MacArthur

After pressing the letter to her lips, Lainey carefully folded it away. She would show it to Jesse when he came in. After that, she would put it in J.D.'s childhood scrapbook, right next to the lock of blond hair she'd kept from his first haircut. She was so grateful for the few reminders she still had of her youngest child.

Her thoughts went to the second drawer in the hutch. She imagined opening it and pulling out the Gold Star. It seemed as if it were waiting for her. Maybe one day…

Later that evening, Lainey carried the mouth watering turkey to the table. "Soup's on!" she cheerfully called out. The smell of the meat and all the trimming wafted throughout the small house.

"Coming, Mother!" Mike hurried into the kitchen, eyeing the dinner with a voracious appetite. He noticed his favorite old family platter was out; the one with the rooster proudly adorning it. It had been a long time since he'd seen it on this table. He rubbed his hands together in hungry anticipation, waiting for the others to join him.

"Mother, you should've called for help. The least I can do is set the table." Elise patted her Mother's arm. She gave the table a quick scan, dreading the ever present empty place set next to her. Tonight it wasn't set. *Had Mother forgotten?* It wasn't set for the first time in four years. Elise looked around at the others to see if they noticed. No one said a word about it. She had a hard time swallowing her food, though it was delicious as always. She was on pins and needles, waiting for her mother to remember the extra setting. Strangely, Mother rambled on about her day and never once mentioned the missing plate.

CHRISTMAS MORNING arrived and as was the custom, the Sommers gathered round the tree to open their gifts. This year, Joe Howard was invited, since he would soon be a real member of the family. Margo's beau was stationed in Germany, still cleaning up the aftermath of the war. Mike wasn't saying much about Patty and from the look on his face, no one wanted to ask.

Lainey clapped her hands for her family's attention. Customarily, the youngest family member, J.D., had done the honors since he was a little boy. Lainey usually pointed out this fact over the past four Christmases.

As Jesse played Santa Claus, Elise began to get the sinking feeling that always overcame her at this juncture of the festivities. After the presents were handed out, all eyes would be on the three remaining unopened gifts-----the unopened gifts that stood there year after year like a festering wound that would never heal.

"That's all I've got folks! Should we let Joe go first since he's our newest family member?" Jesse gave Joe a strong pat on the back. "I never knew how brave you were–takes nerve to join this family!"

Joe chuckled in return, sending a special smile to his fiancée as he began opening. Elise wasn't listening to the playful banter next to her. She was too busy focusing on the bare skirt surrounding the tree. There were no more presents. They had all been passed out. *Where were J.D.'s gifts?* Isn't this what she wanted? All those times she'd ordered Mother to stop the foolishness. She should have felt relieved, but instead she felt only emptiness. She wondered if the others were feeling the same thing.

Soon, the gifts were opened with bows and paper happily strewn across the shiny wood floor.. Again Lainey clapped to be heard above the hubbub. "Before we clean up, we've one more order of business to take care of." Everyone looked expectantly at her. "Elise, Mike, and Margo, please go to the back closet and each of you get one of J.D.'s presents."

I knew it was too good to be true, thought Elise. *She just can't let it alone.* On the way to the back room, she caught Mike and Margo's eyes, shaking her head doubtfully.

Each sibling returned holding a package. *What did their Mother want of them now?* Lainey cleared her throat and fiddled with her hands. "As you're all aware, Daddy and I had high hopes that J.D. would return one day and open these presents himself." She looked fondly at Jesse. He reached over to squeeze her hand. He wasn't sure what was coming, but it was obviously difficult for her to find the right words.

"I've slowly come to realize that J.D. won't be coming home." She stopped to take a deep breath. She didn't want to cry in front of Joe. "Don't you get me wrong. I'll never give up on him---never, ever forget him, as I know you won't. He lives in all of us. He'll live forever right here." She softly touched her heart.

"So----I'm giving you each one of his presents as a remembrance of your brother. I love you very much. Daddy and I are very glad we have you. Go forward with your lives, please."

Margo went first, now that she was the youngest sibling. She very carefully removed the red bow, barely disturbing the green tissue as she pulled the box free.

"A pair of spurs with his initials engraved on them." Her usually bold speech was barely audible. It was her turn to hold them to her heart. "Mother, they're perfect. I'm sure he would have gotten a lot of use out of them. I'll keep them always."

"Tell Daddy, Margo. He's the one who had them custom made right after the war broke out." Margo went over to her father's recliner and hugged him tightly.

Next it was Mike's turn. His package was quite big with white tissue covered in golden flecks. Some gold ribbon festooned the top. In typical fashion, Mike tore into the package, shredding it like he always did. The box was taped so seriously shut that it took a lot of wrangling to open it. Everyone laughed through unshed tears as Mike finally won the fight, pulling out a fine leather saddle. Again it was engraved with the letters "J.D.S.". Mike bit his lip and looked wordlessly at his mother.

"Don't look at *me*, son. That's Daddy again. Had it made, along with the spurs, back when the war started." Lainey crossed the room to hug her surviving son. Buddy wagged his tail at her, waiting patiently for his own pat on the back. "Mike, ride Star with that saddle. The horse is yours now. Take care of her. That's the best thing you can do to honor J.D.'s memory."

Everyone's eyes settled on Elise. She tinkered with the holly fastened lovingly to the card written in Mother's handwriting.

"Well, Sis, what are you waiting for?" Daddy smiled kindly on his eldest daughter.

"Daddy, I-I-think-well-I think I don't want to open it today." Elise picked up the package, hugging it tightly. She looked into Joe's concerned blue eyes. "I'm going to wait until the time is right. Someday, maybe Joe and I will have a little boy, a fine boy just like J.D. Some Christmas morning, we will have it saved just for him and we'll tell him about the uncle he never knew." Joe whisked away a tear that trickled down Elise's nose. An awkward silence fell upon the family.

"Enough of this somber mood. It's Christmas morning! Jesse, put the carols on the phonograph and let's go have some biscuits and gravy. Elise, give me a hand. Margo, could you be a doll and clear out this mess?"

"Mother, why is it always me? Mike, you lazy thing, get over here and help me…"

With that, the Sommers family began the process of picking up Christmas leftovers, along with the broken pieces of their hearts.

Chapter 51

SHE HAD NEVER FELT MORE ALONE than she did on this night of February 14, 1946. After the war, home didn't feel like home anymore. Her fathers and siblings had forged ahead with lives of their own while she'd been gone. She didn't know where she belonged.

The band's version of Glenn Miller classics blared from the Community Center Hall. It was the first peacetime Valentine's Dance in over four years. Mountainview came out to exuberantly celebrate as only they knew how. She personally had never felt less romantic. She idly wondered if her long-awaited transfer to El Paso would ever come through. Clearly, there was nothing here for her anymore.

Looking around, she realized everyone she knew was in the arms of someone they loved. She waved at Margo, appearing svelte and movie star glamorous as ever, holding a long cigarette holder in her tapered fingers, and looking into the eyes of Rob, who was now a local bull-rider. Elise was jitterbugging up a storm with her fiancee, Joe.

Gwen scanned the crowded hall, hoping to find Caroline. At least she could sit with someone she knew. That idea was quickly nixed when Gwen turned and saw Caroline arm-in-arm with Slade. He was so tall, and she so short, yet there couldn't have been a more perfect couple.

Gwen sighed audibly. *What am I doing here?* she muttered to herself. Everyone was paired off, it seemed. Everyone except her. She served herself a cup of punch, almost slopping it all over her new dress.

I'll stay five or ten minutes for appearance sake, then I'm out of here. I couldn't wait to come back here, but I don't know why. Dad's got a new family and my siblings are grown and gone. There's not much holding me to this little town after all. Time to move on---get back my job in El Paso or another big city—write for a magazine or real newspaper.

Pensively she sipped her punch, watching the couples move in synch on the dance floor. She did a double take at a laughing young man in a cowboy hat. He was a dead-ringer for J.D. It seemed like ages ago when the real J.D. had been here, screwing up his courage to ask a classmate for a dance, then awkwardly shuffling his feet to the music.

Poor J.D., she thought, and her eyes welled up. A few days before, she'd noticed that Mrs. Sommers had finally put the gold star in her window. *I've got to get out of here before I start bawling like a sissy. What did I think I'd find anyway?* She wiped her eyes, straightened her dress, and stood to go when a lone male made a bee-line for her across the darkened room.

Not now, she thought, *I'm not in the mood for small talk tonight.* A stab of anxiety made her shiver. She squinted at the figure. No, thank God it wasn't Charlie. He was still in jail, last she heard. Would be for quite awhile. Besides, this guy wasn't as tall as Charlie---he had a more average build. She turned away so as not to stare.

"May I have this dance?"

"I thought you were with someone else now."

He shook his head and looked into her eyes. "I repeat, may I have this dance?"

"I don't know," She bit her quivering lip. "Hasn't there been enough pain between us?"

He dug in his overcoat pocket and pulled out a small jar of pennies. Deftly, he opened the jar and poured the pennies into the ashtray at her table. "You won't dance with me, not even for a hundred pennies?"

She gathered a handful of the coins in her hand, letting them fall through her fingers one by one. "It was *you.* It was always you and I thought it was Charlie."

Not responding, Mike studied his shoes in embarrassment.

"Why didn't you ever tell me it was you?"

"I didn't figure it would matter. You had your sights set on him."

"What do *you* want, Mike, or is it too late to ask?"

"I think you know what I want, Gwen." He looked her hard in the eye. All the war years seemed to melt away in that moment. For awhile, the suffering and the loss were forgotten as he took her hand and held it to his lips. "I want you, Gwen, and I always have."

The band struck up "Moonlight Serenade" and the two old friends and newfound lovers smiled at one another as they began the dance of a lifetime.